Eleanor of South London

GEORGINA
DARTER

Published by Georgina Darter

ISBN: 978-0-6457320-0-9 (paperback)

FIRST LARGE PRINT EDITION, 2023

For book orders and enquiries, contact:
bandgdarter@bigpond.com

 A catalogue record for this book is available from the National Library of Australia

Disclaimer
The characters in this book are fictitious and any resemblance to real persons, living or dead, is purely coincidental.

Dedication

To my wonderful husband Brian
who not only encouraged me
but kept the cups of tea coming.

Acknowledgments

I should like to thank my husband and sons for supporting me in my writing endeavours. Special thanks to Gina Jessop and Di Norman for their contributions. Thanks, too, to Rommie Corso of Hardshell Publishing for taking on board my debut novel and giving it the professional treatment.

1

'Good morning, Eleanor, time to wake up' said the young female nurse, cheerily, pulling back one of the closed curtains over the French windows, allowing the morning sun to stream in, casting dust motes to dance around and exposing the view out to the street and park beyond.

Eleanor did not respond. She had been awake since five o'clock and now it was seven o'clock. She knew the time as there was a large clock, on the wall, opposite her bed. *Tempus fugit*, time flies, she thought to herself. This evoked a happy memory for Eleanor, but she could not give it recall. She had been tempted, if she could reach, to ring for a cup of tea at five o'clock but knew that the skeleton night staff still on duty, would have not had time for her needs. They had so much to achieve before finishing their shift. The nurse fussed around her getting out the clothes she thought Eleanor should wear for the day, never thinking to ask.

Eleanor had other ideas. She would change her dress later, to one of her choosing, she thought.

'Let's have a shower, shall we?' said the nurse. 'Then we can have a nice cup of tea'. A second young nurse came in to assist.

Eleanor hated the use of the word 'we' every time a staff member wanted to get her to do something. It was so patronising thought Eleanor. It made elderly residents seem like young children. Eleanor realised that some of her fellow residents were acting more like children as they aged but they should be treated with respect. She had recently overheard two young nurses refer to her as Mrs Tea Bag. She knew that was a reference to her surname.

Life in Lady Rawlings Home for the Elderly was advertised as being 'just like home' and offering only the best of services. Eleanor and most of the other residents could not agree with these sentiments, but whether they liked it or not they knew they were there for the duration and conceded defeat. She had heard other residents express such views.

The single storey home was nicely situated in a tree-lined street in one of the better areas of North London, close to Burnt Oak, and each room had a nice outlook of either the park across the way or the courtyard rose garden with a birdbath in the centre for rooms at the back of the building. The French doors allowed access to the outside although in the case of the rooms facing the park there was a locked gate to deter would-be wanderers or escapees as Eleanor chose to think of them. She had considered escaping herself but was unfamiliar with this part of North London and knew that she would not get far.

Residential care had not been Eleanor's idea for her final years, preferring to stay in her own home until the end, but the family had consulted with her doctor, and everyone thought it was the best solution for Eleanor's age and medical problems, apart from Eleanor, whom no-one had thought to consult. If she had had her way, and her health issues not so bad, she would be going on a cruise and letting young, mainly Asian staff, tend to her needs and at her beck and call. As a seasoned traveller Eleanor knew cruising would be the answer to her declining years and health. She had once read of an American woman who spent many years moving from one cruise ship to another. The woman had calculated that the total cost of cruising was cheaper than residential care and that the service she received was far superior. The idea had sat in Eleanor's memory mellowing.

Showered, dressed and her short, grey hair neatly combed into place, Eleanor finally had a cup of tea on her small wooden table beside her. The nurse placed a multi-coloured crocheted knee rug on her lap and tucked it in around her legs. Breakfast was still some time away and she would be taken to the dining room past other rooms with the usual strong smell of urine in the morning and past the kitchen with the smell of cooked cabbage at lunchtime. So, she was sitting in her own winged-back armchair, recently reupholstered in sage green velvet, placed by the French windows of her room now with both heavy curtains open and tied back so that she could see the street and park. The nurse had chosen, for Eleanor, a pink floral dress with a matching silk scarf around her neck. Acceptable, for a change, thought Eleanor.

'I'm coming back shortly', called the nurse and together with her assistant they left the room and closed the door quietly, leaving Eleanor alone.

Eleanor then allowed her mind to wander. She had been thinking for some time of writing a book about her family and particularly her life, but her arthritic fingers now meant that she could no longer tap away on her old portable typewriter.

For some unknown reason Eleanor became aware of the silence around her. There was not even a bird singing in the trees. Perhaps it was the warmth of the room that caused Eleanor's eyelids to close and then her memories took over.

2

A very young Eleanor was sitting on the multi-coloured rug, in front of a log fire, listening to her mother Mary, seated next to her, relating family tales. The young Eleanor believed every word that she was told, but, in reality, some was fact some was hearsay, and some was pure embellishment. Whatever, the stories enthralled young Eleanor. Like the one about her paternal grandfather.

Cigar smoking Reginald John Hawkins was tall, overweight and bearded. His greying hair neatly barbered was slicked back with pomade. He was also the epitome of sartorial elegance. As a respected bank manager, he believed that he had to portray a certain image. His daily dress comprised shiny, black leather boots, pinstriped trousers, white shirt with starched birdwing collar and black tie. Also, a grey waistcoat, displaying a thick gold chain, across the front, attached to a gold hunter watch secreted in one of the pockets. Rounding off the look, he wore a black frock coat and when outside, a black silk top hat. He liked to carry a silver topped cane, too. At home Reginald looked the same minus his top hat of course. Only his wife ever saw him in his nightshirt. Although young John had seen the washing on the line, in the garden, and guessed that it must be his father's.

Reginald and his much younger wife Phoebe, who was meek and mild mannered, liable to an attack of 'the vapours', lived in the family home at Wandsworth. It was a three-storey, detached, brick, residence with a large garden. In the basement lived Mr and Mrs Dawes, an elderly couple. Mrs Dawes was the cook/housekeeper and Mr Dawes did the gardening and carried out menial tasks such as cleaning the family's leather boots. There was no familiarity between the Hawkins and the Dawes. Each knew his station in life and to cross the line would mean instant dismissal as far as Reginald Hawkins was concerned. Young John's memory of Mrs Dawes was that she always smelled of lavender water whilst his mother wore expensive French perfume.

Apart from the smell of perfume young John's memories of his mother were vague as she tended to stay in her bedroom much of the day resting, or quietly crying, and only appeared for dinner in the evenings.

Occasionally, during the day, she might come down-stairs to check whether Mrs Dawes had everything organised for Mr Hawkins on his return home from the bank. He recalled that his mother was petite, thin and unsmiling. She always wore long black dresses as though in permanent mourning. Young John could only recall one occasion hearing his mother laugh out loud.

As head of the household Reginald always looked stern, and his word was law in his own home. He was very Victorian in his attitude to life. Children espe-cially should be seen but not heard. Late in his life his son was born, whom he named Reginald John, after himself but warned Phoebe to be more careful in future as he wanted 'no more brats'.

Young John, as he became known, was a disap-pointment to his father. He was not a good scholar and showed little aptitude for anything that might give him future prospect. His father continually told him that he would not amount to much and undermined young John's self-esteem.

Reginald Hawkins had a sister of whom he was very fond and extremely proud. She was beautiful and intel-ligent. His sister married a man involved with the rail-ways in India and soon after their marriage they went to live in India. He used to brag about how well his sister had done for herself by marrying such an influential man in the railways. Occasionally a letter would arrive on the door mat and his mother would say that it was from young John's Indian Aunt. Young John had received a book about the American Wild West, for his last birthday, and loved to read about cowboys such as Buffalo Bill and Wild Bill Hickok and Indians such as Big Chief Sitting Bull and the wives known as squaws. He especially loved to look at the coloured illustrations. However, being young he could not figure out how he could have an Indian Aunt.

One day his mother informed him that his Indian Aunt was coming to visit. Young John sat by the large bay window watching for a woman with her hair in two long, black plaits and a feather in a headband and wearing moccasins. Without warning a horse drawn Hansom cab pulled up outside the house and an elegant young woman alighted. She was dressed in pale grey clothing to the floor, elbow length pale grey kid gloves and wearing a large expensive looking hat with ostrich feathers adorning it. The total look was complemented with a small grey silk bag, hanging by a chain, from her wrist. She was welcomed at the door by John's mother and briefly introduced to young John without naming her, well as far as he could remember. She, too, smelled nice, but spicy, like Mrs Dawes ginger cakes.

The woman handed John a small parcel which he thanked her for and then opened in front of her and his parents. Inside the wrapping was a box with the name of a toy shop written on it. Taking the lid off the box John saw a highly detailed locomotive inside painted black. Carefully removing the locomotive from the box, he looked at the woman and thanked her again with a big smile. The woman was then taken, by his mother, into the parlour for afternoon tea whilst his father stayed next to him. Once the two women were out of earshot John's father took the locomotive and box from John's hands. John would never see the locomotive again. When his father left to join the ladies, John was excluded as per Victorian rules. Young John continued his vigil at the window, but no Indian woman appeared. After the well-dressed lady left John's mother asked him why he was staring out of the window. He told his mother that he was waiting for the Indian Aunt wearing moccasins. His mother laughed out loud to young John's amazement. 'John that lady who has just left was your aunt from India, your Indian Aunt'. It was the only time young John could recall such a reaction from his mother and he would cherish this brief but emotional event forever.

On 22 January 1901 Queen Victoria, Monarch of the Empire died, thus ending the Victorian era and later, a change of direction for young John.

3

When John was only fourteen his father died of a heart attack, at Waterloo Station, about to board a train for Southampton, according to the First-Class ticket found in his waistcoat pocket. A few minutes earlier he had been in conversation with an old friend, from his gentlemen's club, who was still close by, when it happened, so he was able to provide the Police with identification for him as, surprisingly, he carried none. It was noted that Reginald's wallet, silver topped cane and possibly a small, brown leather attaché case were never found.

The train ticket provided a mystery, as no-one was aware of why he was going to Southampton and the reason was never found. This caused the family undue grief. John's mother did not cope too well with her husband's death, leaving all details of the funeral to others. The house needed to be sold according to their solicitor. It transpired that Reginald had many outstanding gambling debts that would take most of the money that the sale would realise. Unfortunately, the rumour mill that can surround a debt-ridden bank manager emerged. Perhaps he was embezzling his customer's funds. Perhaps he had a mistress. What was he doing at Waterloo Station? The shame, rumours and innuendos surrounding young John and his mother were enough for Phoebe to have a breakdown and she was placed in a psychiatric facility where she lived for a short while before passing away. Again, someone organised the funeral arrangements excluding John in any decision making.

John was forced to find work but was glad that his Indian Aunt wanted to stay in touch with him as she felt she owed her late brother that much and had written to the solicitor expressing this.

Strange to say, but John believed his aunt's name was Elsinore, having overheard his parents talking one day. He never thought to check with anyone. With someone interested in his welfare John would correspond with his aunt once or twice a year, updating her on changes in his life. His Aunt would always sign off her letters with a stylised letter E. Their intermittent correspondence would span many years.

Meanwhile, John found a home with his maternal grandmother, who, whilst caring, as though it were her duty, showed little in the way of love. This relationship made John determined to make his own way in life, preferring not to rely on others. At his young age and not well educated he trudged around markets looking for any manual labour that was needed and managed to find enough work to be able to pay his grandmother board and lodging and clothe himself. He even managed to save some money, too, by deciding not to take up the habit of smoking cigarettes. Saving had been instilled in him from an early age by his banker father.

4

After a few years, a chance meeting with Mary Collins, whilst delivering some vegetables to a nearby shop, changed adult John's attitude to life. He and Mary had attended the same primary school in Wandsworth, and he remembered her. She also recognised him. Mary was working in an eel and pie shop near Camberwell Gate, behind the counter. The shop was a favourite haunt of John's, whenever he was in this area, as the meal was cheap and nourishing. Pie and mash being a traditional working-class food, originating in the East End of London since the 19ᵗʰ century. John loved to hear Mary call out *'pies up'* when a fresh batch of pies came out the oven and taken to the front counter.

Mary was a quite a few inches shorter than John, who stood over six feet tall, but had a fresh, open face and her hair was tied back in a neat bun. She was devoid of make-up, but John preferred to see her peaches and cream complexion and discouraged her from 'looking like a clown', in his words. Seeing her now as a confident young woman had a strong effect on him and after a whirlwind courtship, they decided to get married.

The actual wedding was nothing fancy, Registry Office was all either of them could afford, plus the fact that neither of them were regular church goers, which was a pre-requisite for many church weddings. Two strangers, from off the street, were called in to sign the register as witnesses, for them, at the Town Hall. For the occasion, John wore his only brown suit and a clean shirt and one of his father's old ties. Mary borrowed a lacy, cream, full length dress from a work friend and carried a single pink rose. John was filled with pride when they were announced man and wife. There was no celebration after the event as Mary had to get back to work. Neither of them considered that they had a family of any consequence so would start their own. They rented two rooms, with shared toilet, in a tenement block in Penrose Street as their first home but John was determined he would lift their status in a few years.

Prior to the Great War (the war to end all wars, an idealistic slogan) John Hawkins was a gas lamp lighter. His usual work attire being a pair of old suit trousers, held up with a wide leather belt, an unironed grubby white, collarless, shirt, with rolled up sleeves to above the elbow, a mismatched waistcoat, a long, fringed, white silk scarf tied as a cravat, a flat, cloth cap, brown boots and gaiters tied to just below the knee to stop rats running up his legs, a common occurrence in those days. So different to how his father used to dress for work. John went out late in the afternoon and by dusk was lighting gas lamps, in the streets of South London, using an 8 ft long brass pole with a pilot light in the end. At dawn, the next day he would be doing the round again but this time extinguishing the flame. He used to say that electricity would never take over his lamp lighting job. During the day he worked as a labourer for the same gas company, digging trenches for gas pipes to be laid. It was tough work but with his muscular build from physical labouring he could cope well with using a pick and shovel.

When Archduke Franz Ferdinand of Austria-Hungary, was assassinated in Sarajevo, on 28 June 1914 no-one, certainly not the general public, envisaged the serious repercussions. So, when war broke out in 1914 John did not immediately enlist due to Mary about to give birth, but after a few months, when many of his fellow workmates were heading off to war, he enlisted in the Army. After a period of basic training, that all new recruits were subjected to, he was sent to France to fight, leaving his young wife Mary, in London with young twin boys. Mary had no idea when he would be home again, although politicians were predicting it would all be over by Christmas.

It is generally accepted that the First World War or Great War of 1914-1918 killed over sixteen million people worldwide, military and civilian. Military deaths were estimated at nine and a half million, around twenty million were wounded including eight million left permanently disabled in some way. John was one of the maimed. He had returned from the First World War with major internal problems caused by shrapnel wounds. Although his memories of the action that caused his injuries were vague, he could recall a German artillery shell exploding in the mud-soaked trench that he was in. He had some recollection of the noise, almost bursting his eardrums and the screams of his fellow soldiers. He thought he could remember seeing dead bodies and remains of bodies surrounding him. After that he had no recall until waking up in a field hospital some days later. Time had stood still for him. The enormity of the situation did not resonate with John for quite a while. His days were spent in and out of consciousness with unfamiliar sounds penetrating his ears, but mainly screams which were in fact his own. He survived numerous operations in field hospitals in France but was repatriated to London and then medically discharged from the Army towards the end of the war. Hospitalised on his return and more operations performed at a major public hospital, John was sent to the country for convalescence. Secretly he wished that he could have lain in Flanders Fields for Eternity, so bad was his pain and depression. Trauma and the horrors of war had scarred him physically and mentally for life. He would never be the same again and hated the man he had become.

If a world war were not enough to contend with, the Spanish Influenza pandemic broke out in February 1918 and lasted until April 1918. The world death toll was in the millions. The pandemic threw more chaos into everyday life. With John still fighting in France Mary was fearful for herself and the two boys of catching the 'flu. Where possible she avoided associating with family members, neighbours or strangers and protected herself with John's white silk scarf to cover her nose and mouth. She resorted to buying groceries infrequently and reduced her personal food intake in order to be able to feed the boys. So scared was Mary of catching the 'flu that she was continually scrubbing surfaces, of their small home, with carbolic. One day, while she was making the beds the four-year old twins found the bottle of carbolic under the kitchen sink. Being inquisitive, one of the boys managed to open the bottle and they both took a drink. How much they ingested was not known. When Mary smelt the carbolic, she rushed into the room to see what had happened, and she panicked. Believing the boys would die from carbolic poisoning she grabbed her only bottle of milk from the kitchen table and forced each to drink until they vomited. Then, still fearing that the two boys would die, she took a mouthful of the foul liquid herself so that she would die with them. Her automatic reflex was to vomit. Despite drinking a lot of water afterwards she could still taste the carbolic for the rest of the day and each time she burped it would leave a foul taste in her mouth. Mary and the boys survived the possible poisoning but the 'flu was still a worry. Although not a religious person, Mary would give up a little prayer each night for their safety. Her prayers were answered.

5

Finally, John was home again with his young wife and young sons who had now grown so much and in fact did not know their father, being too young to remember him when he went to war. There was a period of readjustment for the boys as well as John.

John was not a well man. He never worked full time ever again. Labouring was totally beyond his physical ability. However, he approached the gas company, for whom he had worked prior to joining the Army, and asked for any type of work that was not too physical. The man in charge of hiring men remembered John and knew that he had a young family to feed. He offered John a night watchman's job. With the gas company digging trenches in every street, to gradually supply gas to every home, there would often be a large trench left open for the night and a dangerous hazard to pedestrians. John's job would entail filling square, red oil lamps with paraffin oil, checking the wicks then lighting them to allow the light to show through the convex lenses, when dusk fell John would position them, spaced a few feet apart, along the side of the trench as a warning to anyone. There was a small wooden sentry box type hut for John, as watchman, to sit in with a view of the length of the trench. If the night became cold, which it often did, John would light a cylindrical metal brazier firstly with wood then stoke it up with coke, just outside the hut entrance. This fire provided him with the means for boiling a kettle as well as keeping warm. Sometimes he would lay a large potato in the embers and ashes under the bottom of the brazier and enjoy a baked jacket potato during the long night. Another time he would put a handful of chestnuts on a shovel and place the shovel on top of the fire to roast the chestnuts. It was surprising how many people, out walking, would stop and have a conversation with John. Behind the hut would be a small wooden shed to house the tools needed by the labourers. Although padlocked each night a night watchman provided additional security. As soon as morning came John would extinguish the light in each lamp and stack them near the hut in readiness for the next evening. He enjoyed being able to converse with the labourers as they started work for the day before he headed off home.

Eleanor had been John's third and final child, born nine months after his return from the Front.

Life in London from 1914 until the early thirties was hard on her family like thousands of others. Abject poverty and hardship flourished everywhere. The Great Depression was another period of history that was hard on everyone with mass unemployment, scarcity of jobs, money, food and everyday commodities. The Great Depression lasted from August 1929 until March 1933. Somehow the Hawkins family did survive but the future was not looking as rosy as it might have been with the advent of yet another war looming, according to the sceptics. Being a child, most of the troubles of the world were foreign to Eleanor and she was more concerned with her doll or helping her mother in the kitchen.

6

After leaving school at fourteen years of age Eleanor's two older brothers, by five years, John and James became the breadwinners. They were twins but a quirk of fate meant that John was born at five minutes to midnight on July 31 whilst James came at ten minutes past midnight on August 1. Mary and John settled on 1 August for their joint birthdays but of course both had to use their correct birth dates on their birth certificates or other important documentation. John was known as Jack, to avoid confusion with his father, after whom he had been named, whilst James became Jim. Eleanor often pondered why people gave children names when later they were shortened, or a nickname applied. From a young age she refused to be known by any other name except Eleanor. She only accepted Jim's name as she had grown up with it. It was some years later that she learned that her father was actually named Reginald John.

Eleanor's mother Mary was about five feet two inches tall in her stockinged feet, a small, rotund woman with a flawless complexion and reddish colour hair worn in a bun at the nape of her neck. Eleanor recalled that she always seemed to be wearing a clean pinafore over her dress. Mary helped supplement the family finances by office cleaning. She would leave home early in the morning to catch a bus over to the West End, but ensured she was home to get Eleanor off to school. Despite the lack of money Eleanor always had something to eat for breakfast even if it was bread and dripping, which she liked. Her mother would save the meat juices left in the roasting pan, in an earthenware basin, from the Sunday roast, and the congealed fat together with a brown jelly, that settled on the bottom would be a treat. A sprinkle of salt on top, when slathered onto fresh bread, really gave it flavour.

Despite their humble life, Eleanor had very, happy memories of her family life. Her parents had never been able to afford to buy a house, so the family accommodation was always rented which was common practice for the poor, in South London, in those days. Unfortunately, moving home was a regular affair. With little furniture and possessions John would borrow a barrow from a market trader and move their belongings on the cart. If they moved at the weekend Eleanor's brothers would help with the heavy lifting of furniture such as beds and a piano, her mother's prized possession, and then push the barrow to wherever the next dwelling would be. Eleanor's parents always tried to find something to rent in the same area so as not to disrupt Eleanor's education more than necessary. Eleanor was a good student. There had never been a shortage of food, as far as she could recall, but then children often do not realise the hardships that adults are enduring.

Her father was at home at lot but seemed to find jobs to do and always seemed to have a hammer or screwdriver in his hand. He sometimes helped the newspaper seller Sid, outside the nearby underground station if the newspaper seller needed time away from his pitch. Sid and John had been soldiers together in France and in fact were in the same trench when the action happened. As a result, Sid lost one leg. His working days were limited so he took the newspaper selling job and it provided him with a small income for his family. At least he could sit down when he wanted to, which was most of the time. Helping Sid, during the day, would provide John with a few pennies for his efforts and selling newspapers was not strenuous. Her mother had a routine of washing, cooking and cleaning but always found time to sit and listen to Eleanor as she recalled her day at school. Mary also taught Eleanor to play the piano during the evening.

Jack and Jim both worked as packers in a garment factory in the East End of London and would travel to work on their bicycles. This would help them save money, although in the winter it was no fun riding in the rain or fog. Occasionally one of them would bring an item or two of clothing home for their mother. Jim said that they were classed as 'seconds' but Mary could never find faults in the garments and was grateful for the boys' generosity.

John Hawkins had a saying. 'Clothe them or feed them and you will always be in work'. Well, the boys were in the clothing industry, but Eleanor was not looking to work in a grocer's shop. She did not particularly like the smell of all the various unpackaged foodstuffs that seemed to blend into unpleasantness to her nose. She preferred the smell of the dairy with the different cheeses. She enjoyed being a machinist when the time came for her to work. The pay was not great, the hours were long, but she stayed reasonably clean and made some good friends.

7

About the age of eleven Eleanor won a scholarship to a local grammar school. Her parents
were thrilled to bits until they found out how much
the compulsory school uniform and incidental costs
would amount to, despite the scholarship. The school
allowed Eleanor to commence term 1 when her uniform comprised of a blue and red diagonally striped tie
and a navy-blue beret with a school badge sewn on but
when her mother spoke to the headmaster about their
financial problem, he suggested taking Eleanor out of
school and enrolling her in the secondary school nearby
which did not require a school uniform. After discussing the matter at home, a devastated Mary and John
agreed with the headmaster's suggestion and Eleanor
changed schools before the end of term. Eleanor never
felt bitter about the need to change schools. She had
an understanding the financial strain it would put on
the household but often wondered what her life might
have been had she been able to continue grammar

school education. Fortunately, her love of reading and a nearby library ensured she was never without a book and this pastime enhanced her learning. Geography was her passion closely followed by history and she found that often the two complimented each other. Due to her reading ability her English comprehension was excellent.

One day, on her way to the local library, Eleanor had seen the words '*Tempus Fugit*' on the face of a grandfather clock in the window of an antique shop. The two words fascinated Eleanor and until she found that the Latin phrase meant 'Time Flies'. She kept the innocent phrase in the back of her memory bank.

After leaving the secondary school at the age of fifteen, with excellent academic results, Eleanor obtained employment as a machinist in the same garment factory as her brothers. She was not ambitious, and her parents did not think girls should have higher education, especially after the grammar school disappointment. She caught the bus to work, took a jam or dripping sandwich for her lunch and avoided spending money unnecessarily. With money tight in the household Eleanor would often draw a black pencil line up the back of her leg from ankle to above her skirt line to look like she was wearing nylon stockings.

She possessed three white blouses, one to wash, one to wear and a spare that she had bought from the factory. She owned two black straight skirts and two pairs of black shoes. Her father would ensure that everyone's shoes were well polished and presentable. The limited wardrobe meant that she looked like a waitress each time she went out. However, this simple dress attire was easy to care for and she always looked nice.

Eleanor was not vain, but her hair gave her great pleasure. It was chestnut brown in colour, like a chestnut just released from its protective covering, and shoulder length with a natural kink. In the sunlight it showed hints of red. When she was a child, her mother had used curling tongs to give Eleanor's hair ringlets. Unfortunately, one day the hot curling tongs, straight from the fire, were accidentally dropped into the crook of Eleanor's left arm and badly, burned her. Using good old-fashioned treatment of butter on the burns and then a gauze bandage Eleanor struggled for days with the pain of the burns. A visit to the doctor was out of the question. Eventually the burns healed but left a nasty scar.

Growing up with two brothers Eleanor had a healthy attitude to men. She treated them as equals, despite the age difference, and hoped one day to find a man as kind and gentle as her own father and brothers. Jack and Jim were both tall with muscular builds and good looks not unlike their father before he went to war, according to Mary. They had similar colour hair, with a natural kink, like Eleanor's. Jack was the more sporting of the brothers and belonged to the local football team and darts team at the local pub. He held the pub record for downing a pint of beer. His father referred to him as a man's man. Jim, on the other hand, was quiet and studious, he also learned to play the piano, taught to him by his mother. He and Eleanor shared a love of books, especially Charles Dickens and the Bronte Sisters, and he would often tell her of his dreams to one day become a writer. He would have dearly loved to go to university but knew it was out of the question for him.

King George V passed away in January 1936 leaving his eldest son David to ascend to the throne. David would take the name Edward VIII with the Coronation set for 12 May 1937. Before he could be crowned David had fallen in love with an American divorcee, Mrs Wallis Simpson. The protocols of Royalty would not allow such a union of a future king and David was advised of this. After much political debate and public anger towards him David decided that he would abdicate the throne in favour of his younger brother Albert. David was never crowned and his official reign lasted 325 days. He married Wallis Simpson and was stripped of his titles, choosing to be exiled abroad. Albert would take the name George VI and together with his wife Elizabeth were crowned on 12 May 1937, the date originally reserved for David.

8

Soon after Eleanor's sixteenth birthday she became aware of a young man who, it turned out, lived in the next street. She seemed to see him quite often, at the library, at the grocer shop and even at the dairy. She had noticed that he whistled popular tunes most of the time, but her favourite was *'Begin the Beguine'*, when she heard him. He was taller than her, with almost black hair but the bluest of eyes as far as she could tell. One day when she dropped her purse, spilling small change over the pavement, he suddenly appeared, as if from nowhere, to pick it up for her. It took a few minutes to collect all the coins, with their hands briefly touching during the collection, but it was enough time for him to pluck up the courage to speak to her. He said his name was Lenny Lipton but added 'and before you ask, no, I am no relation to Sir Thomas', and he apologised for staring at her. He went on to explain that she was the prettiest girl he had ever seen and would she agree to walk with him to the park. During their walk he told Eleanor where he lived and a little about his family, adding that they were not a close family since his older sisters had married.

The incident had affected Eleanor, in an unfamiliar way, like a small tremor, and she realised that she was feeling a little light-headed as they walked. She did not know why. Perhaps it was the embarrassment of dropping her purse. She had only agreed to walk with Lenny for half an hour as she needed to get home. Surprisingly, Lenny knew her name and where she lived. He said that he had recently made friends with her brothers and played darts with Jack. Eleanor should probably have felt uncomfortable but in fact she felt the opposite. She felt safe with this young man.

He asked to see her again the next week to which she agreed, but away from their respective homes.

Lenny had a small motorcycle and often gave Eleanor a ride when they met. It was a guilty secret that Eleanor did not encourage. She tried hard not to enjoy holding him around the waist during the ride but inwardly felt good. He, on the other hand, felt good about having her so close to him. Eleanor did not mention the motorbike rides to her parents as she knew that they would not approve. She had heard the conversation, at the dinner table, with her brothers, that their parents were strongly against riding such terrible machines and her brothers were forbidden to even think of buying one. Cycling was a much safer option, according to her father, and at Eleanor's insistence, Lenny sold his beloved motorcycle without much resistance.

9

A few months later, whilst the family were sitting down to dinner of pork sausages and mashed potatoes, a family favourite, when Jim's face suddenly flushed, and he blurted out that he was getting married. Everyone stopped eating and silence reigned. John looked at his son in disbelief. 'Explain yourself' he said. Jim then had to confess that a girl he had been seeing, recently, said that she was pregnant and that the baby was his. 'You damned fool' exclaimed John, 'what were you thinking?'. 'Do you love her?'. Jim shook his head. 'This is not the time nor place to continue with this conversation' said John, standing up from the table 'we will talk later' and turned and left the room slamming the door behind him. No-one finished their meal. Eleanor said that she was going to her room whilst Jack said he was going down the pub. Mary put her hand out and rested it on Jim's arm. No words were said, but he knew he had at least one ally.

Lily and Jim had met at a dance hall. Jim was taken by her dimpled smile, cupid bow lips, petite frame and flirtatious way of looking at him when he asked her to dance. She had felt so light in his arms and her cheap perfume seemed to stay with him after she left. They had had only a couple of dates before he found himself wanting more of Lily than he dared think possible. When a brief opportunity arose, in her home whilst her parents were out, Lily readily agreed, and so they were intimate, albeit in a hurried and clumsy fashion. It was a heady experience, but Jim hated himself afterwards. Knowing little of love, he knew that lovemaking was special between two people that had a warm attachment to each another and he knew that he did not love or have strong feelings for Lily. She was merely an infatuation, but not having had the experience of a girlfriend before he was feeling very unsure of himself and his actions. Not long after their hasty passion Lily told him of the baby. She said that her mother told her she must get married as she was worried as to what would the neighbours think if she did not. Over 21 years of age Jim did not need his parent's permission to get married and Lily's parents were only too eager to get her married off.

John and Mary had met Lily once, when they were out walking through a park, and happened across Jim and Lily sitting on a park bench holding hands. John had taken an instant dislike to the pretty blonde seventeen years old. John, who normally was not judgmental, told Mary, in confidence, that he thought Lily was a slut and that she had trapped Jim. He even doubted that the child was Jim's knowing what type of man Jim was. Mary, however, although bitterly disappointed, told John that they should support their son and maybe, in time, John's opinion of Lily might soften.

With no extra space in either family's rental accommodation Jim and Lily had to find somewhere to live. A few doors along the same street as John and Mary, lived an elderly widow, alone in a large house. Jim approached her to enquire if she would be willing to let him and Lily rent two rooms at the top of the house but share kitchen and bathroom facilities with her. Luckily, she agreed with the idea and the small rent they could afford. With the accommodation sorted Jim made the necessary arrangements for the marriage ceremony, which took place at the Registry Office in the local Town Hall. There was not going to be a reception after. Being a weekday Eleanor and

Jack could not attend, due to work commitments. John refused to attend the ceremony and Mary supported her husband's wishes. However, Lily's parents did attend. Her mother wearing a cheap imitation fur coat, despite the warm weather and her father in a less than fashionable black suit.

As the summer months moved into autumn and then towards winter John had softened his attitude towards Lily, but he still harboured a strong doubt as to the baby's paternity but started to embrace the idea of being a grandfather. If the baby were a boy, he would take him fishing for tiddlers in the pond at Clapham Common and show him how to make a kite and fly it from a nearby hill. He would teach his young grandson as much as he could about life and encourage education. He regretted not having the time nor energy to do such things when his own boys were younger having spent so much time in and out of hospital. John loved making things out of wood and had fashioned a beautiful wooden cradle, for his grandchild, to which Mary had added some tulle and lace. Mary had also knitted a complete layette for the baby, in white, and Eleanor had bought a small cuddly teddy bear for her new niece or nephew.

A loud banging on the front door early in the morning on Christmas Eve saw Jim standing there panicking that Lily had gone into labour. Mary grabbed her big woollen coat, hanging on a hook just inside the hall, and threw it on over her flannelette nightdress. She barely had time to change her slippers for old shoes. Running, they went to Jim's home. Lily looked very pale and said that she was in a great deal of pain, so an ambulance was called. Christmas Eve was spent with Jim and Mary sitting outside the labour ward of major public hospital. Finally, in the early hours of Christmas Day a doctor emerged from the labour ward double doors and asked if he was Jim Hawkins. He replied that he was. Without sitting, the doctor coldly informed Jim and Mary and that Lily had been delivered of a stillborn son. Showing no compassion, he turned and briskly walked away. Jim and Mary were shell shocked. They both burst into tears and then grabbed each other in an embrace that lasted a few minutes. Neither would recall the bus trip home as they were numb with shock and functioning on auto pilot.

Eleanor's memory of that Christmas was blurred. She recalled that the family did not celebrate. The turkey stayed uncooked and presents unopened. When

Leonard came to the house to see Eleanor and give her a Christmas present, she quickly blurted out to him what had happened and sent him away asking him not to call again for at least a few days. Jim was inconsolable over the loss of his son that day and for some time after.

Months passed. Jim and Lily separated, and Jim moved back in with his parents. Finally, Jim and Lily divorced. Jim vowed never to remarry but seemed happy living at home again. He lost any interest in women, instead preferring men's company, especially at the pub.

10

Time is a healer, so it is said, and late in the following summer Jack and his girlfriend Kathleen jointly informed the family that they were getting married. Happy times ahead. John and Mary were delighted with the news. They had always liked Kathleen and she and Jack had been an item for three years. Jack and Kathleen had met at the local pub where Kathleen had been working, behind the bar, at the time. Jack was taken by her green eyes and Irish lilt in her voice. Her curly hair was Titian red in colour, and she wore it up in a bun with a couple of tendrils of hair falling to her nape. They announced that it would be a traditional white wedding with Eleanor as bridesmaid and Jim as Best Man, if they both agreed, which they did.

They were to be married in the local Church of England and the reception would be in the adjacent church hall. Neither side had many relatives, with most of Kathleen's family still back in Ireland, so it would not be a huge wedding.

Eleanor enjoyed going shopping, in Oxford Street, with Kathleen to buy her wedding dress and a bridesmaid dress for herself in a large department store. The bridal gown was quite simple. White satin falling straight to the floor with a lace front panel. Long sleeves and a high neckline. She would finish the ensemble with a floor length veil and her hair loose. Pastel pink was the colour that Kathleen had chosen for the bridesmaid dress although not Eleanor's favourite colour. She always preferred blue. Making a mental note that one day, if and when, she got married her bridesmaids would wear blue.

Kathleen would carry a large bouquet of pink carnations and gypsophila whilst Eleanor would carry a small posy of pink carnations.

On a Saturday afternoon, at the beginning of Autumn, with the leaves on the churchyard trees turning gold, red and rust brown, Jack and Kathleen were married. There had been a bit of a hiccough at the West Door of the church when Kathleen arrived and got an attack of nerves. As much as she loved Jack, she suddenly had this overwhelming feeling that what she was about to commit to was not what she wanted. Eleanor did her best to calm her down and the vicar became quite annoyed that she was putting on such a display. He had another wedding arranged after theirs and wanted this wedding party to be gone in a timely manner. Kathleen's father, who had arrived from Ireland for the occasion, discreetly pulled a small silver hip flask from his jacket pocket. He looked around before offering it to Kathleen. She readily took a sip. Her cheeks became flushed pink and she shuddered. It was the first, and possibly the last, time that she had tried whiskey, despite working in a pub. The alcohol had had the effect needed and so to the strains of 'Here Comes the Bride' a more relaxed Kathleen and her father set off slowly down the aisle. Kathleen was now smiling and nodding to the small congregation of family and friends, on either side of the aisle, in recognition. Eleanor was a few feet behind them. The incident would remain a secret between the three of them although Eleanor did wonder if Jack detected the smell of alcohol when he kissed the bride. If he did, he did not say.

11

Eleanor's aversion to names being shortened came to the fore at the beginning of their relationship when she told Lenny that she would call him Leonard. At first, he was taken aback. Leonard was on his birth certificate, but everyone knew him as Lenny. Eleanor was adamant. It was Leonard or nothing. He capitulated again, reminiscent of his reluctant motorcycle disposal.

Eleanor and Leonard did not see each other during the week. Leonard had taken an interest in motor car engines as well as motorbikes and spent a lot of time lending a hand at a local garage after work. He also loved to attend New Cross Speedway in the Old Kent Road alone or with friends. He loved to hear the loud crackling roar of the highly tuned racing bikes and smell the engine fuels and burning rubber. The grit, from the cinder track, thrown up into the faces of the spectators on the bends also excited him.

Eleanor, on the other hand, always had things to do at home, helping her mother, doing her own washing and ironing or washing her hair. Recently Eleanor had taken to dyeing the front of her hair blonde. She would pour neat peroxide into a saucer and using an old toothbrush she would brush the liquid through the front of her hair. She knew that if she kept up the peroxide regime, she would eventually have the blonde front to her hair that she was after. Her mother warned her that her hair might fall out, but it never did. Eleanor was always tired after a day at work on a sewing machine but kept up with her regular routines and piano practice.

However, the weekends were different. Friday night Leonard played darts at the local pub but Saturday night he would ensure that he took Eleanor out. One week it would be to the cinema, especially if the film were a musical, whilst the next week would be to a dance hall. On Sunday, he would take her to one of the museums at South Kensington. Although Eleanor enjoyed the Science Museum her favourite was the Natural History Museum. Sometimes they would take a walk along the Serpentine, depending on the weather. Not wanting to push himself on Eleanor they only held hands. Leonard respected her age and did not want to do anything to upset her.

Most parents are astute when it comes to what their offspring are up to so it came as no surprise to John and Mary when Eleanor asked if Leonard could come to tea one Sunday afternoon. They had both noticed considerable behavioural changes in Eleanor who although normally a happy-go-lucky type of person seemed to have an extra something about her. They liked what they saw and had made a joint educated guess as to what was happening with their daughter. Eleanor's two brothers had dropped hints that their young sister may have a suitor and Mary was aware of Leonard hanging around the neighbourhood and heard him whistling.

Telling Eleanor to leave everything up to her, Mary laid the table with her best white, damask tablecloth and set the best bone china on it. The china had belonged to Mary's mother and hardly ever saw the light of day, always packed away in newspaper in a strong wooden crate. Eleanor felt special when her mother went to these lengths for the occasion.

Wearing a new blue and white gingham dress Eleanor greeted Leonard at the front door. He had arrived at the time stipulated by Eleanor and was very courteous to her parents. He shook John's hand and gave a slight bow to Mary. Of course, he knew both of Eleanor's brothers so only offered them a smile and a nod.

The whole family sat down together to eat. The boys had been to a wet fish shop near the Elephant and Castle, for the seafood, lining up, as usual, for quite some time. Sunday tea, in the Hawkins household, was traditionally winkles, shrimps, bread and butter, watercress sandwiches, hot buttered crumpets, angel cake and tea. On this occasion Mary had also made a sherry trifle, with the last of the sherry left over from Christmas. Eleanor could tell by the atmosphere, that afternoon, that Leonard had received her parents nod of approval.

Traditionally, after Sunday tea, the family would gather around the piano and whilst Mary played the tunes the whole family would sing. They all liked the modern songs of the day. On this memorable Sunday, Mary excused herself to wash up the tea things and suggested that Eleanor play the piano, which she did. Leonard was impressed. He made a mental note to buy a piano at some time in the future for Eleanor when they married.

After tea Eleanor saw Leonard to the front door. He turned, took Eleanor in his arms and gave her such a passionate kiss that it took her breath away. At first, Eleanor was taken aback, but she threw her arms around Leonard's neck and returned the beautiful kiss. She was ecstatic. She now knew, deep in her heart, that this was love.

With flushed pink cheeks Eleanor returned to the kitchen to help her mother clear away any crockery and cutlery that had been used. Mary looked with fondness at her daughter. 'I will tell you something' she said. 'Your father used to whistle all the time before he went to war. It was one of the things that I liked about him. Leonard has that same attribute. He will make a good husband'. Eleanor hugged her mother. She had never known her father whistled, as the man she knew was not a well man. Throughout her childhood he had a sullen disposition and did not seem particularly happy with his life, but this was the father that Eleanor knew and loved. In later years Eleanor would learn and understand why he was the way he was.

From now on she would try to see more of Leonard and slowly introduce him to other members of her extended family that they only tended to see at christenings, weddings and funerals.

With Eleanor and Leonard's relationship deepening and time passing, at the age of eighteen Eleanor told

Leonard that she now felt ready for marriage. He had waited patiently for her to reach eighteen and knowing that they still needed her parents' permission for them to marry. Neither had any doubts that the permission would be forthcoming. They were right. There was one stumbling block though. When Eleanor sighted her birth certificate, she thought there must have been a mistake. Up until that point she had celebrated her birthday on the 18th of November only to find out that it was in fact the 19th. Tackling her mother as to the discrepancy Mary could offer no explanation. With her forgiving nature Eleanor accepted that humans are fallible. However, John and Mary wanted a period of engagement first so that they could both be very sure of their feelings. Thoughts of Jim's failed marriage probably came to mind.

12

Shopping for a ring was fun despite the cold weather. Eleanor had been looking in jeweller shop windows previously and, although she did not want to make the final decision, found two rings to her liking in different shops. One Saturday afternoon Eleanor and Leonard went shopping for the ring. Eleanor let Leonard lead the way as they sauntered down the Walworth Road. At each jeweller shop they would stand and stare. A diamond ring, they agreed, was the only type of ring Eleanor should have. Of course, price came into the equation. Finally reaching the first shop, where Eleanor had spotted one of the preferred rings they again stopped and stared in the window. Leonard saw what he thought was the right ring. They went inside the shop to take a closer look and Eleanor tried it on. It was a beautiful solitaire diamond that sparkled in the shop lights. Unfortunately, it was too big. It could be altered but it would take a couple of weeks. Eleanor and Leonard could not wait two weeks, they wanted it now.

Hand in hand they left the shop and continued with their saunter and looking in shop windows until they reached the second jeweller's shop where another ring was to Eleanor's liking, they stopped and stared again. Leonard pointed out a pretty diamond ring with two smaller diamond chips set either side. The price was within his price bracket. He had been saving hard for months.

As they both entered the shop a small bell rang above the door. There was a small, bald man, on the far side of the counter, bent over, examining the inside of a watch and wearing a *loupe*. The noise of the bell made him raise his head and a big smile erupted on this face. At Leonard's request, a black velvet pad of rings was extracted from the front window and Eleanor selected the ring that they had both agreed was the one she wanted to try. The ring fitted perfectly. As Eleanor admired the ring and turned her hand around under the shop lights it sparkled like a million fireflies. This was the ring. Her heart gave a flutter.

Payment made, the ring was placed in a small red leatherette box with a raised dome and the name and address of the jeweller inside the lid. The jeweller invited them back to the shop when it was time to buy the wedding ring. He said that he would give them a good discount on the price. They thanked him for his generosity.

Eleanor was so happy that she could wear the ring immediately, so John and Mary had arranged for a small party, at their house, that evening. Leonard's parents were invited along with a few of Eleanor and Leonard's friends. A few days before, Mary had made a cake, in the shape of a heart, and iced it for Eleanor and Leonard to cut and share.

Eleanor had said that she did not want to wait too long to get married and with Civil War in Spain ongoing she was worried that Great Britain might get involved. There were also rumblings about a man named Adolph Hitler who was causing concern in Europe. Although Europe seemed so far away Eleanor knew that any troubles there could involve British troops being sent to fight and with Leonard and her brothers being in their early twenties, they were the right age for 'cannon fodder' as her father had expressed one evening during dinner.

13

Not yet twenty Eleanor required her parents' written permission to be married, which was not a stumbling block. Eleanor and Leonard set the wedding date for the Saturday 5 August 1939. Like Jack and Kathleen, they too were to be married in the local Church and have a reception in the church hall.

With Eleanor's professional machining ability, she made her own wedding dress. It was white satin, to the floor, with leg o' mutton sleeves and a high, lacy collar. She would wear a circlet of artificial orange blossom on her head with a waist length veil and carry a bouquet of red carnations with Lily of the Valley interspersed. A delicate trail of greenery would hang down from the bouquet of flowers.

Eleanor had originally wanted Kathleen as Matron of Honour, but Kathleen was heavily pregnant with her first child, so it was out of the question. Leonard had a young sister named Ann. She was a shy twelve years old and needed some persuading. The promise of a day at the zoo, after the wedding, changed her mind. The bridesmaid's dress was also made by Eleanor and in blue taffeta with a large satin bow on one hip. A circlet of artificial white daisies would be on Ann's head, and she would carry a small posy of Lily of the Valley.

Local caterers were engaged for the sit-down reception. The wedding cake was to be made by a local baker in Kennington Park Road. It was to be a square, two-tier fruit cake. Iced in white with springs of orange blossom at the lower four corners and a small silver vase (loaned by the bakery) on top with more orange blossom. The cake would stand on a silver and mirror base, also kindly loaned by the bakery.

Leonard had had little to do with the wedding preparations preferring to leave them to Eleanor and her mother but was consulted on a few matters considering he was offering to pay for half of the wedding. He did, however, return to the jeweller shop and purchased a plain gold wedding band for Eleanor called D shape. Eleanor's parents would have loved to have paid for everything, but their finances would not run to it, and they wanted Eleanor to have a wonderful wedding with good lasting memories.

One wedding item that Eleanor would not agree to was a car to take her to the church, which was only a few streets away. She said that she could not condone such a waste of money. She was happy to walk through the streets in her wedding dress and enjoy the looks of neighbours. Her parents were horrified. Leonard took it in his stride. If she did not want a car, then she would not have a car. However, he had other ideas. As Leonard worked as a porter at Covent Garden market, he had numerous contacts who could help him with his request. He had a friend named Joe with a horse and flat-topped cart who agreed to take the bride to the church free of charge. He also said that he would spruce the horse and cart up to make Leonard proud. There would be three chairs on the cart for Eleanor, John and Ann and he would ensure lots of flowers would surround them. It was certainly going to be a surprise to Eleanor as she exited her home.

On the actual wedding day and true to his word, Joe arrived outside the house prior to Eleanor's departure. The black horse's coat was gleaming from hours of brushing and he had small white ribbons tied into his mane as bows. The paintwork on the cart shone and flowers adorned the floor of the cart. Joe had provided a set of short steps for Eleanor and the others to allow access to the chairs. Joe had even dressed up in a morning suit and top hat for the occasion.

The look on Eleanor's face when she came outside and saw it was one of total amazement and she burst into tears of happiness. Leonard had to rely on Joe's animated description of her reaction when he later saw him. From now on everything went to plan. With the horse trotting sedately through the streets Eleanor enjoyed the looks of passers-by and calls of good wishes. She responded with smiles and waves to complete strangers dabbing her eyes occasionally.

Leonard was anxiously waiting in front of the altar but as the organ started up he could not help but turn to watch his beloved Eleanor walk down the aisle looking like a fairy princess. His heart raced and he had a lump come into his throat. She was the most beautiful sight he had ever seen.

The wedding ceremony went without a hitch. Everyone sang lustily to well-known hymns, especially 'All Things Bright and Beautiful', the first of the three hymns. When the vicar pronounced them man and wife Eleanor cried again, but with excitement. Outside the church they were greeted with confetti. It was only a short walk to the church hall, so the horse and cart was dispensed with after some obligatory photographs.

The sight of the church hall laid out with tables, chairs, white tablecloths and decorations brought tears to Eleanor's eyes again. Her mother and friends had taken it upon themselves to see to the decorating and kept it secret from Eleanor. She considered herself the luckiest woman alive that day.

After the meal and cake cutting, tables and chairs were rearranged along the walls so that there was sufficient floor space for dancing. A trio had been engaged for the evening and many of Eleanor and Leonard's friends were arriving to swell the numbers of guests. With alcohol freely flowing and everyone in high spirits it was time for the first dance by the newly married couple. Leonard wanted something lively, but Eleanor asked for 'Begin the Beguine'. This would always be their song.

A couple of months earlier Eleanor and Leonard had secured a small, rental flat not far from her parents in Paisley Road. It comprised three rooms. There was a bedroom, kitchen and living area. They shared the bathroom with other tenants in the three-storey house and the toilet was outside in the back garden. This was common, at the time, in London. Eleanor purchased some green and white gingham material and made curtains for the kitchen, adding their own touches to the flat with simple, basic furnishings.

After the wedding reception Eleanor relented and accepted a taxi ride to their new home. She hated wasting money and considered a taxi fare to be an extravagance. Leonard traditionally carried Eleanor over the threshold and even up the two flights of stairs to their rooms.

Once in their bedroom there was a degree of awkwardness as neither had seen the other naked before. Eleanor was aware of a man's body due to living with three men plus her mother had instructed her on what to expect, but Leonard had had to rely on men's magazines to know about the female form and what his mates had told him about women. Shyly they undressed together and slipped into bed naked. Leonard wanted to make love immediately but knew he had to take it slowly and arouse his new wife with gentle kissing and fondling. The intimacy arrived and despite some small pain Eleanor enjoyed the experience. Lying in each other's arms they both fell asleep.

Next morning Leonard rolled over and could not help but fondle Eleanor's breast. She did not resist, and another intimacy soon followed.

As it was now Sunday Eleanor and Leonard had been invited to a roast lunch at her parents' home. Lovemaking had been such a pleasure to them both that they lost track of time and finally arrived late for the lunch. Fortunately, no-one commented on their late arrival but both Eleanor and Leonard felt guilty.

Due to work commitments, for them both, there was no honeymoon plus Eleanor believed honeymoons to be a waste of money. 'Why pay for someone else's bed,' she would remark.

The newly found excitement of intimacy had no bounds. Their appetite for each other's body, at night, became insatiable. There was not an inch of each other's bodies that had not been explored and kissed.

14

The third of September 1939 saw Great Britain declare war on Nazi Germany. There had been rumblings for numerous years and stories of atrocities coming out of Europe but the invasion of Poland on the first of September brought things to a head. The shock of the declaration caught many Britons by surprise and the thought of their young men going off to war was not easily entertained. At first John talked to Jack, Jim and Leonard about not rushing to enlist. He thought the war would be over in a few weeks and he had bad memories of his own war experiences. He did not want his boys as cannon fodder.

Young, patriotic and undeterred by John's warning both Jack and Jim went to the recruitment office together and enlisted. Jack wanted the Army whilst Jim asked for Navy. Like John in the first World War, Jack was sent off for basic training and then sent to an unknown destination in Europe. Secrecy about troop deployment was crucial if the war was to be won in a shorter space of time as possible.

Jim was assigned to *HMS Wakeful*. It had a deployment of 110, and he soon made friends with his easy-going nature and was far more comfortable in the company of men.

A few weeks passed and Eleanor noticed that she was waking up each morning feeling nauseous. She had missed a period, too. Secretly she knew what was happening to her body and did not want to break the news to Leonard until she felt sure. Another couple of weeks passed and she broke the news to Leonard that she felt that she was pregnant. Leonard had noticed a couple of changes in Eleanor but chose not to comment on them, especially when she did not enjoy having her tender breasts fondled although she was still enjoying nightly intimacy. Leonard did worry that it might not be good for the baby, but Eleanor reassured him that all would be well.

A visit to her doctor in the Walworth Road confirmed her intuition and a date was calculated by the doctor using a formula. Their baby would be born the first week in May. Breaking the news to both sets of parents was easy and the excitement was only overshadowed by Leonard announcing that he would soon join the Royal Air Force. He felt that he should fight for his country as thousands of others but particularly his two brothers-in-law. Leonard was sent to an airfield, somewhere in Scotland. He was a member of ground crew, and his knowledge of motor car engines served him well with aircraft engines.

The next few months were a strain on everyone. No-one knew where their men were, and letters were infrequent and censored. Eleanor continued to work but spent a lot of time with her parents, especially her mother, always wanting to ask questions about motherhood.

It was the beginning of April 1940 when Eleanor woke to strong back pain. She was hoping that the baby was not coming yet as it was not due for at least another month. When her waters broke, she knew she just had to get to the hospital. Unable to contact her mother she gratefully accepted the unexpected offer from a neighbour with a motorbike and sidecar who said he would take her, in the sidecar, the short ride to the local hospital which she was most grateful for.

Alone in the hospital, unable to contact Leonard, Eleanor gave birth to a healthy son, albeit a bit early and underweight. The experience of childbirth was worse than Eleanor had expected but the end result was worth the pain, which was soon forgotten. Eleanor and Leonard had previously discussed names and so the baby was called David. Finally, her parents got the news and visited her. They managed to send a telegram to Leonard via the RAF and he in turn sent a reply. His whereabouts still unknown. The stay in hospital was two weeks, most of which she had to spend in bed with David beside her in a crib. She was breast-feeding David and he took to her breast well.

Back home, in their little flat, Eleanor and David bonded even more. She would count his little fingers and toes daily and kiss his little ears. She enjoyed bathing him daily and cuddling him close when drying him. Dusting him with baby powder reminded her of flouring pastry when she was a little girl and helped her mother making pies. David ate well and slept well. He was a perfect baby. The only thing missing was Leonard. Eleanor hoped and prayed that it would not be long before he could come home to her and their darling new son.

15

Six weeks after David's birth Jim was coming home on a weekend leave pass. He was bringing a shipmate with him who lived in the North of England and would not be able to get home and back to his ship in the period allotted to them. Everyone was delighted to see Jim again. He looked resplendent in his naval uniform. He introduced his friend Arthur Grimshaw, also in uniform. A large man with blond hair and a strapping physique. His nose showed that it had been broken and Jim told everyone that Arthur had been a professional boxer prior to the war. His name was Gorilla Grimshaw in the boxing world.

Both Jim and Arthur were keen to go dancing that night, hoping to meet some pretty girls so Mary suggested they take Eleanor and her friend Rita and make a foursome. At first Eleanor was not keen, she was worried about David and knew that he would need a feed and who would look after him. Mary had it all worked out including having David for the night at her home. She thought it would do Eleanor good to get out for a change instead of staying at home mothering all the time. Reluctantly Eleanor agreed and left some expressed milk for David's feeds.

Wearing a pretty, red floral dress and black, small-heeled shoes, her hair loose to her shoulders Eleanor and Rita went dancing with Jim and Arthur. Eleanor did not expect to be partnered with her brother Jim, so it was Arthur that danced with her, held her too tightly to him and tried to kiss her whilst on the dance floor. Eleanor was feeling repulsed and told Arthur that she was a married woman, pointing out her wedding ring and that she had only recently become a mother. This did not seem to deter his amorous advances and his insistence that they danced every dance.

When the evening was over the four of them started walking home. Jim offered to see Rita to her home, and they turned off a couple of streets before Eleanor's home. Arthur had been treating her better after she had been firm with him about her status but as they neared the front door, she began to feel somewhat uncomfortable. Before she could put her key in the lock Arthur clamped his large sweaty hand over her mouth, hoisted her off her feet and slammed her against the porch wall. He threatened to kill her if she screamed when he removed his hand. With his other sweaty hand he quickly went under her skirt and ripped her knickers off. He fumbled with his uniform and pulled out his penis. Eleanor could not believe what was happening to her. She seemed to freeze. He spread her legs and thrust his hard erect penis into Eleanor so brutally that she felt part of her tear and she began to bleed. Undeterred, Arthur thrust time and again and at the same time managed to squeeze her milk laden breasts, causing her milk to flow with his rough handling. In no time his desires were met. Eleanor's milk quickly darkened the material of her dress. This man was so strong she had no defence against him, and her screams were trapped in her throat.

As quickly as it had all begun Arthur put Eleanor back to the ground and tidied himself up. He thanked her for a pleasant evening and then walked away laughing.

Eleanor was bewildered. She raced indoors with tears streaming down her face and could not wait to take her clothes off. She grabbed a bowl of water and started to wash herself in the kitchen. No time to go to the bathroom. She needed to wash all traces of the incident away. Getting into bed, naked, she felt as though her whole body was hurting. Her head was aching, and she could not stem the flow of tears, soaking into her pillow. Sleep eluded her as she ran the incident through her head continuously.

Next day, after throwing the dress, bra and torn knickers in the dustbin, she went to collect David from Mary's home but avoided seeing either Jim or Arthur. She wanted to tell her mother everything that had happened, but circumstances would not permit. Mary commented that she did not look herself and Eleanor feigned a headache. She would wait until the weekend leave was over and the boys had gone. She even declined a meal with them just wanting to get away from the horrible monster. Jim was disappointed that he did not get to say goodbye to Eleanor but accepted that he did not understand women.

On the following Monday Eleanor was due to return to the hospital for David to be checked and herself to have a post-natal examination. She cancelled both appointments telling the hospital staff that they both had gastric upsets. She avoided making a new appointment, too. She also decided that she would not tell Mary as she did not want it to reflect badly on Jim. This was a dark secret that she would keep to herself forever.

A few days after the traumatic event Eleanor felt much better. She had her regular routine of breast-feeding David and the soreness below had also eased. Thinking all was now well Eleanor did not tell her mother what had happened but did comment that she did not like Arthur and her mother agreed with her. Mary found him obnoxious and overbearing. She could not think how Jim could have befriended Arthur, but Jim was soft-hearted and probably hearing that Arthur could not get home kindly offered Arthur an option, which he gladly accepted.

16

Life in London carried on, almost as normal, considering it was wartime whilst there was a massive evacuation taking place at Dunkirk. HMS Wakeful was involved in evacuating 640 men and heading towards Dover when disaster struck. Two German e-boat torpedoes hit the ship causing massive explosions. The ship quickly sank. Only two of the 640 evacuees survived whilst twenty-five of the crew of 110 also survived. Sadly, Jim was not one of them nor was Arthur. The date was 29 May 1940.

John and Mary were numb with shock when they received the news. Their beloved, gentle son was gone. They had only seen him three weeks earlier and he was so full of life at sea and considering signing on after the war. Telegrams were sent to Jack and Leonard. Eleanor and David moved back in with her parents for a short time whilst affairs needed to be put in order. The Navy advised that there was no chance of his body being returned, he may have gone down with the ship.

No body, no funeral, no last resting place. A watery grave. All that was left for the family was photographs and memories of happier times. The shock seemed to affect John more than they realised.

Back in her own little flat, time had passed, and Eleanor became aware that her body was changing again. She was still breast-feeding David but again feeling nauseous in the morning. Ignoring it for a couple more weeks Eleanor finally came to the realisation that she was pregnant again. A visit to the doctor again confirmed her suspicions. Choking back the tears Eleanor told the doctor what had happened. He listened sympathetically and told her that he could arrange a termination in the case of rape, or she could keep the child. Either way she must tell her husband as soon as possible. Taking pity on Eleanor he arranged, with the RAF, for Leonard to have Compassionate leave, which was quickly granted.

17

Once home, between sobs, Eleanor told Leonard everything that had happened that night and how dirty and ashamed she felt. Compounding the situation was the fact that the father of the child was now dead. Eleanor never thought she would ever have to say the word, but she asked Leonard if he wanted a divorce. Leonard listened in disbelief and shaking his head on hearing such a brutal tale. At first Leonard wanted to hold his young wife but when she raised her hands to stop him, he felt rejected. This made Leonard angry, and he started walking around the room shouting, balling his fists and then thumping the kitchen table. He did not know if he was angry with Eleanor, Arthur or the word divorce. He was confused. His wonderful world was crumbling in front of his eyes. His shouting had woken David who was now screaming. Walking out the door and slamming it behind him Leonard started walking the streets. He thought of going to the pub and getting drunk but instead he roamed the streets until he found John keeping watch over another gaping trench.

Falling on his knees in front of John he told him the sorry tale. John was shocked but placed a caring hand on his shoulder and got Leonard to rise. Sitting together the two men talked through what Leonard had told him. John said that he could not advise how the situation should be handled but Leonard should think about his son David and what a divorce might do to him and his relationship with Leonard in years to come. Accepting a cup of tea with John, Leonard felt much better. His anger had subsided, but he now harboured hate for a man he never met.

When he went back home Eleanor was already in bed and David fast asleep in his cot. Leonard decided to sleep in the armchair fearing that his own wants would not be met tonight.

A hungry David woke Eleanor and Leonard. Eleanor took David to her bed and commenced breast-feeding. Leonard came into the room and was overwhelmed with emotion at the sight in front of him. His lovely young wife and their beautiful son.

Once David was sufficiently satisfied and resettled in his cot, Leonard asked Eleanor if they might talk in the kitchen. He told her how he had spoken to her father, who was equally shocked at what Eleanor had been through but was able to lead Leonard to a decision without influencing him. If it was what Eleanor wanted, and she was the only one who should decide on the baby's future, then he would accept another man's child and raise it as his own. It would mean that family and friends would know it was not Leonard's by the timing, but he was prepared to face the consequences.

With Leonard's short compassionate leave due to end Eleanor informed him that she would keep the child. The thought of a fatherless child given away through no fault of his or her own weighed heavily of Eleanor's mind. At least she could give this baby a biological mother. She knew of a couple of unmarried girls at work who were forced to give up their babies because they could not support them alone. On his final night home Eleanor and Leonard were able to enjoy each other in an intimate way and Eleanor felt that their love was stronger.

18

Although a war was raging in Europe life in London had not been affected too much. People were still able to work, albeit women doing men's jobs whilst their menfolk were fighting overseas. Food rationing was introduced in January 1940 which made people careful in their buying habits and resourceful in their meal making.

No-one knew how long the war would last or what Nazi Germany was capable of inflicting on Britain, but people were encouraged to evacuate to the country, particularly if they had children or to build air raid shelters in their back gardens. Where John and Mary were living there was no possibility of building a shelter, but people were informed that they could make use of the platforms at the nearest underground station should the event arise. The platforms were many feet underground.

Without warning the first of the bombs hit England on 7 September 1940. At first, bombs were falling on heavily industrialised areas and docklands in London and Liverpool. This was the beginning of the Blitz and would continue until 11 May 1941. Loss of civilian life and property was huge.

With the bombing came the blackout. No lights were to be seen anywhere. John's employment as a night watchman was terminated as he would not be able to light lamps around the trenches. Instead, the gas company dug shorter lengths of trench during the day and the labourers had to make sure they were filled in by day's end.

So, John decided that he would be better employed helping his fellow man and became an air raid warden. He could guide people to shelter and assist the fire brigade, if need be, despite his poor health. During his patrol he would call out *'Put that light out'* to any careless people breaking the blackout rule.

The home of Jack and Kathleen was one of the first casualties of the war, as they were living near the docks at the time. With Jack fighting abroad Kathleen decided to take their, now, two children Patrick and Colleen back to family in Trim, County Meath, Ireland. They made a hasty departure, but Kathleen felt that there was nothing worth staying in London for, especially with their home and all their possessions now a pile of rubble.

Similarly, Eleanor thought she might be better off with David and her pregnancy to move back home with Mary and John. At least she would be saving on the rent of their flat and could go down the underground with her mother, if need be, whilst her father was out on patrol. Eleanor bought David an all-in-one suit called a Siren Suit. With him dressed snugly she could grab him one handed and know that he would be safe and warm without needing blankets.

Christmas was only a couple of weeks away when John started to have chest pains and coughing a lot. He was also having difficulty in breathing. He was not one to go to the doctor preferring Mary's home treatments such as cough syrup and paregoric sweets. The sweets had opium in the manufacturing process. He did take himself to an herbalist in the Walworth Road for sarsaparilla believing that his blood needed cleansing. He continued going to work despite Mary warning him to keep his chest well covered and to keep out of any draughts.

David was nine months old when his first Christmas arrived. He was a bonny baby with his father's looks, dark hair and blue eyes. He laughed a lot and got great joy tearing off the wrapping paper on the wooden toy train that John had made. There were none of the usual Christmas festivities in John and Mary's house due to the blitz and Jim's death, but they felt that David should have some festive experience. John's health continued to worry Mary. He seemed to be getting worse. On New Year's Eve John collapsed. He was admitted to the local hospital where he passed away from pneumonia. He was 58 years old. His death reminded Mary of a previous Christmas when her first, unnamed grandchild died. She hoped that she would not start to dread Christmas.

John's funeral was low key with few mourners due to the war. John was interred in Streatham Cemetery where both his parents were laid to rest. It would be sometime before Mary could afford a marble head-stone in his memory.

After John's death Mary was unable to continue paying the rent on the house, they were living in, so another move was on the cards to a smaller house. This meant moving to an area quite away from where she was used to and getting used to new bus routes and shops. However, Eleanor and David continued living with Mary. Mary was still managing to do some early morning office cleaning, but never sure if her workplace would still be standing due to the bombing. She encouraged Eleanor to look for some part-time work, as a machinist, whilst she would look after David during the day. Although visibly pregnant Eleanor did manage to secure a machinist job in a nearby factory that was producing army uniforms and really enjoyed the chance to earn some money, enjoy a change of scenery and socialising with the other women. She had not realised how she had missed female companionship and hearing other's stories of their lives.

19

St Valentine's Day, 1941. A day for lovers. Also, the day that Derek was born. Eleanor looked down at her new son, strong and a healthy eight pounder. Despite the ordeal that she had experienced conceiving him she still had much love for the child. After all, she was his mother. When she told Mary about the name, she had chosen Mary said it was nice but secretly she always thought Derek sounded like earache, or perhaps it was Eric? Leonard was advised of his new son and the name having played no part in the decision making process.

Months passed and Derek grew quickly and always seemed to be hungry. He was even wearing the same size clothing as his older brother David with barely ten and half months between them. When his hair started to grow it was blond. Just like his father's. In fact, Eleanor could see Arthur in her son and tried hard to ignore the strong resemblance.

Eleanor even managed to go back to work but opted for full-time as the money was much needed. She could not expect Mary to earn enough to keep them and pay the rent which she had done on numerous occasions. There was an allowance that came through from the RAF for Eleanor, but it was not great. The lack of money had been a constant throughout Eleanor's life she recalled.

Leonard came home on a weekend pass in July 1942 due to a reposting to another airfield, closer to home, was all he would say. The weekend coincided with his birthday so of course Eleanor and Leonard celebrated in their favourite way. Later, lying in each other's arms they talked about the future and what they would like to do once the war was over. They had no idea how much longer it would continue. Eleanor wanted their own house with a garden for the boys and perhaps a small dog. Leonard smiled as he listened. He loved to hear Eleanor's voice and he would love to give her what she wanted but it would mean getting a good job one day. Still, he knew that dreams could come true.

It did not take long for Eleanor to recognise the signs that her body was changing again. Unlike her two previous pregnancies, though, Eleanor was experiencing severe bouts of morning sickness and munched on ginger nut biscuits throughout the morning until the nausea subsided. She sensed that this might indicate a change of sex for this baby. At least her attitude towards this baby was different. This baby had been made with love and although she did not treat David and Derek differently, memories of the rape often re-emerged when she was alone with Derek. Recognising it was not the child's fault she still had flashbacks.

On May Day, 1943 Eleanor woke to strong contractions and had sufficient time to get a taxi to the local hospital where she was delivered of a beautiful daughter with rosebud lips and a healthy weight. Having discussed names with Leonard, prior to the birth, she was named Diane May Lipton. The family was complete. Once back home with Mary and the boys, life fell into a regular pattern of child rearing, full-time work and trying to exist on food rationing. Unfortunately, another house move had to be undertaken with the help of friends.

20

By the age of two Diane had grown into a pretty, little girl with chestnut brown hair like Eleanor. She also resembled Eleanor. Diane was a happy and bright child and quick to learn like her brother David. Derek seemed to be the odd one out. Diane loved playing with the boys and became quite a tomboy, but Eleanor made sure she still dressed her like a little girl. In fact, she would try to make Diane a new dress each week but had to resort to buying boys-wear for David and Derek.

Schooling for the two boys had been disrupted due to the constant moving houses and the war, so Eleanor and Mary ensured that time was dedicated to them both to learn reading, writing and arithmetic, the basic three R's as it was known. Whilst David showed great promise in his studies Derek was not so bright.

Eleanor would often refer to her three children as the 3 D's. It seemed easier than saying their names in full even though she still had an aversion to shortened or nicknames.

Six years and one day since the start of World War 2 it was finally over. As Leonard was based in England, he was quickly demobbed from the air force but faced the daunting task of being a real father to his three children aged 6, 5 and 2. He sometimes said 'come to Uncle Leonard.' Eleanor used to laugh and tell him to say Daddy. It took a short while of adjustment for Leonard and the children.

Celebrations took place all over Great Britain at the end of the war and there was a good feeling of optimism even though things like rationing would continue for come some time to come.

Leonard and Eleanor decided that they should find their own accommodation and found a small house close to Mary. It suited the situation as Mary would continue to look after the children whilst both Eleanor and Leonard worked full-time. Leonard's ground crew work in the Royal Air Force had given him skills in both mechanical and electrical work. Armed with his new skills he approached an electricity supply company and landed a job as an electrician. Ironically his first job was the wiring of new concrete lamp posts, in each street, to replace the gaslights, unaware of John's prediction years previously 'that electricity would never take over his lamp lighting job'. His mechanical skills were often utilised by friends and neighbours, who were lucky enough to own vehicles, especially those that had been in storage throughout the war and needed servicing.

When Jack finally came home, from serving overseas, it was good to see that he appeared unscathed, but no-one would really know the mental anguish that he endured at the sights seen and the actions he had taken. Like thousands of other ex-servicemen and women it was never mentioned, just bottled up. Jack said that he had to search for the family through previous addresses before finally locating them. He soon informed Mary that he would be going to live in Ireland with Kathleen and the children. Mary was not surprised and after a short stay with them, in cramped conditions, left to re-join his family. Mary sent him away with a heavy heart but put on a brave face. She felt that she was losing yet another son.

21

As if living through a war was not enough, February 1947 heralded severe winter conditions and caused major cuts in power supply due to shortages of fuel in England and Wales. It was the coldest February with a maximum average of 28.6 degrees F, for any month since records began in 1878. Everyone shivered.

Eleanor felt that her life was now complete. Her husband was back home unscathed, remembering how her poor father had returned from war, she had three healthy children and she still had Mary. Life could not be better, could it?

Wrapped up well, Leonard had left for work and Eleanor was just putting coats, hats and gloves on the children, ready to take to Mary's before setting off for work herself. She heard the familiar plop of a letter on the front door mat and went to retrieve it. Eleanor would always remember the day an official looking letter arrived addressed to her although not the date. She looked at the envelope for a few minutes turning it over in her hands wondering what it might be. She carefully slit the edge of the envelope with a kitchen knife and withdrew the single page letter. It was from Sully & Sykes Solicitors, well-known and based in Central London. It informed her that she was the beneficiary of a Will and requesting her to make an appointment to attend their offices, in the very near future, to hear of the bequest. She should bring along evidence of her birth and marriage to the interview. Eleanor was confused. Who did she know that would leave her something in a Will? They must have the wrong person she thought and left the letter on the kitchen table whilst she went to Mary's. She mentioned the letter to Mary who was as equally perplexed. That evening she showed the letter to Leonard who could throw no light on the contents. He said that the only way she would find out would be to make the appointment as requested, joking that she might become rich like winning the football pools.

Needing to take a day off work, without pay, Eleanor attended the Solicitor's offices arriving before her appointment time. The building was large and daunting, and the interior was mainly a very dark panelled wood. The offices were on the first floor, so Eleanor took the tiled stairs rather than enter the small, gated lift. The female secretary showed Eleanor to a leather covered chair, outside one of the offices, and told to wait until Mr Sully was ready to see her.

After a few minutes, the door opened, and Eleanor was ushered in and asked to be seated. Dressed in her best brown houndstooth checked, short jacket, over a brown corduroy skirt, cream coloured cotton blouse and wearing cleaned black shoes, Eleanor was seated across a large mahogany desk from Mr Sully. Charles Sully reminded Eleanor of a kindly old headmaster. Guessing that he could be aged about 60 or more, he had thinning grey hair, a nicotine-stained moustache and very blue eyes. He placed his gold rimmed *pince-nez* on the bridge of his nose. Before proceeding, he asked Eleanor for her proof of identity documents. Eleanor produced her birth and marriage certificates and asked for an explanation as to why she was there, telling Mr Sully that she thought they had contacted the wrong person. Mr Sully examined the two certificates and told Eleanor that he was satisfied that she was the right person.

He then picked up a document and commenced to read out. '*This is the last Will and Testament of Mrs Eleanor Beauchamp, widow, of Hillside House, Lucknow, India*'. Eleanor let out an audible gasp, which caused Mr Sully to stop reading. He asked Eleanor if there was a problem. Eleanor gave a little laugh and explained that the lady he was referring to was always known as the Indian Aunt. She went on to add that it was, in fact, a family nickname which came about when her father was a young boy and when told that his Indian Aunt was coming to visit imagined her to be a North American Indian squaw. His imagination fired by a Wild West book in his possession. Despite the passage of time Eleanor said that she was unaware of the lady's real name until he had just said it. Mr Sully smiled when he heard the story.

Once she had composed herself Mr Sully continued. The lady, in question, had died in 1942 but with disruptions to the mail service and difficulties in locating John's family that everything had taken much longer to finalise. In fact, a private investigator was hired to locate Eleanor due to her constant moving around after it was established that John had passed away. Mrs Beauchamp had not been aware of the death of John and therefore the Will was not as straightforward as Great Aunt Eleanor would have liked. Mr Sully continued. Without disclosing the other bequests, he told Eleanor that in the event of her father pre-deceasing Mrs Beauchamp then his bequest of an amount of money would automatically go to Eleanor, and this, in fact, had been the case.

In addition to the money, Mrs Beauchamp had left Eleanor a valuable gold bangle. Mr Sully actually had it in his safe and went off to retrieve it. On his return he handed Eleanor a red leather rectangular box with a tooled gold trim. With trembling fingers Eleanor lifted the lid on the box and lying in a bed of silk was a beautiful gold bangle encrusted with precious stones of different colours in a line. Eleanor removed the bangle carefully and turned the bangle this way and that to catch the light. There were seven stones and Mr Sully watched Eleanor's frown. By way of explanation Mr Sully pointed to the first stone, a diamond and said to Eleanor to remember the initial D. The next stone was an emerald. This time he said E. The third stone was an amethyst and he said A. This still was making no sense to Eleanor. The fourth stone was a ruby, and the initial R. Another emerald and another E. The sixth stone Mr Sully said was a sapphire and the initial S. Finally, the last stone was a topaz and the initial T. Mr Sully asked Eleanor if she had been remembering the initials and she said she had. They spelt the word DEAREST. Mr Sully went on with the story of how Mr Beauchamp had presented the bangle to his wife on their 25th wedding anniversary, having bought it on one of their rare trips back to England. Eleanor replaced the bangle back in its box and placed it carefully on Mr Sully's large mahogany desk.

Still unsure of what was happening to her and trying to still her shaking hands by holding them tightly in her lap Eleanor asked what the next steps were. Mr Sully said that he would draw up some papers and contact her again now that they had her address but added he would appreciate being notified should she move again. He would retain the jewellery until everything was finalised, and if she needed guidance on how to sell the bangle, at a later date, should she wish, he would be only too willing to assist her in that field. Eleanor asked about the rest of the estate. 'Was it left to Great Aunt Eleanor's children?' she asked. Mr Sully explained that Mrs Beauchamp failed to have any issue, due to a health problem, but always felt that her nephew John had named his daughter in her honour. She had received informative and descriptive letters about all the family members, from John, over the years, and felt a special bond and interest towards the child despite never ever meeting her. His final remark was that any monies left after all fees, etc was to be given to the Red Cross, a charity that Mrs Beauchamp had supported most of her life.

Eleanor rose and shook hands with Mr Sully before leaving. She could not explain how she felt. Her mind was in turmoil with the information she had received and could still visualise the bangle and the gleaming stones. Almost on auto pilot Eleanor made her way home again awaiting Mary to bring the children back and Leonard to come home from work.

Trying to hold back her exciting news Eleanor prepared tea for Leonard and the children and had invited Mary to stay. Despite Leonard's insistence to know what had happened that day Eleanor kept putting him off. Not wanting to speak in front of the children Eleanor told Leonard and Mary that she would reveal all about her appointment after tea. Despite an appetising meal, that she had prepared, Eleanor found that she had little appetite. The news she had was almost bursting inside her.

Finally, when the meal was over, she sent the children to play in the bedroom and closed the door on them. Shaking and trying to remember the sequence of events Eleanor told Leonard and Mary of her sudden and quite substantial inheritance. Leonard and Mary just sat there. Words failed them whilst they tried to digest what they had just heard. Leonard was first to get up and hug Eleanor tightly and then Mary pushed him aside so she could hug her daughter. The news was certainly going to change a lot of things in their lives and needed some careful thinking plus guidance from Mr Sully as to the best way to handle such a windfall.

22

Eleanor and Leonard talked about the inheritance every day when they were together out of earshot of the children. Leonard insisted that as it was Eleanor's inheritance, she should make the decisions regarding how she would spend it. Eleanor was generous to a fault and said that she considered the inheritance a belonging to all the immediate family but certainly would not squander it.

Writing down a 'wish list' Eleanor considered a house with a garden was the main priority. Closely followed by a small second-hand car, although Leonard enjoyed riding his pushbike to and from work each day. Eleanor would not leave her mother out of any changes in lifestyle and if they could not find a four bedroomed home to accommodate them and Mary then she would look at buying a small flat near to them for Mary. She had not thought about how much she would send to Jack and Kathleen, but they would get something considering part of her inheritance was also their late father's share.

Eleanor and Leonard started scouring the houses for sale sections of newspapers. Eleanor's preference was Herne Hill or Brixton Hill. She thought about Dulwich but decided that would be beyond their reach before knowing how much she would have.

Some weeks later Eleanor received a letter from Mr Sully inviting her to attend his office again. This time Eleanor would take Leonard.

Leonard looked around the wood panelled office, noted the large mahogany desk and felt some trepidation. He had never had dealings with solicitors before and was unsure what to expect and decided to keep his mouth closed and let Eleanor and Mr Sully deal with everything. The one item of office decor that did surprise Leonard was an aspidistra, in a brass pot, in a corner of the room by a large opaque glass window. It reminded Leonard of his grandmother's home. So old fashioned, he thought.

To begin with Mr Sully informed them of the final amount of money that could be written on a cheque, in Eleanor's name. With this information both Eleanor and Leonard gasped. The amount was beyond their wildest dreams and would certainly pay for a substantial home in Dulwich Village. Mr Sully then suggested some types of investments that might suit Eleanor's windfall, but a bank manager would be better placed to advise her, when she deposited the cheque.

The conversation then turned to the bangle and Mr Sully withdrew it from his desk drawer to show Leonard. Again, Leonard gasped. He was almost afraid to take it from the silk lined box. Mr Sully asked Eleanor if she had made a decision on what she wanted to do with the bangle. Eleanor told Mr Sully that she and Leonard had discussed the bangle and as much a she would like to keep it, she could never see herself wearing it and would worry constantly that it might get stolen. Mr Sully said that if she trusted him to sell the bangle, through a reputable auction house, he believed that she would receive yet another considerable sum. The amount of money that was now running through Eleanor's head was making her feel dizzy. She asked for a glass of water, but Mr Sully had arranged for a tray of tea to be brought in with an undetected touch of a button on his telephone. When the secretary brought the tea in Mr Sully asked for water, too.

Mr Sully asked Eleanor and Leonard to be patient. The bangle would need to be sold and any outstanding fees would also need to be recovered from monies.

Eleanor said that she understood, but she would like to start looking for a house for them all. Mr Sully told her that it was, quite in order, for her to do that, but to keep him informed to ensure she did not overcommit herself. Eleanor did not feel that was a possibility now that she knew the amount of money coming her way.

23

The London Olympics was happening in 1948 and the cycling events were to be held at Herne Hill Velodrome, built in 1891. As Herne Hill was an area that Eleanor was interested in, she increased her endeavours to find a suitable house mainly through trolling through the newspapers. Leonard was interested in cycling, and he encouraged her to look at houses in Herne Hill. With their name lodged with three real estate agents it was not long before they had several suitable houses to look at. There were two houses that would suit their requirements, but one was in Burbage Road. The Velodrome was located off Burbage Road and house prices were beginning to rise due to the Olympic Games venue. Undeterred by rising prices, Eleanor and Leonard knew that they had the final say but on a second viewing of the Burbage Road property, they took Mary and the children with them. Being a sunny, Saturday they were able to look around the surrounding area first and in particular the velo-drome. The two boys were so excited.

The house was two-storey red brick with a tiled roof and a single attached garage on one side. There was a small wall between the garden and the pavement with a small wooden gate to the gravel path. There were two more low gates across the gravel driveway. The window frames were painted dark green. Opening the door of number 36, light seemed to stream in from all directions. The lounge was situated on the right with a staircase on the left. Next to the lounge, along the hall-way was a dining room with French doors to the large rear garden, just right for growing vegetables, thought Mary, and straight ahead was the kitchen which also led out to the garden through a back door. Upstairs there were four bedrooms, one quite small located over the front porch with an interesting round shaped window. David commented that it looked like a ship's porthole. Diane immediately claimed it as hers, whilst the two boys wanted to share one of the two rear bed-rooms which overlooked the Herne Hill Velodrome. Eleanor and Leonard would have the front bedroom and Mary said that she would be content to be any-where. Although happy with the house Eleanor had decided that each room would need to be wallpapered as she was not keen on the existing wallpaper and perhaps the paintwork could be updated from green to cream. The outside window frames would also need repainting in another colour at some stage, but that was a job for Leonard. After informing Mr Sully of their intentions and getting his approval, it was now left to the real estate agent to finalise the paperwork and give them a date when they could move in.

24

Back home and the weather warming Eleanor suggested to Leonard that they might be able to afford a week's holiday in a caravan. Eleanor had never stayed in a caravan before but had conjured up how much fun it would be for the family. Unfortunately, Mary would not be able to come due to the small size of the caravan. An advertisement in the window of a local newsagent sounded just the thing they were looking for and would not cost too much. The caravan was situated on-site at Southend-on-Sea, a coastal town that Eleanor had never visited before but then she had not travelled anywhere, apart from London, and the family could get a cheap fare with Winter's Coaches, a local coach company, to get them there. There was also a train that would get them there but was dearer. Eleanor was struggling to spend her newly acquired wealth after years of penny pinching and this holiday would be no different.

On a Saturday morning, with the sun shining brightly and spirits high it was time for a new adventure. Despite her misgivings about wasteful expenditure, Eleanor agreed with Leonard to take a taxi ride to the bus terminal where the coach would be waiting. Leonard was thinking about carrying suitcases not cost. The children were thrilled at the experience. Packed for their holiday the family set off dressed in their 'Sunday best'. The children were well behaved never having travelled in a coach before, but then Eleanor had always instilled good manners in her three children. The family sat on the back seat of the coach as it had five seats across. She let the boys sit either side so that they could enjoy the view out of the side windows whilst Diane sat looking down the centre aisle.

The coach trip only took a couple of hours and soon they were standing on the Promenade breathing in the ozone. Diane did not like the smell, she thought it was fishy. Eleanor looked at the beach and where the sea should be but did not express her disappointment. She was unaware that she was looking at a tidal estuary for the river Thames. The tide was out, and Southend showed its famous mud flats. She was surprised to see an extremely long pier and decided that would be a destination on one of the days of the holiday. At least the sun was shining.

Leonard carried the two large suitcases, borrowed from a workmate, the short walk to the caravan park which fronted the Promenade. The caravan was sited with a view to the mud flats. The bottom half of the caravan was painted dark green whilst the top half was painted cream. Leonard banged his head on the top of the door frame when entering. He would make a mental note to duck his head in future. The interior of the caravan was compact but cosy with pretty chintz curtains. The boys quickly opted for the two side beds which were seating during the day, each with a side window. Diane would sleep in the large, pull down, bed beneath another window, with Eleanor and Leonard. All beds needed to be made each evening. Lack of storage meant that after unpacking a few things they would need to live out of the suitcases for the week. There was a small gas stove an oven and a sink. All very basic, but Eleanor had nothing to compare it with, so she was impressed. There was a toilet block nearby, too. The children thought it was fun having to walk to the toilet block in their pyjamas.

Eleanor decided that it was time for them to take a walk and explore the new surroundings. A short walk along the Promenade brought them to a row of variety retail shops. The two boys ran on ahead and stopped at the ice cream shop. Eleanor could not help but smile as she ordered ice creams all round and paid for them without a qualm. The boys then found a shop that sold buckets and spades as well as comic postcards. The saucy Donald McGill postcards, on a revolving stand, put a smile on Eleanor and Leonard's faces, some were quite naughty. Eleanor relented again and bought the children a bucket and spade each, of their choice, and a picture postcard to write and send back to Mary. Walking further along the whole family stood mesmerized at the window of a shop watching a man make seaside rock from a long sausage shaped piece of candy. He pulled it and twisted it, threw it over a large metal hook and contorted it in many ways, making the large sausage shape slimmer each time. The piece of candy and how the man was handling it reminded Eleanor of a large python that she had once seen on a cinema screen. Eleanor's emotions were soaring. This was going to be a very, special week.

Sunday dawned overcast and Diane woke early. She opened the push out window above the bed. She could see a flock of turkeys on the other side of the nearby fence and started to call out to them. The turkeys erupted in a cacophony of gobbling noises which woke everyone in the caravan and probably other caravans, too. Diane was asked not to call out in future but to wait until she could stand by the fence and call.

The children were dressed in shorts and cotton tops for a short walk to the beach again, but at least the tide was coming in and the day was not too cold. The family walked down some steps to the beach. The children changed into their swimming costumes and armed with their colourful tin buckets and spades, with wooden handles, soon started digging in the mud and making sandcastles. Unfortunately, they were also getting quite dirty as there was a lot of oil in the mud. Eleanor suggested they walked into the sea to wash the dirt off, but they just seemed to get dirtier. Back at the caravan site Eleanor took all three children into the toilet block and washed them thoroughly. She would need a rethink about the beach.

Monday brought the rain. Undeterred and having bought plastic mackintoshes for them all on their way, the family headed for the pier. Apparently, it was the longest one in the world, but Eleanor was not interested in statistics. The children seemed quite happy to be walking and walking and walking, but the return trip was a different story. Diane refused to walk back so Leonard had to carry her on his back, piggyback style. The boys were too big to be carried but moaned constantly about how tired they were feeling and that their feet were hurting. Trying to cheer everyone up it was unanimously decided that fish and chips would satisfy everyone. It did for a short while.

Back at the caravan Eleanor started to dry any clothing that had got wet whilst they were out. It was not an easy task in such confined quarters and only the oven to provide sufficient heat. The condensation soon fogged up all the windows and the children enjoyed drawing pictures, on the fogged glass, with their fingers.

Leonard had thought to bring a pack of playing cards, so whilst Diane played with her doll Leonard and Eleanor taught the boys some card tricks and card games. The game of Snap soon has everyone laughing and shouting. Eleanor and Leonard made sure that the boys won every game.

Tuesday, Wednesday and Thursday brought more rain and more unhappy faces, especially the children. Leonard went to the shops and bought a couple of jigsaw puzzles and an early reader for Diane. The cramped environment was beginning to take its toll. The boys wanted to go home. Eleanor and Leonard were trying to make the best of the experience and had everyone sing songs or play charades. Diane could not fathom charades.

Friday brought out the sunshine again. A short trip to the beach but without the children entering the water. It was too hard cleaning them up afterwards. Eleanor sent Leonard to a nearby shop for a beach tray. This consisted of a tray, a pot of tea for two, two cups, two saucers, a small jug of milk and a small bowl of sugar. The cost was reasonable but there was a hefty deposit of ten shillings for the beach tray. This ensured that the tray was always returned. No-one could afford to lose out on ten shillings. The children shared a bottle of fizzy drink using some cups borrowed from the caravan.

More walking for everyone and some souvenir shopping. Eleanor and Leonard treated themselves to some cockles and whelks served on small saucers from a street stall. The children preferred candy floss and Diane had some stick to the front of her hair when she tried to take a big bite. Returning to the seaside rock shop Eleanor bought each child a small stick of rock with the words Southend-on-Sea printed through it. She also bought one for Mary together with a pretty, ceramic vase, with a picture of Southend Pier emblazoned across it and the words 'Souvenir of Southend-on-Sea'.

Eleanor had seen, next door to the fish shop, an advertisement sandwich board for a palmist, Madame Enid. Eleanor's curiosity got the better of her and she left Leonard minding the children whilst she went in to have her palm read. The interior of the shop was dark and there was a strong smell of incense which made Eleanor cough at first. Madame Enid sat at a small table dressed as a gypsy with gold coins around the edge of her headscarf. She ushered Eleanor to sit and took Eleanor's left hand in her studying it for what seemed ages. Finally, the silence was broken, and she informed Eleanor that she had tragedy awaiting her that she could not stop. Madame Enid could also see much water, as in oceans, that would cause Eleanor heartache in the future. She predicted marriage and three children, although Eleanor was indeed married with three children so that was not a surprise. The reading was over in minutes and Eleanor had to cross Madame Enid's palm with silver. A bit unnerved, Eleanor related the story to Leonard who just laughed it off as hocus pocus and poppycock. However, the dire predictions would stay with Eleanor for many years and prove prophetic.

Eleanor regretted that she had not done any research on Southend and promised herself that the next holiday would be researched by asking friends and borrowing books from the library. She thought Brighton sounded nice, but that could wait.

Everyone was awake early on Saturday morning and the children kept asking what time the coach was leaving. Eleanor explained that the coach had to bring another group of holidaymakers to Southend and that they would be on the coach going back. Leonard offered to take the children for a walk whilst Eleanor finished the packing and cleaned the caravan. She did not want the caravan park owner to think badly of them.

Back home, with Mary, and surprisingly the children were full of exciting stories to tell her. Eleanor had thought the holiday was a disaster, but to hear the children telling Mary of the fun they had perhaps Eleanor had read the situation differently. Mary told the children how much she liked the souvenir they had given her and yes, she had received the pretty picture postcard.

25

A few weeks passed and Eleanor was advised to collect the keys to their new freehold home from the real estate agent's office. Moving day was timed for a Saturday so that Leonard, Mary and herself did not have to take time off work. Although Leonard no longer worked at Covent Garden Market he had stayed friends with Joe and was quick to ask for his help with the removals. Joe still had his flat-topped cart but now he had another horse, much younger and stronger and able to climb the hill. Joe was only too willing to help the young family. He was promised a couple of beers for his efforts at The Plough public house in Dulwich afterwards.

Moving day went without a hitch as the family had little in the way of furniture or ornaments. Eleanor had bought herself a sewing machine and already had bolts of material to make up into curtains for each room. She was seriously considering giving up work now that money was not an issue and could spend her time productively making the house a home.

Eleanor had taken Monday morning off work, without pay, in order to enrol the two boys at the local primary school. Diane would be going there a few months later due to intake dates. Mary had said that she would be glad to get the children to school each morning and collect them in the afternoon as it fitted in with her cleaning jobs. This arrangement worked well and one day Mary announced that she was giving up her cleaning jobs as she had found employment at the school, as a dinner lady, but did not reveal that she had taken a few years off her age when applying.

The next few months passed without incident, apart from David catching chicken pox quickly followed by measles. Childhood illnesses were common-place, usually caught at school, and most children recovered very quickly after the correct treatment. David seemed more prone to catch childhood illnesses than Derek and Diane who were not affected. Everyone had slipped into their new lifestyle with comparative ease. The children were unaware of the change in fortune, and Eleanor continued to keep a tight rein on expenditure.

26

2 0 November 1947 was a big day in London with the marriage of Princess Elizabeth to Prince Philip, the Duke of Edinburgh. The whole country was certainly in need for some cheerful news as the end of the war had not solved many of the problems such as unemployment and food rationing. The general public were somewhat sceptical about a lavish wedding at such a time of austerity, but Princess Elizabeth was determined and despite being impressive, did not overdo the extravagance. Eleanor and Leonard took the three children to London and found a position where they would be able to get a good view of the procession and perhaps get a wave from the royal couple. Each of the children was given a small Union Jack flag to wave. The whole day was both exciting and tiring for the five of them and there was no resistance from the children when it came to bedtime that night.

Then, some exciting news from Mr Sully. The gold bangle studded with precious stones had brought a handsome sum at auction. Eleanor could hardly believe her eyes when she read how much. Mr Sully's letter enclosed a cheque made out to Eleanor. With their finances now securely in place Eleanor might allow herself a little more spending.

Christmas 1947 was to be the best Christmas ever for the family. Eleanor and Leonard decided that the boys were old enough to have two wheeled bikes, a blue one for David and a red one for Derek, whilst Diane would have a green three-wheeler. The cycle shop said that they could hold them until Christmas Eve. Leonard was keen to introduce the boys to cycling as he had ridden a bike most of his adult life and was riding his bike to a from work each day. With the Velodrome so close he enrolled them in a junior cycle group there which they enjoyed immensely. He hoped that one of them might become a champion one day like his idol Reg Harris.

With Christmas presents sorted Eleanor and Leonard bought a real fir tree, four feet high, for the lounge and lots of coloured lights and decorations. Leonard fixed some decorations across the ceiling, too. There would be decorations on the table, something Eleanor had never done before but had seen in a magazine some years before and remembered how it looked. She kept thanking her lucky stars that her life had taken such a wonderful turn and regretted not knowing Mrs Beauchamp. Christmas lunch was as traditional as Eleanor could make it due to the food rationing. Mary had helped out some weeks earlier by making a Christmas pudding and a Christmas cake.

As to be expected, Christmas Day was a hit. Each of the children had a Christmas stocking filled with small presents and a small amount of confectionery as well as an orange. Leonard gave Eleanor a pretty marcasite brooch in the shape of a bow. The jeweller, where they had bought the engagement and wedding rings, was delighted to see Leonard again and once again offered him discount on the brooch. The jeweller pointed out that the bow shape was called a lover's knot. Eleanor gave Leonard some cufflinks. They gave Mary some new slippers and winter gloves. After lunch they all went for a long walk, with the children on their bikes, to get over their big lunch. Tea was turkey sandwiches followed by Christmas cake. The children made no fuss about going to bed that night as they were all so tired.

27

L ife was ideal. Eleanor decided that she should improve her skills and enrolled in a typing school. She had visions of an office job one day although financially she need never work again. The original idea of learning a new skill had come from talking to her next-door neighbours, two spinster sisters, Gertie and Mildred. They were both much older than Eleanor, but she enjoyed their friendship, and they were always giving the children little treats or baking a cake for the family. They had enrolled in a course and encouraged Eleanor. Using an Imperial typewriter and a Pitman's book Eleanor found that she could soon touch type and with practice had a good error free speed.

The typing teacher Miss Morgan suggested to the class that for a reasonable cost there was a week's trip to Switzerland available through the Ministry of Education for students. At first Eleanor said that she could not possibly consider going away and leaving her family for a week but when Gertie and Mildred said that they were going she gave the trip more consideration. Sitting down, after tea, with Leonard one evening she told him of Miss Morgan's trip. He was delighted and told her she should go. Money was not an obstacle and he, with Mary, could cope with the children for a week.

Firstly, Eleanor needed a passport size photograph for the passport she would apply for. A local photographer took four photos, but Eleanor thought that their price was a bit exorbitant for what she got. However, she needed the photos. Submitting her completed claim form and photos Eleanor had to wait a couple of weeks for the official passport to arrive. She had already given up work so asking for holidays was not an issue. Unsure of the clothing she needed she went through her wardrobe and drawers selecting her newest clothing and ensuring that she had cardigans in case the weather was cool. She would still need to buy some strong walking shoes, however. Eleanor would be flying for the first time in her life and was apprehensive about the flight. Gertie had flown before and said that she had nothing to worry about. She was right. Strapped safely in her seat Eleanor barely noticed that the 'plane had taken off. She compared it to sitting in a very comfortable armchair. A quick look out of a window at the tiny houses below made her stomach lurch so she buried her head in a magazine for the rest of the journey. Back home, the children stood in the back garden on the evening that Eleanor flew out. They waved to a 'plane that was flying overhead believing Eleanor was on it.

A smooth landing convinced Eleanor that flying was the only way to travel great distances. She would fly again. Switzerland was everything Eleanor could dream of. She had read some books from the library and was determined to see as much of the country as possible, although limited by the tour leader. The tour party was based in Interlaken, in a quaint typical Swiss chalet, surrounded by snow-capped mountains. Eleanor felt like a child in fairyland. The highlight of the week, for Eleanor, was a visit to the *Kleine Scheidegg* and the *Jungfrau*. Souvenirs for the family filled her suitcase for the return journey plus lots of reels of used film. She had taken a small camera with her and spent many happy hours taking photos of people and places. Eleanor had not only seen sights she had never seen before but tasted foods she had never tried before. Her favourite was apple strudel. This first trip abroad had certainly whetted Eleanor's appetite for travel, but she would need to wait a few more years before she could venture abroad again.

28

On 29 July 1948, Leonard's birthday, the London Olympic Games commenced with great fanfare. The Games would last until 14 August and the whole family could not wait for the track cycle racing at Herne Hill to begin. They were able to get a good view from the back bedroom windows and Leonard had his father's old binoculars to get a better look at the riders. Knowing how much Leonard wanted to be close to his idol Reg Harris Eleanor purchased a ticket for Leonard to attend, as a birthday present on the day that Reg was racing. He was overjoyed at the opportunity and witnessed Reg Harris win an Olympic Silver medal in the Men's Tandem and another in the Men's Sprint. He even managed to get an autograph from him.

Another year passed. The house had been repainted outside from green to cream and the front garden boasted a fantastic show of rose bushes in various colours. Around the borders of the garden Eleanor had planted white alyssum and blue lobelia alternately. The effect was quite striking when the flowers bloomed. This was Eleanor's domain. Whilst out in the back garden Mary had created a productive vegetable garden, with Leonard's help. Leonard had planted a couple of fruit trees as well. Eleanor had requested a lemon and an apricot, telling herself that she would make lemon curd and bottle the apricots.

Whilst out digging over the soil for Mary to plant more vegetables he heard a woman scream. He thought he knew the direction of the screaming and his hunch was right. He raced next door and knocked on his neighbour's door. Gertie was distraught when she opened the front door. Mildred was still lying at the foot of the stairs. Fortunately, she was conscious but said she was in a lot of pain. Leonard tried to make her comfortable but did not move her if he could help it. The deformed leg indicated to Leonard that it was broken, and he expressed this opinion. An ambulance was called, and Leonard offered to go with Mildred as Gertie was in no fit state. She was in shock herself so Leonard sent her to his home where he knew that Eleanor would look after her.

On his return from the hospital, he was able to reassure Gertie that everything was alright. She had, indeed, broken her leg but would soon be home. The main reason they needed to keep her in hospital for a few days was her age. She had whispered it to the doctor not wanting Leonard to hear, but he had. He decided that he would keep the information to himself, the gentleman that he was. Gertie and Mildred referred to him as their *'Knight in Shining Armour'* after that episode.

At Gertie's request, Leonard moved Mildred's bed to the downstairs front room in readiness for her return from hospital. She would not be climbing any stairs soon and would be able to watch the world go by out of the front window to where he also moved a comfortable armchair.

29

One day a letter arrived for Eleanor with the company name Sully and Sykes printed on it. Eleanor cautiously opened the letter only to read that Mr Sully had passed away, unexpectedly in his sleep. His partner, Mr Sykes, felt that Eleanor would like to be informed as he knew how much Mr Sully had become part of Eleanor's life and had watched her life flourish with his help. There had been a private funeral, but Eleanor quickly wrote to Mr Sykes expressing her and her family's condolences to Mr Sully's family, if he had one, and to thank Mr Sykes for letting her know. The letter left a strange feeling in Eleanor's stomach that she could not shake off. She felt that she had lost someone close, almost a friend. He had certainly provided her with more assistance than she would have expected, but never overstepped the mark.

No-one would ever know the secret that Charles Sully carried in his heart and to his grave. He had never married, as the one woman he loved deeply had married another and moved to India. Miss Eleanor Hawkins, as she was known then, studied music with Charles. From the first day he saw her he just knew that there could never be another woman for him. Eleanor had thought of themselves as good friends and Charles was too shy to tell her of his true feelings even after she told him of her upcoming engagement. After Eleanor became Mrs Beauchamp she stayed in touch with Charles, but in a professional manner, choosing him to be her solicitor. She would never know how much he looked forward to her infrequent visits to London and would always advise her to call in and see him, on the pretence of reviewing her Will. The few hours he spent with her were so precious to him although a torture. It was no wonder then that Charles Sully had taken such an interest in Eleanor Lipton when their paths finally crossed. He had hoped that the two Eleanors would have a striking resemblance, but sadly no.

30

Just prior to his 11th birthday David sat a school examination known as the eleven plus (11+). This exam was sat in a child's final year at primary school and consisted of general knowledge questions. It was a way of streaming children into a more suitable form of secondary education according to their abilities, such as Grammar, Secondary Modern or Technical Schools. David comfortably passed his 11+ and was accepted to start at the nearby grammar school in September 1951. Derek would sit his examination the following year. Before the start of the school term Eleanor took David to the school uniform shop in Dulwich. The cost of the entire uniform was not cheap, but money was no longer an issue and Eleanor was keen for her children to be well educated.

Wearing his new uniform Eleanor took David to the local photographers and had a series of photos taken. These would be framed and hung on the dining room wall. In time, photos of Derek and Diane, in school uniform, would be hung alongside.

31

1951 heralded the Festival of Britain which was opened by King George VI. An idea to commemorate the Centennial of the Great Exhibition of 1851, but without international or Commonwealth exhibits. With much of London still in ruins, from the bombing, the South Bank of the River Thames was chosen as the most suitable site whilst at Battersea the Festival Pleasure Gardens were to be built. The concept was embraced by the British at a time when there was still austerity and gloom, following the war. The project promised employment and the exhibition sights created sheer wonderment when finished, something for all. There was a *Festival Hall*, the *Dome of Discovery* and a cigar shaped structure known as the *Skylon*. There were so many exhibits to see that Londoners could easily spend a day there seeing the inventiveness and genius of British scientists and technologists. Other cities around Britain held their own much smaller exhibitions. The Pleasure Gardens contained lots of fairground type rides and numerous things for children to enjoy. The whole idea really took off and lifted the spirits of the people and was deemed a 'triumphant success' and a 'beacon for change.' Such was the positive impact. Eleanor, Leonard, Mary and the children made a couple of visits to The Festival site and the Pleasure Gardens as there was so much to see and learn. Whilst there they purchased, for five shillings, a commemorative coin for each of them.

32

Mary loved her dinner lady job and especially the children that she daily came into contact with. The other women were so friendly, and each day would bring a lot of laughter. She learned about peoples' families and in turn regaled them of tales of her own, past and present. Late in November she was carrying some boxes out to the industrial dustbin, in the school yard, but did not see a large metal mop bucket in her path. As a consequence, she tripped over the bucket and badly grazed her right shin on its edge and injured her arm. At first, she thought she had broken her arm, but it seemed okay once she was standing up and trying to move it. Giving her shin a quick wipe with her handkerchief, which she had just wetted under the nearby tap, she picked up the boxes and deposited them in the dustbin before returning to work, without telling anyone what had just happened.

A few days later the wound on Mary's leg started to weep, was very red and angry, possibly infected. Mary had never been one to see a doctor first, she would always try a home remedy and generally was successful in healing or ridding herself of an ailment. Home remedies did not work on this occasion and when Eleanor saw the infected wound insisted that they caught the bus to the hospital on Denmark Hill for treatment. After a long wait in the Emergency area Mary was seen by a doctor. He was not happy that she had tried to heal herself and the fact that the wound had not been thoroughly cleansed when she first injured the leg. Now she was 68, in the doctor's opinion, a couple of days hospital stay was required, admitting her immediately.

Eleanor returned home to tell the rest of the family and said that she and Leonard would go back to the hospital at visiting time but preferred that the children did not attend with them. Eleanor had only been gone a few hours before visiting her mother, in a ward, and was shocked at what she saw. Mary showed her a rash on her body and said that she felt a strange sensation as though she was swelling up. The doctor had administered penicillin to combat the infection. Mary had never received penicillin before. The result of the drug was that Mary appeared to be allergic and it would be some time before the medical staff realised her predicament. As well as the rash she constantly scratched her arms and legs due to an outbreak of hives, too. Eleanor told Mary that they would speak to the doctor and return the next day.

The next day Eleanor and Leonard arrived to find Mary's face so swollen that she was hardly recognisable. There were slits where her eyes should have been. She was having difficulty speaking due to the swelling and the medical staff were not quite sure how to deal with the infection if they could not administer penicillin. Eleanor spent most of the day with Mary whilst Leonard went home to the children. Sometime during the night Mary had a loss of consciousness and Eleanor called for the night sister. The doctor arrived after what seemed a long time to Eleanor, and he stood looking at Mary and shaking his head. He warned Eleanor that Mary might not survive the night as she appeared to be going into anaphylaxis. Eleanor was shocked. How could a healthy woman with a small wound on her shin be so ill. The situation did not change over the next few days and finally Mary succumbed to the chronic infection which had shut down her vital organs, without regaining consciousness.

Now Eleanor was beginning to dread Christmas as she knew Mary used to. They would lay Mary to rest at the West Norwood Cemetery. Eleanor's brother

Jack had been informed of Mary's death and had said that he and his family would attend. Unfortunately, a heavy fall of snow meant much of the public transport system was shut down and even expensive flights from Ireland were cancelled. On the day of the funeral the only people able to attend, due to the weather conditions, were Eleanor, Leonard and three of Mary's dinner ladies. The children were spared the trauma of an interment, staying at home with Gertie and Mildred, the next-door neighbours, making sandwiches and cutting up cake for everyone's return.

With Mary's death and burial before Christmas, but it was hard to celebrate without her as she was such a big part of everyone's lives and the children took her death hard. The two boys did not shed tears in public, but Diane seemed to cry constantly. The veil of gloominess that hung over everyone was very hard. Christmas Day lacked fun despite Eleanor's best efforts.

33

It was well into the New Year before Eleanor felt she could deal with clearing out Mary's wardrobe and disposing of clothing and her bed to the Salvation Army. Mary had very little in the way of jewellery, but Eleanor kept what little there was, especially Mary's wedding ring. Not wanting to appear over eager, both boys asked if they might take over Mary's bedroom as they had been sharing one bedroom for a number of years and each wanted their own space. Leonard said that a toss of a coin would decide who got the room. With Leonard flipping a penny, Derek called heads whilst David called tails at the same time. The coin came down heads up, so the room would be Derek's. Leonard redecorated the room as the wallpaper had been rather feminine with large Redoute roses all over it. Leonard also put up an extra shelf to accommodate Derek's cycling trophies. In fairness, he redecorated David's room, too.

Whether it was because of Mary's death but when Derek sat his 11+ examination he failed to attain a good score that would get his admittance to a grammar school. Eleanor was surprised as both boys seemed to be of equal standard, despite Derek's poor start. The school headmaster said that it was quite common to fail at his age but there was a second chance called the 13+ so perhaps he would do better then. A local comprehensive school was found for Derek where he thrived with the education provided. As predicted by the headmaster, when Derek sat the 13+ examination he passed quite easily and so off to the grammar school, with David, when the time came although one year lower than David.

As Eleanor had promised, a photograph of Derek in his new school uniform was hung on the wall next to David's.

34

With King George VI's death on 6 February 1952 the whole country went into deep mourning. On the day of the funeral, the 15th, the whole of the nation stopped for two minutes silence in honour of the King. After ascending the throne in controversy, he had steered Great Britain through the horrors of war but to his own health detriment. His daughter, Princess Elizabeth would now be Queen and the date of the Coronation was set for 2 June 1953.

Eleanor had certificates for her typing skills and thought that she might like to find a part-time job. She saw an advertisement in the *South London Press* for a typist in an insurance broker at Camberwell Green. Frank Gold was the owner of the company and was impressed with Eleanor's credentials. He offered her three days per week as a typist sending out insurance renewal letters. He introduced her to Doris and Gwen in the office where she would be situated. The previous typist had left for maternity reasons. Leonard was thrilled with the news, as were the children.

Life fell into an easy rhythm. Eleanor's job was going well, and she had learned the duties of Doris and Gwen in order to be able to cover for them when they were on holiday. Frank Gold was impressed with her abilities and gave her a small pay rise to show his appreciation.

A regular caller at the business was Mrs Masters. She was an elegant looking woman in her mid-fifties who always looked like she had just come from a beauty parlour. Her platinum blonde hair and make-up were impeccable, and her clothing suited a woman of her age. One day she came in wearing a Canadian ranch mink coat and a pair of Deed's expensive leather gloves. Eleanor was impressed. When Eleanor made a comment to Gwen and Doris about Mrs Master's visits Doris informed her that she was Mrs Gold's sister, Frank Gold's sister-in-law. Oh, thought Eleanor, naively, nice of her to call in to see him so often.

Leonard had received a promotion to foreman and would spend much of his day driving around the locale, in a little van, seeing his workers and directing work to be done. He still whistled, but now it was the latest tunes that he had heard on the radio. His workers would listen out for his whistle and ensure that they were working whenever his visited. Leonard was aware of this and used to smile to himself. Leonard had learned to drive during the war and his time with the RAF. He and Eleanor talked about the possibility of them buying a car to save Leonard the daily cycle to and from work. They settled on a second-hand, black, sedan that Leonard bought from his old friend, from market days, Joe. Leonard's knowledge of car mechanics would come in useful, and he would be able to carry out his own service on the vehicle. It was however, a reliable vehicle and the family were able to enjoy weekend trips through the countryside, apart from one trip when the engine overheated and Leonard had to knock on a cottage door and ask to borrow a watering can in order to top up the radiator. He made sure that his vehicle was roadworthy before any future trips, but also carried a large bottle of water in the boot.

Working back, one evening, after Gwen and Doris had left, Eleanor did not hear the main office door open and close or Frank Gold's open door close. She was too engrossed in the letter that she wanted to get into the post that night, after Frank Gold had signed it. Frank would often work very late, as it was his business, and he had much to achieve. Letter finished and checked for errors Eleanor did not bother to knock on Frank's door to go in.

'Oh, sorry' she exclaimed. There was Frank Gold and Mrs Masters, in a close embrace having a passionate kiss.

Quickly retreating and closing the door behind her Eleanor put down the letter, grabbed her coat and handbag and left the office.

Once home Eleanor told Leonard what she had seen.

'Stay out of it,' he said 'none of your business'

'But he is a married man, Mrs Masters is his sister-in-law' Eleanor went on.

'Just forget it Eleanor, what other folks do is not of our concern,' said Leonard.

Next morning, she found it hard to look Frank Gold in the eye, and nothing was said between them. Her pay packet, that week, had an extra ten shillings in it and she would continue to receive the extra money for the entire time she worked there. Leonard called it 'hush money'.

35

Both boys were doing well with their studies and winning trophies for their track cycling. Although both boys were competitive at the track, they did not mind which one won a race so long as the other came second. Rewarded with trophies they did not mind whose name was on it either. However, they were not competitive at home, being supportive of each other especially with homework. Diane would soon be sitting her 11+ examination and spent her time reading books, particularly Enid Blyton's books.

At the end of April, Leonard drove the family to a bluebell wood at Badger's Mount in Kent. Unbeknown to Eleanor he had spent much of the war at Biggin Hill, a nearby aerodrome so, he knew the area well. The children whooped and laughed as they went deeper and deeper into the bluebell wood despite plenty of bluebells at their feet. Native bluebells have a strong sweet smell and Eleanor just adored breathing in their fragrance similar to hyacinths. The children gathered armfuls of flowers and placed them in the boot of the car. Leonard then drove them to a nearby tea shop called 'The Cottage'. As they entered Diane pulled at Eleanor's skirt and pointed to two ladies seated at a table.

'That's my teacher' Diane said.

Eleanor recognised Miss Bolin as Diane's teacher and the other woman was Miss Parr, the headmistress. Eleanor took Diane over to say hello and Leonard and the boys followed. Eleanor introduced Leonard and the boys individually and they each said 'hello'. Miss Parr commented on the good looks of the two boys and asked about their schooling. It was a brief conversation, but Eleanor was glad that they had not ignored the two ladies.

Leonard made sure that they found a table away from the two ladies in order to give them all privacy. Eleanor then ordered tea for two and three lemonades, scones, jam and cream for them all. It had been a wonderful day out and the bluebells ended up in vases of water as well as jam jars filled with water once they were back home. The house smelt beautiful.

36

In late May the family had managed a week's holiday at Brighton, driving to the destination, and staying in a bed and breakfast establishment, in a back street, but within easy walking distance to the seafront. It was a huge improvement on the Southend experience, but with some differences.

Eleanor was complimented by the landlady on how beautifully polite the three children were and a credit to their parents. This made Eleanor swell with pride, both she and Leonard had worked hard at good parenting and their efforts were reaping rewards. The children's futures seemed destined for success.

The children had taken their buckets and spades with them to Brighton and were bitterly disappointed that the beach was all pebbles, so no sandcastles on this holiday. The weather was still quite cool so there was no going into the sea either, but everyone managed a paddle on the water's edge during the week. They all walked a lot, particularly around the shops in The

Lanes, and Eleanor relented and gave the children a few pennies each to test their skills in the Penny Arcade.

Diane showed a lot of interest in the grand houses along the seafront, many of them hotels and was fascinated by the Royal Pavilion. The building was a former royal residence, beginning in 1787 and built in three stages. It was a seaside retreat for George, Prince of Wales who became the Prince Regent in 1811 and King George IV in 1820. The architecture being Indo-Saracenic, with onion shaped domes and minarets, a style prevalent in India for most of the 19th century.

Back home again and Leonard decorated the outside of their house with red, white and blue bunting whilst Eleanor had planted red, white and blue plants in the garden in readiness for the Coronation. Eleanor, Gertie and Mildred set about organising the neighbours for a street party and games for the children as well as a small gift to remind them of the occasion. Every UK school gave each child a souvenir Coronation book, with a royal blue cover, and a pseudo coin showing through the front. Leonard had gone out and bought a small television set so that they could watch the first televised Coronation. Life was indeed good.

37

It was no surprise then that Diane easily passed her 11+ examination and was accepted to a grammar school for girls, starting first term in September 1954. Another trip to the uniform shop for a complete uniform and another photo for the wall. Eleanor could not be prouder of her three children. They were all academically gifted and she knew that their futures would be secured with good educations.

Unbeknown to Eleanor, Leonard arranged to get a passport for himself. He thought that it was time he and Eleanor enjoyed their life together instead of continually worrying about other people. He did not know just how soon he would make use of his new passport.

With all three children attending two local schools David and Derek were allowed to ride their bikes to school and were very proficient riders, due to their cycling abilities on the velodrome where they were affectionally referred to as The Lipton Boys. Both boys were evenly matched in their physical attributes although Derek was the bigger of the two. Diane needed to take the bus for a couple of years as her two-wheel cycling ability was not as good as the boys. Cycling gave the teenage boys the freedom they wanted and the exercise, especially when climbing hills. They could ride to Camberwell Green or Brixton or catch up with friends scattered around the area. One of their favourite rides was to Brockwell Park, especially in the Autumn where they could collect conkers from the horse chestnut trees, marvelling at the colour of the beautiful chestnuts inside the prickly green outer casing. They would take some conkers home, pierce a hole through the centre, push through a shoelace and knot it at one end. Hanging down this would be their weapon to knock out another's conker. The game was very popular with boys at the time, but it caused a number of bruised knuckles with the gusto used to beat the foe.

On a cold but dry Saturday in late January 1957, David and Derek went for a casual ride. Derek was riding just ahead of David, on a busy, main road to Camberwell Green, when a large black dog ran out from the left-hand side of them and crashed into Derek's front wheel. The force of the impact sent Derek flying over the handlebars and catapulted headlong into the windscreen of an oncoming car. David was momentarily frozen with shock, jumped from his bike, then burst into tears before rushing to his brother's aid. People ran from a nearby shop, and someone called for an ambulance. David cradled his brother's head in his lap, oblivious of the blood, and could not stop shaking. It seemed an eternity until the ambulance arrived together with a Police car. The ambulance people treated Derek where he lay and after loading him into the back of the ambulance suggested that David travelled with them as he was obviously in shock. David had given his and Derek's details to the Police before being taken away to the nearest hospital.

Being a Saturday both Eleanor and Leonard were at home. The ringing of the doorbell interrupted Leonard's reading of the daily newspaper. He answered the front door to see a Police officer standing there. He was puzzled. The officer confirmed that was the residence of the Lipton family and Leonard nodded. The officer showed his warrant card and asked to be let in which Leonard complied with all the time wondering what it was all about. Hearing voices Eleanor, who was in the kitchen with Diane, making sandwiches for lunch, came out to see who their visitor was. She was shocked to see a uniformed Police officer and wiping her hands on her apron asked what he was doing there. The office suggested that they all sit down, including Diane. He then broke the news to them of the serious accident, and what was known of the circumstances that had occurred, and the untimely death of Derek due to horrific head injuries. Eleanor went numb with shock. Leonard was stoic, holding back the tears, and put his arm around his wife whilst Diane screamed and ran upstairs sobbing. A few minutes of silence passed whilst the enormity of the situation sunk in. The Police office told them that David was in hospital under sedation and observation due to severe shock. The police officer told them that there was a car outside to take them to the hospital.

All three were seated at the hospital bedside of David as they tried to make sense of the situation. David felt that it was his fault as he had suggested the ride to a cycle shop to look at new models of bikes. They would need to keep a close eye on him whilst his mind was in that state. Leonard was angry that an irresponsible dog owner had let their dog roam freely. Diane just sat there with tears running down her face and sniffing. Eleanor tried to retrace the morning's events before the boys left for their ride. They were in such good spirits ribbing each other about an upcoming bike race and which of them might win. Eleanor then had a flashback to Southend and the ominous prediction of Madame Enid. Could this be the tragedy she referred to?

David was kept in overnight, and Leonard collected him in a taxi to go home. Leonard had requested the taxi driver to take an alternate route so that they would not pass the scene of the accident lest it should upset David even more.

Arrangements for the funeral were left to Leonard. Derek would be interred at West Norwood Cemetery where they had lain Mary to rest a few years earlier. Despite being school holidays, the school principal was advised of Derek's death and he, along with Derek's class teachers, would be in attendance. There would also be Derek's friends. Leonard would book a small hall to cater for the anticipated large number of mourners to take refreshments after the interment knowing that their home would not be big enough.

Gertie and Mildred had door knocked every house in the road and collected money for a wreath. On the day of the funeral, they stood a beautiful floral wreath, on a kitchen chair, by their front gate for all to see. The funeral director would place it in or on the hearse at the appropriate time along with the other wreaths and dozens of sheaths of flowers from family, friends and associates.

Following three days of rain and again waking to pouring rain, the dreaded day had arrived. The day of the funeral was Thursday 14 February 1957, which would have been Derek's 16th birthday. Eleanor and Leonard had felt the need to have the funeral then. Eleanor wore a black two-piece suit, which she bought especially for the sad occasion, whilst Leonard wore a dark suit, white shirt and black tie. Both David and Diane wore their respective school uniforms. School had returned but all students were given the day off in order to attend the funeral, if they so wished. Gertie, Mildred and a couple of the neighbours attended as did Frank Gold, Doris and Gwen. Mr Gold had closed the office for the day and also told Eleanor to take off as much time as she needed after such a devasting event. After the church service the cortege moved to the cemetery, with rain still pouring down, and where only a handful of people stood around the empty grave. Eleanor was holding Leonard's arm and they were both sheltering under a large umbrella. David and Diane were standing next to them also sheltering under a large umbrella. After a few words from the clergy the rosewood coffin was slowly lowered into the abyss. It

146

was then that Eleanor noticed the grave had been half full of water and the coffin went below the water. She came over faint but holding on more tightly to Leonard's arm she managed to hold herself up. She suddenly thought of Derek's father and his death beneath the waves of the English Channel. Could this be an omen or just a nasty coincidence? Whatever it was, the sight of her son going under so much water would stay with her forever. A handful of dirt and a few flowers were tossed into the open grave site, and everyone left for the hall and refreshments. Later the grave would be filled in and numerous wreaths and floral sheaths laid on the top. A headstone would come later when the ground had settled. Eleanor and Leonard had already selected a stonemason and the wording for their son agreed upon.

Derek's room would stay just as he left it, for the time being. Eleanor closed the bedroom door, and no-one entered the room for a few weeks. Diane felt that she could not move into a room which contained so many happy memories but so much sadness, despite it being much bigger than her box room.

38

Against her better judgment Eleanor accepted Leonard's suggestion that they take a short holiday together. He had been to see a travel agent and they would get a week's holiday flying to Lucerne, Switzerland, in the first week of March. He remembered how Eleanor was so enamoured with Switzerland, but they would visit a different part. The weather would still be a bit cool and some snow still around, but a change of scenery might do them both good. Gertie and Mildred stepped into the breach when Eleanor told them that she was worried about leaving David and Diane for a week. She was assured that they were two very sensible children and Gertie and Mildred would supply them with a hot meal each evening as well as keeping an eye on them.

The City of Lucerne was like a picture postcard, a well-preserved medieval core amid snow-capped mountains on Lake Lucerne. There was a covered bridge built in 1333 and called the *Chapel Bridge* which linked two parts of the city. The air was fresh and clean. Eleanor and Leonard both liked the rock relief *Lion Monument* commemorating the Swiss Guards who were massacred in 1792 during the French Revolution in Paris. Their hotel was quaint but comfortable and they enjoyed exploring the eateries around the city.

They also took a cruise on the Lake. The experience certainly helped both of them to overcome the past few weeks and they couldn't wait to tell David and Diane of their experiences, show them photos and give them souvenirs. Eleanor ensured that there would be gifts for Gertie and Mildred, too.

On the last day of their holiday which had, in part, rejuvenated their love and need to go on with life, Leonard said that he had been thinking. The children were not so dependent on them now although they still had needs which would be met. Money was not a big issue as there was still plenty of Eleanor's inheritance invested and earning a good interest. Leonard wanted to have his wife to himself and suggested they both take another holiday during the first two weeks of July. Eleanor was hesitant saying that any holiday would need to fit in with Frank Gold's needs. Leonard did not have the same reservations. He believed that every-one would understand them needing further time off from work and would have no hesitation in requesting two weeks from his employer. He had already decided that Spain and a good dose of sunshine would be the best tonic.

39

It was shortly after their return home from holiday, and as they finished dinner, one evening, that Eleanor told David and Diane that she had something of importance to tell them. Leonard placed his hand over Eleanor's on the table and gave it a little squeeze. Taking a deep breath Eleanor began to speak.

'Shortly after David's birth I was viciously raped'.

Diane gasped. David raised his eyebrows.

'I will not go into detail apart from saying that after a great deal of agonising and lengthy discussions with your father I decided to keep the child and named him Derek'.

Both children were sitting there looking stunned.

'Derek?' said Diane 'what our Derek?

Eleanor nodded 'your half-brother'.

Eleanor continued. 'Unfortunately, Derek's father drowned, along with Uncle Jim in the English Channel. They were shipmates. Their bodies were never recovered. With no father but a biological mother I felt duty bound that he should be raised as ours, mine and your father's. Of course, there were people who knew of this but were sworn to secrecy such as your grandmother. For years I have wanted to tell you both, but it never seemed to be the right time. But finally, I think it is the right time now to bring this all out into the open'.

With tears welling in his eyes and his chin quivering David said, 'he will always be my brother'.

'I love him, I mean loved him' said Diane correcting herself. 'No, I still love him and always will'.

'Did Derek know, Mum?' said David

'No, I never told him, and we will never know if he suspected anything'. Wiping away tears, she continued 'I am so, so sorry not to have told you before, but the time just never seemed right. I do hope that you can both find it in your hearts to forgive me and close an unhappy chapter'.

David and Diane nodded. They both rose from the table and went round to hug and kiss their mother. Leonard squeezed her hand again. It was if a huge weight had been lifted from Eleanor's shoulders. She so hated secrets.

40

Flying to Spain for two weeks, together, was going to be a second honeymoon said Leonard when Eleanor reminded him that there was never a first honeymoon. They both laughed at this. A small hotel in the harbour area of San Sebastian gave their holiday some authenticity. There were unfamiliar sounds and smells that added to the experience. Someone somewhere always seemed to be playing a guitar. Strange, thought Eleanor, just like in the movies.

In contrast to Switzerland, Spain was very hot. July is the hottest month. Eleanor wore sleeveless cotton summer dresses, a large straw hat and sunglasses every time they went out. Leonard enjoyed the freedom of shorts and a cotton shirt teamed with sunglasses but no hat. There was a need for sunglasses to avoid the glare of the whitewashed houses and the sun reflecting off the sea. Neither of them keen swimmers so paddling their feet in the water's edge was their limit.

Trying local delicacies was fun and sitting at a bar one day, quietly enjoying a beer, Leonard decided to try, what appeared to be, crumbed onion rings that were placed near him on the bar top. He bit into one and found it quite chewy but bit into another one soon after having enjoyed the first one. He offered one to Eleanor, but she declined saying that she did not like the look of them. The barman, in broken English, asked Leonard if he liked the food to which Leonard said he did but chewy indicating his jaw. The barman laughed and started to try and demonstrate an animal, waving his arms around. Leonard frowned, not understanding. Another customer nearby, Spanish but spoke English, told Leonard that he was eating octopus. Leonard nearly vomited, but then realised that he had actually enjoyed eating 'onion rings'. Everyone in the bar laughed. This was a good story for the children and the men at work when they got home.

At a local market they saw peaches, at a very cheap price, and unfamiliar with metric weights and measures thought they had to buy a kilogram as advertised. A kilogram is equal to two pounds, two ounces in Imperial weight. Delighted with their purchase they probably ate too many peaches, each, in one go. Their stomachs and toilet visits told them the error of their ways.

Due to the hotel's proximity, they could wander easily to *La Concha Bay* and look across to a large island, in the bay, that looked like a turtle when seen from nearby *Monte Igueldo*, after taking the funicular railway to the summit.

Booking a couple of side trips with a local tour company, they spent two days, travelling overnight, with a bus load of Spaniards to Pamplona for the *Running of the Bulls*. The actual running of the bulls first thing in the morning was enjoyable but Eleanor did not enjoy watching the bullfights later in the day but did enjoy the Paso Doble music played by the band. Leonard was swept up in the euphoria, but Eleanor could only see the blood and cruelty that the so-called spectacle brought. However, a day in Biarritz proved so very different. The playground of the rich and famous appealed to Eleanor who had been a film fan for most of her adult life. Unfortunately, they did not see anyone who fitted into the category of rich or famous, but the elegant seaside town in France was very impressive. Leonard finally submitted to the power of the sun and bought a white cotton cap which he wore at a jaunty angle on his head. There were plenty of stories, photos and souvenirs to share with the children and the neighbours.

Back home and feeling refreshed, after the past few months, it was time to settle back into normal life.

However, Leonard warned Eleanor that holidays abroad were now going to be a regular occurrence. He was determined to see more of Europe, with the South of France and Italy high on his list but he felt they ought to fit in a trip to Ireland to visit Eleanor's brother Jack and his family as they seemed to have drifted apart through no-one's fault. With other commitments the idea of a visit would sit on the back burner till much later.

41

Once more the passage of time was a great healer. Prior to leaving school David was appointed Head Boy for his final year and the honour was not lost on him. He gave excellent speeches when required to do so and played an active part in chairing the Student Council as well as the debating team. He finished school with six passes in GCEs and obtained a position in a bank. Diane had also excelled in her studies and like David, also obtained six passes in GCEs. Diane chose to be a teacher and was accepted to study at a teacher's college.

David, understandably lost interest in cycling after the accident. Both boys' bikes were stored in the garage to collect dust. As soon as he was able, David bought himself a small car and had driving lessons with a local driving instructor until he passed his driving test, first time, which was quite quickly. David encouraged Diane to learn to drive and willingly loaned her his car after she passed her test, first time, too.

At the age of eighteen David was called up to do his National Service, a requirement at the time for all able-bodied men aged between 18 and thirty. He was looking forward to the challenge. He approached the Personnel section of the bank and they assured him that he would have a job waiting for him on his return after two years. Surprisingly, David failed the medical examination. The medical team cited a mild hearing loss due to mastoiditis as a small child. David had never thought that his hearing was impaired, but the authorities' decision was final. Many of David's friends were also called up and he used to listen to their boastings, at the pub, when they came home on leave, of the great times they had in Germany or Cyprus. He felt that he had missed out on a great opportunity in life and was envious of them. It was if life had a mind of its own.

Whilst at teacher's college Diane obtained some part time employment in a small café in Brixton. She was quite happy making tea and sandwiches and the money that she earned meant that she had a healthy bank balance for one so young. Unsure just what she would do with the money she just kept saving, undecided between a car or travel overseas. One day she met an Australian man, a couple of years her senior, who was in England as part of his 'see the world before you settle down'. Diane had met numerous Australians before but this one took her eye. He was over six feet tall, had blond hair and blue eyes and a beautiful healthy-looking tan. His name was Bruce Dawson and he currently lived in Earl's Court. The suburb was commonly known as Little Australia or Kangaroo Valley, due to the number of young Australians that lived there. Although he was keen to see more of Diane, she resisted by saying that she needed to concentrate on her studies but would see him occasionally and would love to stay in touch during his time in London. They went out together on a few occasions but nothing serious developed in their relationship.

After completing her teaching degree and again attaining good results Diane started to look around for the type of school that would interest her. She settled on a nearby secondary school, which was close to the teacher's college, and where she had done her practical training. She had continued to stay in touch with Bruce who had by now returned to Australia and was living in Adelaide, South Australia. Despite her wide knowledge of geography Diane had to look up Adelaide in an atlas. It was a long way from Herne Hill.

42

In 1964, at the age of 21, Diane decided that it was time to spread her wings. She had been making enquiries at Australia House about an assisted migrant passage to Australia and with Bruce's help had secured the names and addresses of some prestigious schools in Adelaide. When she broke the news to her parents of her intentions to leave home, for Australia, they were shocked. Eleanor remembered the dire prediction of Madame Enid regarding great amounts of water such as oceans. Could this be what she was referring to? Leonard went to the local library to get books on Adelaide and see if he could deter his daughter in taking such a leap of faith. Despite their joint protestations Diane pressed on and finally received notification that her application for assisted passage of ten pounds had been accepted. She would be advised when arrangements had been made for her passage. The assisted passage came with the proviso that she would stay for a minimum two years or else repay the Australian

Government for her outward passage and pay for her own return. Undaunted, Diane felt she could honour this two-year arrangement quite easily. She had a healthy bank account and good credentials for employment so she felt very confident that she would succeed. Although the family had a telephone installed it was agreed that the 'phone would only be used, by Diane, in an emergency and that letter writing would be their way of keeping in touch. Albeit a delay of some six weeks each time.

Leonard insisted that the four of them would drive to Southampton to see her off. At the end of school term in July 1964 Diane waved goodbye to her parents and brother, on the docks, as she set sail on the *'Fairsky'*, a one-class Italian-styled passenger ship taking migrants to Australia to start a new life. The ship departed Southampton. Its route would take it via the Suez Canal, stopping at Aden before proceeding to Fremantle. Although the ship was well designed for long voyages, with numerous open decks, a swimming pool. Areas for deck games, three dining rooms and various other facilities such as a cinema and hospital Diane found herself located on a lower deck and sharing the cabin with an older woman who snored, going to join her family. Six weeks was certainly not going to be a pleasure cruise, so she made sure she stayed out of the cabin during the day and involved herself in outdoor activities such as quoits. There were lots of children aboard, too. Diane seemed to be saving a child from going overboard at least once a day. Parents were enjoying the trip whilst ignoring the supervision of their young. Children also dined at a different time to adults so at least there was a time of day that she was not on tenterhooks regarding someone else's offspring. It was not long into the trip that there was an outbreak of chickenpox amongst the children. Instead of confining infected children to their respective cabins there was a general attitude that herd immunity was the best policy and spotty children abounded. Most wearing calamine lotion camouflage.

The ship made its first Australian call in Fremantle, Western Australia, where numerous passengers disembarked, including Diane's cabin companion. At last, a decent night's sleep lay ahead. Bruce was on the quayside when the ship docked at Outer Harbor in Adelaide. It was so nice to see a friendly face although she had to admit that she had made a few friends whilst on board the ship and had names and addresses of where they would be staying in the interim, to look up once she had settled.

The first thing that struck Diane was how cold it was in Adelaide although the sun was shining, but then it was winter. She had expected a hot climate all year or at least warmer. Thank goodness she had thought to put a winter coat in her luggage. The drive, with Bruce in his car, from Outer Harbor to his parents' home at Glenelg did not take too long. Glenelg was a seaside suburb of Adelaide and very popular, in the summertime, with tourists as a tram service ran from Adelaide to Glenelg and return.

Mr and Mrs Dawson were most welcoming. Mr Dawson was also a teacher whilst Mrs Dawson was a nurse. They appeared to be in their mid to late fifties. They showed Diane to a small, but comfortable room, at the top of their three-storey home overlooking the sea on the Esplanade. Impressed, Diane could not wait to write to her family and tell them of her first days and the voyage.

The next day, being a Saturday, Bruce was able to show Diane around the immediate vicinity in the morning and Adelaide in the afternoon except all retail shop closed at 12 noon, a far cry from going shopping with her mother, in Peckham Rye, on a Saturday afternoon. It seemed that most people were more interested in going to the footy. This transpired to be

Aussie Rules football. Bruce offered to take her to that day's match at the Adelaide Oval. Diane accepted, unsure what to expect. She had attended a few football matches in London over the years but struggled to understand Aussie Rules and how anyone could get a score from missing the goal and hitting an upright or get a score by getting the ball through the outside posts. Surely, most games had one goal but this game seemed to have points for near misses. Strange. She couldn't wait to tell David.

Spending enjoyable time with Bruce had Diane feeling good about this big move and her feelings towards Bruce had heightened.

On Sunday, after breakfast, Mr and Mrs Dawson announced that they were going to church and Diane was welcome to join them. Although not a churchgoer Diane thought it might be nice to see new sights and meet some people. With Bruce and his parents in Mr Dawson's car they set off for St Peter's Cathedral in North Adelaide, near the Adelaide Oval where she had watched the footy game the previous day. Mrs Dawson explained that the cathedral was a landmark and an important part of the City's heritage. A beautiful historic building on the outside Diane could not wait to see the interior. She was not disappointed. Awed by the beauty of the interior of the cathedral Diane could hardly keep her attention on the service. At the conclusion of the service, they made their way outside shaking hands with the clergy and other friends. A young woman came up to Bruce and gave him a kiss on the cheek and asked him to introduce her to his new friend. He introduced Diane first, saying that she had just arrived from England and then he introduced Sheila, his fiancée. Diane was mortified. At no stage had Bruce ever mentioned a fiancée and although he had not pursued a strong relationship with Diane, she believed that, given time, there could be something between them. She certainly hoped so. This revelation had certainly turned Diane's hopes on their head, and she now needed to think carefully about her future.

43

After taking the tram to Adelaide and deciding that employment was her first priority, early on a Monday morning, Diane presented herself to a couple of school principals in the hope that she might obtain a position as soon as possible. The first schools she approached were impressed by her credentials but wary of giving a position to one so young and, in their words, inexperienced. Undeterred Diane walked around Adelaide trying to think of a way of getting employment so that she could leave Bruce's parents' house quickly. The answer came in a café in Rundle Street. She was sitting alone, with a cup of tea and a piece of home-made cake, according to the price ticket, with tears running down her face when one of the waitresses saw her. Sitting down at the same table the waitress asked her why she was crying. Diane will never know why she told this complete stranger of her dilemma, but Julie, the waitress, offered her a solution.

'There's a spare room where I live, although it is not opulent', she said. 'The boss is an old Italian man, but he has a good heart and a soft spot for young damsels in distress. When he comes in the shop I'll see if I can get you a job. Go for a walk and come back in an hour'.

Walking along tree-lined North Terrace and past the War Memorial towards the Botanic Gardens Diane could not get over the grandeur of the City of Adelaide and some of the majestic buildings. She turned down a side street only to find herself by the river Torrens and walked some way along the riverbank. She liked this city, it had a welcoming feel about it despite her current situation. She was determined to get through two years and go back home but taking it one day at a time.

As Julie had said, good news awaited her back at the café. There she met Mr Conti, a lovely man in his sixties, portly and sporting a big black drooping moustache but with a bald head.

'Call me Tony', he said 'everyone does'. 'Now young lady you tell me about yourself and convince me I can use your talents in my business'.

Diane began by telling him of her work experience in a café in Brixton but suddenly burst into tears and poured out her woes whilst Tony dragged on a cigarette and sipped black coffee. Then a big beaming smile crossed his face.

'Julie, meet your new assistant starting tomorrow' he shouted.

Diane was overjoyed and wanted to kiss the old Italian but thought better of it. Telling her to come back at the end of the day Julie said that she would take her home and see if the accommodation would suit her.

Deep in her thoughts Diane had not taken much notice of the café when she first entered it. Now she had a chance to look around. The shop was quite small and located in the heart of the retail district. The floor was black and white tiles in a chequerboard style. Halfway up the walls were gleaming white tiles and the top half of the walls were painted Azure Blue. There was a large, framed scene of Venice on the wall opposite the high counter. The shop was appropriately name '*Tony's Café.*'

The café was open five and half days per week, but Tony only employed his two staff for five days preferring to work on his own on Saturday morning and once the shop had closed at 12 noon he would do his accounts and get the orders ready for the following week. His wife Maria would come in just before closing and spend the afternoon giving the café a thorough clean. The arrangements had worked well for years.

44

Diane surprised herself by not being nervous about being taken to a strange house in a strange town. Her desperation overcame all fear. With Julie by her side, they sat on a bus heading north-east out of town. They were going to the suburb of Paradise. Julie told her that it was the only place in the world where you could catch a bus to Paradise. Diane had to smile. She would make mention of this comment in her next letter home. A short walk from the bus stop led them to a single storey brick house which Diane recognised as a bungalow back in England. Julie opened the green painted front door to a long passageway with rooms off to each side. Towards the back was a kitchen and then a built-on room before the back garden. This built-on area was the accommodation that Julie could offer her as the other rooms were taken by other tenants. Julie explained that everyone paid a share of the rent, shared communal areas, cleaning and bought their own food. They either had jobs or were students and their paths rarely crossed unless they all wanted the shared bathroom at the same time. The landlord of the property was Tony.

Diane said that she would think about it and tell Julie of her decision the next day when she started work. Julie then walked Diane to the bus stop having explained which bus would take her back into Adelaide where she should catch the tram to Glenelg. Sitting on the bus tears began to well up again. Diane felt so lost and alone. In this country people spoke the same language, had the same money, pounds, shillings and pence, drove on the left-hand side of the road and had so many things in common with England, but she felt so alienated.

It was dark by the time Diane arrived back in Glenelg. Trying to put on a brave face, on her return to the Dawson house, and standing in the floodlit garden whilst Mr Dawson cooked a barbecue, Diane related her day to Bruce and Mrs Dawson, although not the full truth, especially the job and possible accommodation. That night she packed her few things and early the next morning, before anyone was awake, she left the house. She had written two letters, one to Mr and Mrs Dawson thanking them for their hospitality and one to Bruce saying that she wished he had been truthful with her about Sheila. Of course, she gave no forwarding address as she could not exactly remember it, but she would not have told them anyway.

It was too early to go to her new job, so she sat alone on a bench looking out to sea and imagining England just over the horizon. Of course, had she known her geography better she would have known that the nearest landfall was Antarctica.

45

The first day working in the café helped to lift Diane's spirits and she told Julie that she would like to stay for a short while in the house. She learned that Julie was in fact from country South Australia, where job prospects were poor, so she moved to the City. She was two years older than Diane but understood the feeling of alienation that was felt. After a long day, on her feet, Diane was feeling exhausted but knew that she would cope. Julie packed up some unsold pies and pasties together with a large piece of home-made cake telling Diane that Mr Conti approved of her taking leftover foods and it would help eke out their food bill. They would also share their bounty with the other house residents. Julie and Mr Conti were beginning to be the guardian angels that Diane so desperately needed then.

After a week of work and living in George Street, Paradise, Diane finally felt she had the courage to write to her family. She did not want them to know how unhappy she was so made her letter sound upbeat and her choice of work only temporary. The last thing she wanted to do was worry her parents, especially knowing how against this adventure they were.

Mr and Mrs Conti were about to celebrate their fiftieth wedding anniversary and Diane, Julie and the other tenants were all invited to a party in the Conti's Campbelltown house, not far from Paradise. The day was warm and sunny but still not hot. Diane and Julie got a lift with Pete, one of the other tenants in his old, battered van.

Diane had managed to meet the other tenants during her short time in the house. There was Pete, an Adelaide university student in his final year, studying engineering, Margaret a hairdresser's apprentice in a well-known Adelaide salon, which Diane was yet to find in her travels, Michael a bank teller in King William Street and Rosemary a nurse at a major Adelaide hospital, who always seemed to be on night shift and sleeping during the day. Margaret and Rosemary were in fact sisters and shared the largest room in the house which was located at the front overlooking the overgrown front garden. Pete had the room opposite theirs whilst Michael's room was next to Pete's along the hall and Julie's next to the sisters. Diane could not help but notice that Rosemary had bright auburn hair whilst Margaret's was black. She would later notice that Margaret's hair colour changed on a weekly basis as other apprentices used her for a model when doing colouring at the salon.

Diane could not believe how many people were at the two-storey Conti house, with a large ornate fountain playing in the front garden, and how many had spilled out into the back garden. She thought every Italian in the neighbourhood must have been there, and she was probably right. The amount of food that was provided was eye popping. There were several types of pizza and even a pig on a spit as well as huge bowls of pasta and home-made Italian sauces. The cakes and desserts were mouth-watering, and Diane found out that it was Mrs Conti who was responsible for the home-made cakes sold in the café. Music soon started. A couple of men played accordions, and people started to sing along with the Italian tunes. Diane found that she knew '*Volare*' and sung along swaying her body. Later she heard one of the men, with a beautiful voice, sing '*Till*'. Diane decided that whenever she heard '*Till*' would always take her back to one of the best days of her life.

Quickly filling a letter, to her family, Diane could not wait to tell them of the fantastic day she had spent, also some of the background she had learnt about her fellow house mates. Having had so much fun that day Diane suggested to Julie that the house mates might have a regular get-together to eat pizza and drink beer, which she had now grown accustomed to. With the weather hotting up the house mates agreed that Friday nights, after work, was the best time to socialise.

46

Sponsored by a large department store in Rundle Street, not far from the café. Julie told Diane that on Saturday there would be a big Pageant, and she should really see it. It was not only for children, but adults loved it, too. Bright and early on a sunny Saturday morning Diane and Julie caught the bus to town and Julie said she knew of a good vantage point where they could watch the Pageant. Thousands of people crammed the many streets where the Pageant would wend its way. There were bands, floats, people in various costumes and children seated on large, toy horses. The whole Pageant ended with Father Christmas and a King and Queen dismounting at the store entrance on North Terrace. The colour and atmosphere overwhelmed Diane. She could honestly say that she had never seen anything like it before in her life. It was something special.

Christmas was looming and Diane was feeling homesick imagining her parents decorating a tree and buying presents. She had sent a small parcel back to family comprising an Adelaide souvenir tea-towel for Eleanor, an Adelaide souvenir keyring for Leonard and a box of hankies, with the initial D on them for David. She knew that the parcel seemed paltry but was not prepared to pay the expensive cost of parcel post. She would have to console herself with the fact that she had survived a quarter of her imposed two year stay and that life could not really have been better than it was at present.

The last Friday get-together before Christmas with Julie, Pete, Margaret, Michael and Rosemary gave Diane an opportunity to hand out some small gifts that she had bought. Julie had suspected that this might happen, knowing Diane was buying gifts during her lunch break and not showing her, so had told the others what to expect. Diane handed out her presents and then was surprised when everyone did the same. Diane was shocked but delighted. Julie noted that there had been a special look between Diane and Pete. Could there be something about to happen?

Working right up until Christmas Eve Diane did not have plans for Christmas Eve or Christmas Day. Julie was going home to the country and although she asked Diane if she would like to come Diane declined. The thought of seeing a happy family at Christmas-time would not help her homesickness.

Sitting in the kitchen, on Christmas Day, waiting for the kettle to boil, she did not hear Pete come in. She believed that she was alone in the house over the Christmas period. Pete explained that he had van troubles and would not be able to go home after all. Diane and Pete sat talking over a cup of tea. Diane felt comfortable with Pete and showed interest in his life story before telling him of her situation. Pete suggested that they pool the food supplies and make the best of Christmas, after all not everyone eats beans on toast followed by Anzac biscuits for Christmas dinner. They laughed at their situation and Diane felt good. Later they went for a long walk and enjoyed the sunshine and the gardens that they passed along the way. Perhaps Paradise might live up to its name.

On Boxing Day Pete asked Diane to go for a walk again. This time he took her up into the hills not far from where they lived. The highest point offered a view of the Adelaide Plains which Diane had not even known. As they walked, they talked more about their lives. Pete told her that his correct name was Pieter Schneider and that he was German. As a small boy, he and his three-month old sister Leisl and his parents had migrated from Germany soon after the war as just like in England, much of Germany was in ruin. Pete's

parents lived in Hahndorf, an early German settle-
ment, in another part of the Adelaide Hills. He promised that he would take Diane there once his van was
fixed, which would not be for a few more days due to
the Christmas break. Diane like his easy manner and
felt very comfortable in his presence. She was already
looking forward to the trip to Hahndorf and possibly
meeting his parents and sister.

The next week passed slowly as the house was empty
apart from Diane and Pete and he had a lot of studying to do and assignments to write. He apologised for
his absence, but Diane understood as she had had to
study hard, too. However, Diane would cook for them
both in the evening. Pete introduced her to drinking a
glass of Moselle with their dinner each evening.

Finally, everyone was back in the house and life
got back to normal. At their first Friday get-together
everyone told of their Christmas festivities and showed
off some of the gifts they had received. On Saturday
morning Pete found Diane in the kitchen and asked
her if she was free for the day and would she like to visit
Hahndorf. Trying to hide her enthusiasm she raced off
to change into something a bit more presentable and
touched up her makeup.

47

The drive in the old van was a bit uncomfortable but Diane was taken with the beauty of the Adelaide Hills in summer. When they reached Hahndorf Pete drove straight to his parents' house which was located away from the main town along a deeply rutted dirt road. They drove through a pair of large white painted wooden gates, over a cattle grid, which Pete had to explain was an obstacle to prevent livestock from wandering as the cattle were reluctant to walk over the gaps in the metal grid. Continuing the drive they followed a long dirt road up to the house. It was another bungalow, as Diane referred to the single storey houses.

Greeted by a tall, striking looking man with a mop of grey hair, a large grey beard and holding a Meerschaum pipe, Pete introduced his father Johann. 'Call me John' he told Diane. She watched Pete shake his father's hand. Not a gesture she had seen with her own father and brother. Walking through the house Diane was struck by the difference in décor and furnishings of her own home just as the cuckoo clock struck one and the little bird poked its head out with a '*cuckoo*'. This amused Diane but neither Pete nor his father seemed to take any notice. There was a large, framed certificate above the fireplace regarding naturalisation. Diane could not recall, at first, where she had seen a similar one. Finally, she remembered. Mr and Mrs Conti had a similar framed certificate over their fireplace.

Mrs Schneider was also tall and elegantly slim with her iron-grey hair pulled back in a bun. She held open her arms to Diane and embraced her. Diane was taken aback, not expecting this type of greeting from a stranger. Pete introduced Diane to his mother Hildegard saying everyone called her Hilda and she would like Diane to do the same. Both Mr and Mrs Schneider spoke good English but with a definite German accent unlike Pete whose English was flawless. Unbeknown to Diane they had been invited to lunch and Hilda provided a most delicious array of cold meats, German potato salad with ham, sauerkraut and other German food items that were new and strange to Diane, but she enjoyed trying them, not wanting to upset anyone. For dessert Hilda had made an apple strudel smothered in thick, fresh cream.

After lunch Pete took Diane for a walk along the main street of Hahndorf, down one side and back along the other. Diane was intrigued by the German architecture of the buildings and the quaint foreign atmosphere the town had. During their walk Pete explained that his father was a commercial orchardist. He grew apple trees on fifty acres of land and sold his crop to a local co-operative. His mother did not work per se but involved herself in voluntary work for her community. At this point Diane felt she had to ask about his sister as she had expected to see her there.

Finding an empty bench for them both to sit on Pete took a deep breath before he spoke. On the voyage to Australia, he was very young. He recalled a day whilst the ship was at sea that a small group of people gathered on deck. The women were crying, including his mother who was holding his hand. The captain was speaking but Pete did not understand English at that age so had no idea what was being said. A small white box slid over the side of the ship and disappeared into the water. Flowers were thrown onto the water. The women hugged each other. The men touched Pete's father on the shoulder and said words in hushed tones. It would be many years later that Pete realised that he had witnessed a burial at sea and that it was his sister

Leisl. When he asked his parents about the incident, they confirmed that his assumptions were right but for them the pain of the loss was unbearable, and they were not prepared to talk about it. His father closed the conversation by saying that the subject was closed and must never be referred to again. Diane moved closer to Pete and hugged him. She knew that they were now kindred spirits forged by the loss of their siblings but felt that the time was not right to unload Derek's death on Pete. He was obviously upset.

Back at the house the four of them sat and drank percolated coffee with a delicious cake, made by Hilda, that sounded like Bee Sting, although that was not quite the German word that Hilda had said. Hilda had said *'bienenstich'*. Diane could not help but comment on their beautiful home and hoped that she might visit again. John asked Diane about her family and told her that he thought she was very brave coming to Australia at such a tender age. Diane felt comfortable enough to admit that her introduction to life in Australia had not all been smooth sailing and she was terribly home-sick but meeting people like them had given her hope that she could find a new life in Australia. Her newly found knowledge about their daughter tied knots in her stomach when she spoke.

On the drive back to Paradise Pete said that he was unaware of how she was feeling regarding homesickness, but it was understandable. His mother had once admitted that she wanted to return to Germany on many occasions but something good always turned up to change her mind. He hoped that something similar might turn for Diane. Secretly, Diane was already having better thoughts about her situation with Pete the focus.

The next day Diane asked Pete to sit in the garden with her whilst she needed to tell him something important. He was curious, not knowing what she could be serious about, but once she had told him about her brother Derek and his untimely death, he hugged her close. They both knew what loss meant and understood the pain and grief that each had to bear. Now they were soul mates.

48

Work at the busy café was routine with early morning starts and a lot of washing of cups and plates, and at times mundane. Diane had noticed that Michael was coming in each day for his lunch and sometimes sitting and having a coffee until it was time to return to the bank. Diane enjoyed the opportunity of seeing him and would spend a few minutes chatting but noticed Julie seemed more happy than usual when he came in. She insisted on making his sandwich and was heavy handed with the fillings. Diane just thought it was a friendly gesture.

Weeks rolled into months. Pete had graduated from university with a degree and secured himself a good job with an engineering company. Margaret had finished her apprenticeship and was moving out to Sydney where she believed she had a better opportunity of finding work. Rosemary had decided to move into the nurses' quarters at the hospital where it would mean no travel at odd hours of the day and night. Diane had asked the remaining house mates if she might move into the sister's room, at the front of the house, when they left. They all agreed, knowing how she had coped with the smallest, coldest room in the house apart from the toilet or bathroom.

49

A whole year had passed with Diane having many different experiences but learning the Australian way of life. She had supplemented her income by tutoring students in their homes. The experience had let her meet new people and learn how many were British migrants and how they too had struggled adapting to their new life.

Diane sat, and passed first time, the South Australian written driving test for her driver's licence. Licence in hand she went to a dealership and bought herself an economical, small, used car, green in colour, reminding her of a frog, to help her get around the suburbs, especially visits to the many sandy beaches that Adelaide boasted. She and Pete had already visited the Barossa Valley and Victor Harbor in his van.

With her ability to drive instead of relying on public transport Diane even caught up with a young couple, she had befriended, that had moved to a satellite town, north of Adelaide, called Elizabeth. They had bought a new house for themselves and their two small children, which Diane likened to a Council house in England. She was pleased for them. Diane was feeling much better now about herself and her situation.

Her friendship with Pete was definitely getting more serious and he had kissed her for the first time on her 22nd birthday as well as giving her some of her favourite perfume, which she had mentioned she wore. Pete took Diane out to dinner at a local Chinese restaurant that night. They had visited his parents on two more occasions and on one of them Diane tasted Wiener Schnitzel for the first time. Must learn to cook this she thought to herself.

On a warm and balmy Saturday evening, the house was empty apart from Diane and Pete. Julie and Michael had gone to a drive-in theatre. Diane could see nothing unusual about two friends going out for the evening. They had, half-heartedly, invited Diane along as they knew she had not been to a drive-in before. Diane declined saying that she wanted to write home. Pete suggested that they sat on the front porch and talked. He brought out a couple of cold beers from the refrigerator for them both. Talking to Pete was the most natural thing in the world to Diane. She felt so comfortable with him. How and exactly how it happened Diane could not recall, but soon they were naked in his single bed and Diane lost her virginity. She had found the experience thrilling and so natural. Afterwards they both fell asleep and as dawn broke Pete woke Diane with his hands fondling her breasts. She did not resist, and lovemaking once again took place having explored each other's bodies with kisses.

Next morning whilst washing the breakfast things, in the kitchen sink, Diane was smiling to herself. Julie saw this and asked why she was so happy.

'Oh, nothing', said Diane.

Julie took her by the shoulders and turned her around to face her.

'You've had sex' she said. 'I know that look any-where'. 'First time?'. Diane nodded.

Julie hugged her. 'That's great, welcome to the club'.

'The club?' said Diane naively.

Julie then told her that she and Michael were an item and they had been having sex for months. 'Be sure to take precautions though' she added, before turning and leaving the kitchen.

50

Just when life was looking good and letters between Diane and her family were full of exciting news a tragedy occurred. Tony Conti had a heart attack, at home, and had died. Unsure of what might happen to her job and her accommodation Diane asked Julie what they might do. Julie said that she had spoken to one of Mr Conti's sons who said that the business could run until Probate was granted and also until the Will had been read they would not know what would become of the properties that Mr Conti owned including George Street.

The café was closed for the day of the funeral. Diane, Julie and the others attended the lavish funeral which was like something out of a film. Everything seemed to be on a grand scale not unlike the wedding anniversary celebrations.

Probate took a few weeks and the Will had been read leaving everything to his wife, but she was no business-woman and said that she would make arrangements, together with her sons, to sell the cafe and the properties. Apologetically she advised Diane, Julie and the other to start looking for new accommodation and Diane and Julie to look for new jobs.

Eleanor had always read Diane's letters but looked for regret between the lines. She knew her daughter well and despite her upbeat writing Eleanor could sense the unhappiness she was experiencing. Leonard suggested that Eleanor write to Diane telling her that she would like to visit, but instead of Diane jumping at the opportunity she begged her mother not to come. She felt that she had been living a huge lie in her time in Australia. Sure, some of it was true but there were a lot of bits missing in her letters. Eleanor was bitterly disappointed that her daughter did not want her in Australia but accepted the fact, plus had told her that she would be coming home for good and not to waste the money.

Diane and Pete had discussed their future living arrangements and Pete apologetically said that his parents would not allow Diane to live at their Hanhdorf home. They were very old fashioned in their views, so Pete would be heading home to live with his parents in the interim but offered to help Diane find a job and accommodation. Diane and Pete now knew about

Julie and Michael being an item so it came as no surprise that they would be looking for a flat to share plus Julie had already found work in another cafe.

With no job and nowhere to live Diane was once again at her wit's end. Although Julie had offered for Diane to sleep on their lounge room sofa Diane was determined to find her own accommodation. A long drive to Elizabeth gave her a chance to think. She knocked on the door of Brett and Sue's house and they greeted her warmly. Sitting, talking over a cuppa and eating biscuits Diane spilled out her predicament to them. Brett and Sue looked at each other.

'You could stay here for a while', said Sue. 'You can sleep in Emma's bed and she can sleep with Mandy. It will only be temporary though'.

'That would be great Sue', said Diane 'but I think I should be honest with you and say that I shall be returning to England as soon as my two years are up'.

So a move to Elizabeth changed Diane's direction again. She secured employment as a relief teacher at the local high school and continued her relationship with Pete. Another teacher at the school had a spare room that Diane could move into, which she accepted.

It was November and Sue and Brett's two little girls had not seen the Christmas Pageant before, so Diane suggested that she take the children for the day leaving Sue and Brett time to themselves. The children enjoyed the day, and both fell asleep, in the car, on the way home.

51

Traditionally German people celebrate Christmas on Christmas Eve and Hilda and John were no different, despite the number of years that they had lived in Australia. Pete told Diane that his parents had invited Diane to join them to stay overnight. Diane bought Hilda some hand cream and a tin of shortbread whilst John got some of his favourite pipe tobacco. Pete and Diane agreed not to open their presents in front of his parents as both had bought intimate apparel for each other, having gone shopping together.

The German Christmas fare was more than Diane could ever imagine. After a hearty meal, and as the clock was getting towards midnight, Hilda asked Diane if she would attend midnight mass with them and then they would open their presents on their return, Diane readily agreed. This was going to be a new experience in a Lutheran church, and St Paul's did not fail to impress her.

The New Year was spent with Pete, Julie and Michael at their flat. They had dinner, at the flat, and then all four went into Elder Park to watch the fireworks at midnight. Pete held Diane close and said that he wished for a better year for them both and possibly an even closer relationship. Diane knew what he meant.

52

14 February 1966 would have been Derek's 25th birthday. It was hard to believe that he had been dead so long. However, the big change in Australia on that date was the introduction of decimal currency. Out with the pounds, shillings and pence and in with dollars and cents. For weeks, there had been advertisements in newspapers and on television with Dollar Bill spreading the word. Diane actually found the change-over quite easy. And the new coinage attractive. She was glad that she was not working in retail at the time as it might have been a bit daunting.

Diane was watching the calendar. Her two years would be up mid-September so she started to make enquiries with a travel agent. She could get a reasonably priced passage back to England sharing a cabin again. Hopefully there would not be so many children on a return trip.

Life with Pete was blossoming. Diane imagined her future with Pete and the children they would have together. They made use of his parents' house when they went away on holiday and Julie and Michael's flat whilst they were away visiting Julie's parents in the country. Julie had given Diane the key on the pretence that someone needed to feed the cat. They didn't own a cat!

Diane had always believed in honesty with Pete, and she told him that she would return to England when she could, but would he be prepared to follow her? Pete said that he would need to seriously think the offer through as he believed he could obtain work but was worried about his father's failing health. He was confident that by mid-September they would have something worked out.

Booking her passage Diane finally had a date. She would leave Outer Harbor on the *Fairsky*, again, on 20 September. Pete had written to a number of engineering companies in England who all replied that they would interview him, once he was on English soil, with the intention of offering him a position. Pete had broken the news to his parents that Diane was returning to England and that he was making plans to follow her. Although disappointed that Pete would be going so far away they realised he had his own life to lead and they would give him their blessing.

The ship was due to sail on a Tuesday, so the weekend before, Pete booked them both into a hotel in North Adelaide for two nights under the name of Mr and Mrs Schneider. Arriving at check in at two o'clock in the afternoon they tried not to giggle when they were shown to their room. Door closed and locked, they fell onto the bed laughing. They may not be married but they were certainly going to act like a honeymoon couple. Their room had a lovely view over the city and parklands, but Diane giggled when Pete said that they would not be spending much time looking out of the window.

Pete said that they couldn't have sex all the time, that they should see some sights, eat and then lots of bed. Diane thought this was hilarious. Holding hands, they walked down to the river Torrens, past St Peter's Cathedral to which Diane gave a brief glance trying not to think of Bruce and his treachery. Crossing over the bridge they headed for Elder Park. There was a Sound Shell, a Rotunda and a round building that was a cafeteria, where they devoured scones and jam and cream, followed by a trip on a tourist boat as far as the Adelaide Zoo where they disembarked. Another walk back along the river to the bridge and then back up to the hotel.

Pete arranged for dinner in their room. He said that he could not care less how much this weekend cost him as she was worth it. What a lovely thing to say thought Diane.

Dinner and champagne over, it was time. How long they made love they had no idea, but finally sleep overcame them. The next morning there was more lovemaking and tickling and licking and kissing. Never had Diane felt such sensations in her body before.

Pete insisted that they showered, had some breakfast in the hotel restaurant and went for a walk again. Holding hands and out in the fresh air Diane felt exhilarated. As much as she wanted to return to England, she would never forget Adelaide. This time they walked to the Adelaide Zoo and spent a couple of hours there before venturing into the Botanic Gardens where they were able to get a sandwich and coffee.

Back at the hotel they showered before going down to the restaurant for dinner. Pete was true to his word regarding no expense spared. They had lobster and caviar, crepe suzettes and champagne.

Back in their room Diane realised that this was going to be the last chance to spend quality time with Pete until he could get to England to join her. Not bothering with nightwear, they were soon in bed and letting their love take over.

Next morning at 10 o'clock, after breakfast in their room, they checked out of the hotel, where the receptionist wished them a long and fruitful marriage. Pete drove Diane back to Elizabeth in his latest car. Diane had given Sue and Brett her car as they did not own a reliable car. Diane had said goodbye to Julie and Michael on the previous Friday night not saying what her plans were for the weekend. Julie would have guessed.

53

Standing on the quay at Outer Harbour Pete held Diane close. He whispered something in her ear which she did not quite get and had to ask him to repeat it.

'Will you marry me?' he said again, but louder.

Diane jumped for joy. 'Yes, yes, yes', she screamed.

Other passengers on the quay turned to see what all the noise was about.

'We will buy the ring when I get to England' he added.

It seemed all too soon, but passengers were being ushered towards the gangplank for boarding. Pete held on to Diane for as long as possible making her the last to board.

With the gangplank lifted the ship started to pull away.

Deep in thought and watching the ship get smaller and smaller Pete felt someone touch his arm. It was the security guard telling him that he must leave the area immediately as they were about to lock the gates. Pete complied and having time on his hands decided to catch up with some old university friends in the city. There was a hotel that many of them frequented, and he was pleased that there were so many there on a Tuesday. Having a couple of beers but ensuring that he had food as well Pete spent an enjoyable, few hours catching up on everyone's news.

There was no moon that night as he made his way to Hahndorf, along twisting and turning roads, but he knew his way and darkness proved no problem for him. His mind was still on Diane as he drove. Along the dirt road and then turning into the home driveway disaster struck. A very large kangaroo jumped out from his right-hand side of the car, hit the vehicle and caused Pete to get thrown hard against the steering wheel. At the same time Pete threw the car to the left and a deep rut caused it to overturn, trapping him.

Hilda had retired to bed to read, whilst John stayed up to finish watching a television programme, expecting Pete home at any time. He heard a noise but could not make out what it was. It was then he heard a horn blaring and looking out of the window could see car headlights at an unusual angle.

Still wearing his slippers John rushed outside and realised that he was looking at Pete's car and that Pete was still inside moaning. Running back inside the house he told Hilda to call for an ambulance whilst he went out to Pete again. He saw the large dead kangaroo nearby.

The ambulance came, as did the Police, but there was nothing anyone could do for Pete. A Coroner would later record that he died from multiple injuries.

A few days later Leonard was walking to the front door, past the telephone on the hall table, when it rang. He picked up the receiver and heard a lot of static noise and someone in broken English trying to tell him something. Amongst the static the caller's words were intermittent and all he could make out was Australia, death and kangaroo. Unsure if this was a hoax call, he hung up the receiver after telling the caller that he had the wrong number. He then dismissed the call, going out to clean his maroon coloured car parked on the driveway

Eleanor was home alone when the telegram arrived. Most unexpected, she turned it over a couple of times in her hand before she carefully opened the envelope and removed the telegram. It read 'Pieter dead STOP Inform Diane STOP Letter following STOP'. Eleanor read and reread the brief message before sitting on the bottom step of the stairs to steady herself.

54

With her arm aching from all that waving and blowing kisses Diane went down to her cramped cabin. There she met Pam who described herself as 'fair, fat and forty, but in fact only thirty'. Before Diane could introduce herself, Pam had launched into her story. She was a nurse who had migrated to Australia to find a husband having been unsuccessful in England with men. She had taken up a nursing position in a mining town called Broken Hill believing miners were rich and probably looking for someone like her. She soon became disappointed and disillusioned. She found that mates, beer and sex, not necessarily in that order, was the common theme amongst Australian men. Plus, of course, their cars. She knew that this was a blanket statement and there probably were some decent men in Australia, but she tried for two years to find one, but without success. She had, though, her fair share of sex romps which she could not complain about. Diane was aghast. Could she cope with this sex crazed chatterbox for six weeks?

Finally, Diane was able to say that she had found a beautiful German man who was coming to join her in England so that they could get married. Pam told her of her envy.

Life on board was a lot more pleasant this time around. As expected, there were fewer children and fellow passengers seemed a lot more relaxed that many of them were heading 'home'. Diane had noticed a couple of familiar faces from her voyage out to Australia and would talk to them about their experiences and what had made them decide that it was not the country for them. She often bumped into Pam who was always talking to someone, especially the Italian crew members.

Towards the end of the trip Diane started having feeling nauseous in the morning. She mentioned it to Pam, who, being a nurse, had her suspicions, but suggested she buy herself some ginger nut biscuits from the ship's shop. They seemed to help. There had been a small outbreak of gastro on board, but Diane thought seasickness probably the cause although she could not recall being seasick on the way out. A couple of days before docking at Southampton Pam strongly recommended that Diane visit the ship's doctor. 'Don't want to take gastro home to the family, do you?' she said.

Telling the male doctor that she felt well apart from the nausea she asked for some tablets. The doctor then asked her a few personal questions before directing her to the small bathroom to produce a urine sample. Sitting back in front of the doctor she watched him carry out a couple of tests on her sample. Watching her face closely the doctor quietly informed her that she was pregnant. Her initial reaction was shock then disbelief. The doctor continued watching her and then asked if it was good news. She said it was, so he congratulated her and gave her an approximate date of late June. Leaving the doctor, she went up on deck and found a seat away from everyone. She then thought of Pete and relived some of their carefree lovemaking at the hotel when she must have conceived. Keeping the knowledge to herself Diane decided that no-one must know until she had told Pete and she was sure that he would be delighted. Such a pity that they had to rely on letters, but she would telephone him once home despite the cost.

Eleanor showed Leonard the telegram when he came home, and they sat and looked at each other trying to decide what to do. Leonard was for contacting the ship to tell Diane, but Eleanor did not want Diane to find out that way without any family around to support her. Plus, said Eleanor they needed to wait for the letter to know the full facts. Reluctantly Leonard agreed with her. They informed David when he came home that evening who also agreed with their decision.

55

The next few weeks dragged for Eleanor, and it was only the day before Diane was arriving home that the letter from John Schneider arrived. She gave it to Leonard to open and read out. John started off by saying that he had found their address and telephone number among Pete's effects and that he had tried to ring them but to no avail. At this point Leonard had to confess that he had taken the call but dismissed it, not even mentioning it to Eleanor at the time. The letter continued outlining the events that led up to Pete's death on their property. John went on to say how much he and his wife had enjoyed meeting Diane and although their son had not told them directly, they believed that the couple were in love and had a future together. By this time tears were streaming down Eleanor's face and Leonard was choked up.

Bright and early the next day Eleanor and Leonard set off for Southampton. David could not join them due to work commitments. Most of the trip was made in silence. Each of them running through the contents of the letter and how they were going to break the news to Diane.

Once Diane was through Customs and Immigration the three of them were reunited. Eleanor thought how well Diane looked, especially with her tan and an inner glow about her. Sitting in the back seat for the one-and-a-half hour journey home Eleanor and Leonard encouraged Diane to talk about her life in Australia. People she met, experiences she had, places she'd seen. To Eleanor it was one of the longest journeys of her life with her stomach churning all the way home.

Apart from lots of lovely flowers, from the garden, adorning the place Diane was surprised that there was not a welcome home banner. She kicked off her shoes and once more hugged her mother who seemed somewhat cool. Sensing that all was not well Diane asked what was going on.

Sitting with Diane on the settee in the lounge, Eleanor took both Diane's hands in hers 'Pete's dead' she said, quickly followed by the words, accident and kangaroo. That's all Diane heard before running to her room screaming, just as she did when Derek died.

For the next few hours Diane lay on her bed sobbing. She would not allow anyone to come in and refused all food and drink. Her world had just crashed. She eventually cried herself to sleep.

Waking the next morning and realising where she was and why she was still dressed Diane tried to make sense of what she had heard. She still wasn't ready to face her family, nor could she think what to do next.

Taking a shower and changing her clothing Diane unpacked but still refused to see anyone angrily telling them to stay away from her. Eleanor and Leonard were unsure of how to handle the situation but would give Diane a little more time.

Finally, after lunch time, Diane came downstairs, hugged her parents and then asked for the full story and some tea and her favourite biscuits. They handed her the telegram and then the letter. At first, she was angry with Leonard that he had dismissed the telephone call, and also the fact that they had not tried to reach her on the ship. Eleanor explained that they wanted to be with her when she got the bad news in order to support her.

The next few days passed in a blur. Diane kept the telegram and letter under her pillow and read it many times a day. Eleanor tried to encourage her to go for a walk or have a shopping excursion with her. Diane declined.

Eleanor took a couple of weeks off work in order to home with Diane as she and Leonard feared that her mental state was unstable. Diane was suffering from a severe bout of depression and Eleanor knew that she might need medication. Eventually Diane admitted that she might need help and agreed to attend a doctor's appointment.

Unsure if she should have her mother with her Diane entered the doctor's surgery alone. She started to explain her mental state but suddenly was telling the female doctor of her pregnancy. At this point the doctor suggested that Eleanor come into the consultation.

The news of the pregnancy came as a big shock to Eleanor, and she was unsure whether to be delighted or disgusted that her unmarried daughter was about to make her a grandmother. Telling the whole story to the doctor and her mother helped Diane face the realisation of becoming a mother herself. The doctor explained the ante-natal procedure from now on but suggested that they get the pregnancy reconfirmed in the light of the distressing news that she had received about the baby's father.

Leonard was taken aback but happy with the news. He was going to be a grandad and couldn't wait to tell everyone. Eleanor urged him to be cautious until they knew for sure that Diane and the possible baby were okay.

With strong family support and an ever-changing body shape Diane's depression slowly lifted. Eleanor had suggested that she write to Mr and Mrs Schneider and offer her condolences and tell them of the baby. Diane felt that she could not write due to the passage of time, since Pete's death, and certainly she could never tell them about the baby.

56

In May it was suggested, by Diane, that after redecoration she would take over Derek's old room and her small box room be decorated as a nursery for her baby. The wallpaper chosen for the nursery was bright and predominantly yellow as the sex of the baby was unknown. Eleanor and Diane went to a large department store in Brixton and chose an expensive pram with a sage green hood and apron. The saleslady said that it would be kept until after the birth of the baby in case there was any unforeseen change of plans. Very diplomatic thought Eleanor. Eleanor and Leonard would pay for the pram whilst David offered to buy a cot of Diane's choosing. Diane's packed suitcase, for the hospital, would be left in the nursery.

Waking in the middle of the night, with back pains, Diane knew the birth was imminent. She had been attending ante-natal classes and knew the signs. She also knew that it could still be hours before the baby was born so she would not wake the rest of the family just yet. Gritting her teeth with each contraction she just had to call out for someone to call an ambulance. David heard her, as she was in the next room to him, and he leapt out of bed, running downstairs to the telephone. The noise also woke Eleanor and Leonard who hastily dressed.

A short ambulance ride to the hospital and barely an hour afterwards Diane was delivered of a healthy son weighing eight pounds. Despite his red wrinkled face Diane swore she could see Pete in him at this early stage.

Four days later Diane was back home with her son whom she would name Peter, an anglicised version of his father's name. With the wrinkled look gone he did indeed look like Pete.

Baby Peter did not want for attention. Diane breast fed Peter, ensuring lots of bonding time, and his grand-parents doted on him. He was hardly ever put down as there was already someone ready to hold him, even David.

Watching Peter grow, over the next few months, made time pass quickly. He was a good baby in all respects. He slept well, ate well and after the initial flurry of attention would happily lie in his cot or on a rug on the floor gurgling.

Eleanor was happy with the ways things had panned out but she was anxious that Diane should start making a life for herself and Peter. She was happy for them to live with them but would need to convince Diane that she needed to get back into the workforce.

57

About the beginning of November Eleanor sat and had a good talk to Leonard about how she was going to tackle Diane and the question of her moving her life on. Leonard listened attentively. He had nothing to add to his wife's plans knowing that she always found the right words for any situation.

Diane's need to go early Christmas shopping gave Eleanor the opportunity. Leaving Peter with Leonard they headed off to Regent Street and Oxford Street. First stop for Diane was a toy shop and a large teddy bear was bought for Peter. Eleanor preferred to buy him some educational building blocks and a recent toy on the market. Sure, he was too young at this stage for the interlocking bricks, but she would keep it in the cupboard until he was older. More shopping brought them up to lunchtime and Eleanor suggested lunch in a department store. Over a bowl of hot tomato soup with a crusty buttered bread roll Eleanor broached the subject of Diane's future. She was prepared to give up work and look after Peter if Diane was to find full time employment. This came out of the blue for Diane as she thought everyone was happy with the current situation and said so. Eleanor went on to explain that everyone was happy but that the long-term needs of everyone had to be discussed. Feeling awkward by Eleanor's comments Diane excused herself from the table and went and bought two pieces of cake for them both. She needed a couple of minutes thinking time. Returning to the table she said she understood where Eleanor was coming from but did not need Eleanor to give up work, she would put Peter into a day nursery. 'No way' said Eleanor indignantly, 'I am going to care for our baby', with the emphasis on the word our. Diane smiled and reached out to touch her mother's hand. She knew her mother was right, as always, and she would take steps to work out her and Peter's future.

Back home and Diane started ringing the principals of a number of local schools asking for employment when school resumed in February. A number of schools said that they had a one term vacancy but another had a whole year that they could offer her. They invited her to attend an interview although she pointed out that she had taught there before but the principal Mr Perkins said that he had recently taken over as principal and would like to meet face to face.

Good news arrived with a batch of Christmas cards, including one from Australia. The good news was from the school confirming an appointment commencing in February 1968 and the other was from Julie and Michael. The letter inside surprised Diane. Julie and Michael had gotten married and were expecting a baby. Julie teasingly said that they had done things in the right order! Diane had written to her about Pete and the baby some months earlier.

It was a good Christmas that year. Not surprisingly David brought a girlfriend home for Boxing Day. Eleanor had suspected that there was romance in the air noting behavioural changes in her son. David's choice was a lovely young lady called Pauline. She was the same age as David and worked alongside him at the bank. They had known each other for quite a while but it was only now they felt comfortable enough to meet both sets of parents and express their joy of being together. Christmas is always a good excuse to break good news thought Eleanor thinking back to sadder Christmases.

58

Just before start of the February term Eleanor resigned from her job. Frank Gold was disappointed to see her leave but once again understood that her family came first. Gwen and Doris took her out to lunch and gave her a beautiful crystal vase knowing how she liked lots of flowers in the house.

Peter continued to grow big and strong and although Eleanor had never met Pete she took Diane's word for it that he was the spitting image of his father. Eleanor approached Diane about her writing and telling Pete's parents about the baby, but again Diane refused offering no explanation for her decision.

Coming home from her first day back at teaching Diane was bubbling and could not wait to tell the family of her first day and who she had met. She had forgotten how much she enjoyed teaching if you had good students and a school community behind you. She remembered some of the staff from her previous short time there but met two newcomers, like herself.

Val had taught at a couple of schools in Yorkshire but had decided on a change to London hearing opportunities for teachers were abundant. The other newcomer was Rob Winter. A nice, looking young man with jet black hair and a moustache to match. Diane thought he looked dashing and could imagine him in a Hussars uniform. She always did have a fertile imagination. It was not until the afternoon break, sitting in the staff room that Diane got an inkling that she had met Rob somewhere before. She brazenly asked if he recognised her. He said that he didn't. She asked him a few questions and hit the jackpot when she asked which school he had attended. When he said, then she was on the right track. She asked if he knew David and Derek Lipton, who both attended the school, he replied that he was good friends with Derek. Bingo, she had seen him at her home when Derek had a few friends over during school holidays and she had seen him again at Derek's funeral. He seemed puzzled. She obviously knew him, but he could not place her. Her trump card was when she said that they were her brothers. Rob stared at her.

'Don't tell me you were that little girl who wanted to play cricket with us boys and we said no'.

'The very one' she replied, 'and you wouldn't let me play board games with you either'.

They both laughed. Rob then apologised that he had not recognised her and for being so mean as teenage boys. He said that she had changed so much in the intervening years.

On hearing about Rob Winter, David said that he knew him well but after school everyone drifted away to jobs and never stayed in touch.

'You know his father owns Winter's Coaches' David said over dinner.

'No' said Diane 'I didn't know', but then remembered the holiday to Southend and the coach trip.

59

March brought good news for David. He had won a promotion to a branch manager's job with the bank. He would be one of the youngest to attain such status. The downside was that he would need to move to Bristol. David and Pauline had been engaged for quite a while, choosing to wait until he got a promotion. The move to Bristol meant that David and Pauline could now plan to get married and settled for September that year. Whilst in Bristol David would try to find a modest house for them to buy and Pauline would see to much of the wedding arrangements. At least David could drive home each weekend to help.

Peter turned one year old and to commemorate the event Diane and Eleanor took him to a well-known photographer's studio for a couple of portraits. Diane thought that she might like to do this each year until he was about sixteen. Two of the photos were stunning. In one he was sitting in a big wicker chair looking directly at the camera and in the other photo holding the reins of a large rocking horse. He was standing for this shot and slightly looking up towards the horse's head. His hair was almost platinum blond and his large eyes so blue. He was indeed a miniature version of his father.

Eleanor had been troubled for months about the fact that the Schneiders knew nothing of their grandson. Eleanor had tried to put herself in their shoes. They had lost both their children and yet here was a grandson looking so much like their son. She agonised over whether or not she should contact them. She didn't even consult with Leonard on this occasion, something she always did when she had a problem.

60

David and Pauline got married in a large church at Romford, where she lived with her parents. The weather was beautiful and warm for September, and it turned out to be a big wedding mainly due to the number of friends that they invited, many from the bank and some from their respective school days.

Pauline's dress hemline came just below the knee. It was white taffeta with elbow length sleeves. She wore a small diamante tiara and short veil, white high heeled sandals and carried pale pink carnations for a bouquet. Diane was Matron of Honour in Oxford Blue satin with a Cambridge Blue cummerbund whilst Pauline's sister Penny was the opposite in Cambridge blue with an Oxford blue cummerbund and white high heeled sandals. They also carried posies of pale pink carnations. Both dresses were of a similar style to Pauline's whose idea was that they could all wear the dresses again at other functions in the future. Ever practical was Pauline.

David wore a navy-blue suit, white shirt and matched his tie and pocket handkerchief in pink. The reception was held upstairs in a pub and was well catered for. David and Pauline were going to Majorca the next day for their honeymoon so did not encourage their guests to stay too long ushering everyone out at closing time.

As promised David had found a suitable house to buy and with Pauline's approval, they obtained a mortgage from his bank. Pauline was able to obtain a transfer to a branch in nearby Bath.

61

Towards the end of the year, and in secrecy, Eleanor obtained two enlargements of Peter's photos and one day when Diane was at work rifled through her desk drawer until she came across the letter from John Schneider telling them of the accident. She was looking for their home address in Hahndorf.

Feeling guilty she carefully penned a letter to Mr and Mrs Schneider and enclosed the two photos. She stressed in the letter that Diane had no knowledge of her actions but as one mother to another she felt they were entitled to know of their beautiful and utterly irresistible grandson named Peter. If they wanted, she would happily keep them informed of his progress and send the occasional photo. Stressing once again that she felt that she had betrayed her daughter but at the same time believed they had the right to know of their son's wonderful gift.

Quickly she received a response from the Schneiders. They were overwhelmed by what they read in

Eleanor's letter and indeed their shared grandson was the image of his father at the same age.

62

R ob Winter was given the task of arranging the
staff Christmas party that year. His parents had a
big house in Crystal Palace so with their permission he
arranged the party there one Saturday night, before the
end of term. His mother graciously provided plenty of
finger food and his father supplied a copious amount
of beer and spirits.

With the party in full swing Rob was able to get
Diane off to one side. He was cautious in his words
but asked her why she was 'playing hard to get'. Diane
looked him straight in the eye and said

'I am a single mother, with an eighteen-month old
son, whose father, whom I dearly loved, died in a car
accident over two years ago.'

There, she had said it. For quite some time she had
wanted to tell Rob the truth but in a school environment they had always acted in a highly professional
manner towards each other. This was their first social
occasion.

There was silence between them. Rob was lost for something to say. Finally, he uttered 'I'm sorry, I had no idea'.

Diane's reaction was to pick up her handbag and leave. Rob watched her drive off and turned and kicked a large potted geranium. It hurt his foot, but also his ego and his heart.

Diane avoided Rob for the last couple of weeks of term staying in the classroom marking books instead of going to the staff room. Rob could not help but notice she was avoiding him and was unsure of how to right the wrong.

Christmas was quiet for the first time in years. David had gone to Pauline's parents leaving just the three of them and baby Peter. Peter ripped the paper off his gifts and seemed more interested in the wrappings than the gifts. He was now walking well, and the Christmas tree had a fireguard around it to stop him pulling at the decorations and possibly pulling the laden tree down over himself.

Eleanor had noticed the Diane had been rather quiet since school finished and spent a lot of time in her room. This behaviour worried Eleanor and she hoped that it was not heading to another bout of depression for Diane.

Eleanor was usually first to pick up the letters on the front door mat after the postman called. That way she could slip Mr and Mrs Schneider's letters in her apron pocket without anyone else seeing them.

63

When the school term started in February Diane still acted cool towards Rob. He was desperate to tell her that he did not know and would do anything to regain her friendship 'with no strings attached'.

It had come to the notice of Mr Perkins, the Principal. He arranged for Diane and Rob to attend a weekend conference in Brighton. Rob was keen but Diane declined the offer saying that she had commitments at home. Mr Perkins was adamant. He was of the opinion that the information they gleaned at the Conference would benefit the whole school and he had especially chosen them as ambassadors for the school of which he was so proud.

When Diane told her parents that she would be going away for a weekend to a Teachers' Conference they were pleased for her. She did not mention Rob.

Knowing that Peter would be fine whilst she was away, she packed a small suitcase and asked to borrow her father's car. Normally he would say yes but he wanted to take Eleanor and Peter to the zoo. He would gladly drop her at the train station.

On the Friday before leaving Rob cornered Diane in the playground and asked how she was getting to Brighton. 'By train' she replied. Rob said he would be honoured if she would accompany him, in his car, to the Conference and promised he would not make advances or take advantage of her. Diane did not know whether to be happy spending time with him or guilty remembering Pete. Suddenly her mind was in turmoil and there were butterflies in her stomach. Not wanting to sound eager she calmly said 'thank you, that would be nice'. Phew thought Rob one hurdle over.

Rob came in his red sports car to pick Diane up early on Saturday morning. It was the first time Eleanor and Leonard had seen Rob since the boys were teenagers together.

As they drove off Eleanor looked at Leonard and smiled.

'I hope you are not thinking of matchmaking, my girl', Leonard said. Eleanor just gave him a wry smile and they went into the house.

Diane had been to Brighton as a child so was not overly keen to go out and see the sights. The seafront hotel was large and very ornate, and the ballroom was packed with teachers from all over Great Britain. Not wanting to be alone Diane stayed close to Rob's side, which pleased him. During the day they sat together when required to work on a set project. Diane then agreed to sit with Rob at the dining table that evening but continued to make small talk with him whilst he was dying to know more about her situation but was afraid to ask.

On Sunday the Conference stepped up a notch and they were paired off with other teachers to share their knowledge and experiences with children from diverse backgrounds. Diane struck up a conversation with a man, from Edinburgh, who had been teaching in Australia and she found it so easy to talk to him about the cultural differences she found. He agreed with her. At the break Rob found her, still talking animatedly, and felt a pang of jealousy.

On the drive back to London Rob could not help himself. He pulled the car over into a lay-by and turned off the engine. Diane just sat there. Rob took a deep breath before saying

'I have been wanting you since the first day we met again in February, and I have now reached a stage where I must know if you and I could have a future. If not, just say and I shall get a transfer to another school and get out of your life for good'.

Diane still sat there. She had been fighting her feelings for some time towards Rob. Each time feeling guilty that she was letting Pete down. There was no set time that a person should grieve for a lost love, and this made moving on, for her, so much harder.

Finally, she spoke

'I shall be honest with you Rob. I met a man in Australia, and we fell in love. He was everything I could ever wish for, and he was coming to England so that we could get married. Unfortunately, he was killed in a car crash just a I left Australia, and I did not know. I also did not know that I was pregnant to him. His legacy is my beautiful son whom I named after him'.

Silence.

She spoke again

'I have developed feelings for you Rob and am struggling with my conscience about whether it is too early to move on with my life. If you are prepared to take me as I am and be prepared for me to slowly move on, with your help, then I should love to be part of your life'.

Silence again.

Rob took her right hand in his and kissed the back of it. He then reached out, in the cramped confines of the sports car, and put his arm around her. She leaned forward and they kissed gently.

How long they sat there in silence they could not remember.

When they saw each other at school they tried not to show any special interest in each other, but Mr Perkins and the other staff had noticed a change in both of them, for the good.

Weeks turned into months. Outside of school Diane and Rob would often have a quick meal in a café or restaurant before heading off to their respective homes.

64

One Saturday morning, Leonard had gone out and Diane was coming down the stairs just as Eleanor picked up the letters from the door mat. Diane espied an Australian stamp and assumed it was from Julie for her. Eleanor thought Diane had not noticed her slip the letter in her apron pocket.

'Is that letter for me?' said Diane, startling her mother.

'Er, no.' she replied heading off towards the kitchen.

Diane followed her. Reluctantly Eleanor held out the envelope. Diane did not recognise the writing immediately, then the penny dropped.

'It's from the Schneiders' she said.

Tearing open the envelope she started to read out loud

Dear Eleanor

Thank you so much for your latest letter giving us news of Peter and the latest photos. He is so much like our

Pieter, and I cannot thank you enough for letting us know of his existence. I shall be forever grateful.

Sadly, I have to tell you that John has passed away with cancer. It was quite sudden. The doctor thinks it was triggered by finding Pieter at the accident site and then his death. They are together now in the Hahndorf Cemetery.

Before he died John set up a Trust for Peter's education and upon my death, he will become a rich young man.

I am sorry to end this letter with sad news but know you would want to know and maybe you can tell Diane, one day.

Regards, Hilda

The two women stared at each other. Diane was first to speak.

'How long has this letter exchange been going on? She asked

'A few months' replied Eleanor

'How dare you go behind my back. You know I did not want them to know.' said Diane

'I felt that you were wrong, and as a mother just had to help them at their time of grief.' Eleanor said.

Taking the letter with her Diane stormed out of the kitchen and upstairs taking them two at a time.

This was the first time ever that the two women had had words with each other. In the past they had always been able to talk things through, but this was going to need careful handling.

When Leonard came home Eleanor told him everything. He sat quietly, thinking over what he had heard. He did not agree with his wife's actions but in fairness he said he would want to know if they had a grandson. He then went upstairs to see if Diane would talk to him.

After an hour he came downstairs again and sat with Eleanor who was drinking a cup of tea.

'Would she speak to you?' she asked

'Yes, basically her reasoning was that she did not want to upset the Schneiders, who have strong religious convictions and are very traditional in their views regarding holy matrimony. They thought the world of their son and by telling them that their wonderful son had fathered a child, out of wedlock, would destroy their memory of Pete.' he said.

That made sense to Eleanor, but she felt vindicated in her actions. The Schneiders had taken the news well and she would now encourage Diane to send her condolences and write regularly to Hilda.

It took Diane a few days to come to her senses and then she apologised to Eleanor and hugged her close.

'I was wrong, but I was angry with the world when I lost Pete, and I know how his parents thought so highly of him' she told her mother.

With the secret now exposed Eleanor made sure that regular correspondence ensued between Diane and Hilda.

65

It hadn't taken long for Rob Winter to start coming around to the house, to see Diane, on the pretence that it was work related. Eleanor told them to put away the lies, and that she and Leonard were pleased that Diane had moved on and that they thought Rob was a suitable match for Diane. He was welcomed into the fold.

Another Christmas came and went and as good news should be told at Christmas, David and Pauline announced that they were expecting their first baby.

Many months later they announced that they were expecting twins.

A few more months and Lisa and Michelle came into the world. Healthy babies. Eleanor would have loved to have gone to Bristol to help Pauline with the babies, but that role fell to Pauline's mother, which was only natural.

Life was indeed good. Eleanor started to think that she was the luckiest person in the world. Sure, there had been ups and downs but then every family have them.

Leonard could not remember when he first noticed the indigestion and eating peppermints to ease the discomfort. He was starting to eat a couple of packets a day when his own conscience told him it was time to see a doctor. Thinking it was nothing serious he finally got to see his GP, Dr Grant, who sent him off for blood tests and an x-ray. He did not tell Eleanor for fear of worrying her.

Sitting across from the doctor he was told that the results were not good and that he would prefer that Eleanor was with him. Leonard tried to make light of the conversation, but the doctor's face was serious and not given to smiling. He would not tell Leonard the full extent of the diagnosis without Eleanor present.

That evening Leonard mentioned, at the dinner table, that he had had some problems and had seen a doctor. It was nothing to worry about, but the doctor wanted Eleanor to attend the next appointment with him. This worried Eleanor but she did not say anything, apart from the fact that she wished he had mentioned his problem to her earlier. She agreed that she would accompany him next time.

66

Peter had just turned three years of age and Diane and Hilda regularly corresponded. Eleanor suggested that Diane take Peter to Australia during the summer school holidays. She was sure that Hilda would love to see her grandson and he would be of a good age to travel and enjoy some of the experience. At first Diane declined stating that money was an issue, but Eleanor said she and Leonard would pay. Diane was also a bit reluctant to leave Rob as their relationship was on a good footing and definitely heading towards the aisle.

The first week in August 1970 Diane and Peter left Heathrow Airport bound for Australia, flying first to Sydney and then on to Adelaide as there was not a direct flight. Peter was good during the flight and the cabin crew fawned over him. There was nothing they would not do for Diane and him.

Hilda met them at the airport and once Peter was in her arms would not let him go. In fact, she suggested that Diane drive back to Hahndorf so that she might hold him.

A month of holidaying in Australia with Hilda and catching up with Julie, Michael and their little girl Jenny, were the highlights of the trip but she had to take Peter to the cemetery to Pete and his father out of respect. She also saw the spot on the driveway where Pete had died. Hilda had erected a bird bath just off to the side. As Diane and Peter were at the airport, ready to board their 'plane Hilda held Diane close and whispered to her to get on with her life, Pieter would have wanted her to find someone else and Peter needed a father. 'You have my blessing' she said then kissed her. 'Stay in touch' she called as the distance between them grew.

Coming back refreshed and full of happy stories, lots of photos and gifts for everyone Diane barely stopped talking for the first few hours that she was home.

With Leonard out of earshot in the garden playing with Peter, Eleanor sat down and broke the bad news to Diane that Leonard had cancer and it was terminal. Diane was shocked. Not her father. It could not be possible. He was always so healthy, and he was still relatively young. No, the doctors must be wrong.

Eleanor went on to tell her that whilst she had been away, they had done the rounds of x-rays, ultrasounds, doctors, specialists, etc. It was true. He had only a few months to live.

Whether the doctors had said months, in order to make everyone feel good, the predication was totally wrong. As school resumed in early September Leonard passed away, in hospital, with Eleanor, David and Diane by his side. Everyone was devastated. How could the doctors be so wrong?

Diane took a week off work whilst Rob took a day so that he could attend the modest private ceremony at the funeral director's premises. Leonard and Eleanor had talked about the end and Leonard was not one for fanfare, and the cremation was carried out to his directions. His ashes would be interred in Derek's grave and the headstone changed to give Leonard's details, too. Despite not being Derek's biological father Leonard had loved and cared for the boy as his own son, and his wishes to be with him were honoured. Eleanor felt comforted that they were together.

67

Diane had been aware of her biological clock ticking and although it seemed so soon after Leonard's passing, she and Rob got engaged. He had chosen a beautiful oval sapphire and diamond ring for her knowing how much she liked the colour blue and sapphires. A small engagement party was held at Eleanor's house with a few friends and Rob's parents, Ken and Liz Winter came. The couple had decided to get married on Christmas Eve. They opted for a registry office wedding and the reception was to be held at Rob's parents' home.

Eleanor did not express her disappointment in the arrangements. She had always dreamed of a big, white wedding for her daughter, in a church and a lavish reception at a golf course after. Now, of course, Leonard was not around to walk Diane down an aisle. Not wanting to upset her daughter's plans she put on a brave face and asked how she could be involved. Surprisingly, Diane and Rob declined her help with the wedding arrangements, but they said that they had a proposition to put to her.

Sitting in the comfortable lounge of Eleanor's home the three of them started with talk of the wedding before Diane made the opening remark that totally floored Eleanor.

'Rob and I have decided that we could live here until such time as we find a suitable house to buy' she said.

'I thought that you might move into David's old room, and we will have the master bedroom' she continued.

At first Eleanor did not speak. She was unsure how to react. This was not a consultation, more of an ultimatum she thought. A *coup d'état*, a takeover bid.

When she did speak Eleanor stayed calm and kept her voice low and even.

'That has come as a surprise to me, but if you would like to stay here, with me, I shall be delighted' she said, trying to make it sound like an invitation.

She went on to say 'however, I shall not be vacating my room, not now or in the near future'.

Silence.

Diane looked at Rob and shrugged her shoulders as if to say, 'I tried'.

Diane then hit Eleanor with a knock-out blow.

'We will be staying the wedding night and Christmas night with the Winter's, who will take us to the airport on Boxing Day. Mrs Winter has offered to look after Peter until we return from out two-week honeymoon.'

Eleanor was dumbfounded. She had brought Peter up from birth and now she was being pushed aside for new grandparents who did not know him. Did not know his food likes and dislikes and she needed Peter now more than ever in her grief.

Taking a deep breath Eleanor said

'You have obviously had time to talk about this and made your decisions. I guess I shall just have to abide by your wishes, but I shall tell you that I am deeply hurt.'

Diane countered with

'We understand how you feel about Dad and so we thought we would take some pressure off of you and allow you time to yourself.'

There were no Christmas decorations or tree at Eleanor's house that year, nor would there be festive food. She could not face the thought of sitting alone with no-one to share the excitement of opening presents or the smell or roasting turkey. She would be opting for a frozen dinner for convenience.

On Christmas Eve and wearing a simple cream coloured dress with a matching collarless coat Diane looked beautiful. Eleanor chose a sombre navy-blue outfit, still grieving, she struggled to be the happy mother of the bride. The wedding went ahead in front of a small group of family and friends and the reception at the Winter's was top class. They had engaged caterers. A lot more people attended the reception especially friends of Diane and Rob. Eleanor hardly knew any of them and felt isolated. She was even denied the presence of young Peter, as a baby-sitter had been engaged by the Winter's to take care of him and keep him away from the festivities.

Eleanor excused herself early from the reception feigning a headache and drove home to a cold and empty house. Once indoors she sat down and sobbed.

The five stages of grief had only just started for Eleanor. She was still raw from Leonard's death. She was angry at how both David and Diane had moved on so quickly from their father's death, but she was understanding enough to realise that David now had family commitments and Diane was keen to start a family, but she personally, felt discarded, worthless.

David, Pauline and the girls were going to Pauline's parents at Romford for Christmas, straight after the wedding reception. Diane and Rob were going to stay with the Winter's for Christmas Day and then fly out to Switzerland on Boxing Day for their two-week skiing honeymoon.

Although both Pauline's parents and the Winter's had invited her over for Christmas Day, Eleanor declined. Saying that she needed time to herself. She had previously given David and Diane money to buy the children some Christmas toys, on her behalf, not able to face going Christmas shopping. The mere thought of happy people spending lots of money and enjoying the experience did not appeal to Eleanor. Thoughts of Christmas past raced through her head.

68

Staying in bed until eight o'clock on a very cold Christmas Day, Eleanor tried to make sense of her life, without Leonard, although it was already three months on. The wedding had distracted her and looking after Peter each day had also provided her with distraction, but now she was totally alone.

Since Leonard's death she had been unable to part with any of his clothing or personal effects. Today would be the day and would keep her occupied against her time of loneliness. She also lamented that Leonard did not live long enough to draw his old age pension from the Government.

Taking a long, relaxing bath, liberally dosed with fragrant lavender bath salts, and then cooking herself some scrambled eggs on toast and yet another cup of tea Eleanor decided that she would start by emptying Leonard's sock and handkerchief drawer. She would be able to part with these items without too much sentiment although she could still smell traces of Leonard's aftershave on some of his clothing, especially his thick jumpers.

Leonard always kept his socks and handkerchiefs in the same drawer as his underpants. Taking the pile of handkerchiefs out of the drawer first a piece of paper fell to the floor. She picked it up and in Leonard's writing saw '*I love you*'. Taken aback, she rummaged in the sock drawer and there she found another piece of paper saying, '*for better or worse*'. Now she was intrigued and grabbed at the neatly piled underpants looking for another message. There it was, '*until we meet again*'. Just three bits of paper, but in Leonard's neat handwriting were messages of love that he must have written knowing of his impending death. Eleanor sat on the bed. How beautiful she thought, wiping the tears that were running down her cheeks. Carefully she checked his socks, underpants, handkerchiefs and the drawer itself to make sure there were no more messages. Then she placed the articles in a large plastic bag ready to donate to the Salvation Army.

Vests and tee shirts were next. She knew what she would find, and she was right. More short love messages, all different. Leonard's shirts were hanging in the wardrobe. Taking each one separately Eleanor checked the breast pocket, found a message, before carefully folding the shirts and placing them in the bag. The messages just kept coming and so did the tears. His suits yielded more messages in both the breast pocket and the inside pockets.

Thinking that she must have all the messages by now Eleanor removed Leonard's shoes from the wardrobe. Tucked into each pair were more messages. Up until this time Eleanor had not counted how many there were, but at least two dozen.

Deciding it was time to have another cup of tea, a couple of sweet biscuits, and to look through the messages of love again, Eleanor took herself downstairs. Counting the pieces of paper there were thirty-one of them. The same number of years that they would have been married, in November, had he lived, she thought. Leonard had really put a lot of thought and effort into his final farewell.

Feeling better and refreshed, she went back upstairs. In the bedroom Eleanor now had five large bags of clothing that she was ready to part with. Telling herself that she still had so much more to remember Leonard by and that it was only clothing. Albeit clean and good quality. Hopefully some needy persons would benefit.

Now it was time to look in the drawer of the bedside cabinet on Leonard's side. It had not been opened since his death, as there had been no need and Eleanor wanted that part of Leonard's personal life to stay intact a little while longer. Carefully taking out his spare reading glasses, medications, cufflinks box, watch and wallet she saw an envelope and a box wrapped in Christmas paper. Opening the envelope first she pulled out a beautiful Christmas card '*To My Darling Wife*'. Leonard's handwriting telling her how much he loved her. She was shaking now as she carefully unwrapped the box. It looked vaguely familiar, red leather with a tooled edge. Holding back from opening it Eleanor's mind was racing at a million miles an hour. Where had she seen this box before? Lifting the lid oh so slowly, Eleanor's eyes went to the size of saucers. There, lying on a bed of silk was a gold bangle encrusted with precious stones that read out the word DEAREST.

Eleanor sobbed. Where had this come from? How long had Leonard had it? She slipped it on to her wrist. She would swear that this was the very one that Mr Sully had said he sold. Perhaps Mr Sully had been the secret purchaser but how on earth did Leonard get hold of it. She would never know the truth. The two men who did know were now both dead.

The next few days passed in a frenzy of housework. The bags were in the boot of the car, ready for when the charity shop opened in the New Year. She missed Peter but busied herself cleaning out cupboards and drawers in the knowledge that Diane and Rob would probably want more storage space. Rob, what a name, why can't he be called Robert, she thought.

Her moods fluctuated going from high to low and back again, but everyone said it was a time thing and that she would gradually get over Leonard's death. She thought back to Derek's death, but she had Leonard by her side all through that terrible period of their lives. Now she had no-one.

When Diane, Rob and Peter returned Eleanor tried to put on a happy face but reserved her tears for when Diane and Rob were back teaching and she had Peter to herself.

69

Just as Peter turned four years of age Diane announced that she and Rob were having a baby, due at Christmas. There was that word again. Eleanor was sure it would haunt her. How her mother had detested that time of year and now Eleanor was finding that she had a similar phobia.

The months passed quickly. With the fine weather lasting longer than usual Eleanor still preferred to walk to the shops, with Peter in his pushchair, as opposed to driving the car. She was not the most confident of drivers having let Leonard do most of the driving over the years.

Diane and Rob had a healthy baby boy at the beginning of December 1971. Eleanor took Peter to the hospital to meet his new brother. When Diane told Eleanor that they had decided to name the new baby James, Eleanor commented

'That was the name of my brother who died in the war'.

Diane said curtly, 'He is named after Rob's grandfather, the founder of the business.'

Peter was moved into Diane's old room, previously Derek's, and the baby took over the newly decorated nursery.

Christmas was a quiet affair as it was so soon after the baby's birth, but Eleanor had put up a tree and let Peter help her with the decorations. She managed to go Christmas shopping, too. Eleanor was a good cook and did not mind cooking for them all.

With Diane and Rob living in the house and not showing any signs of moving out Eleanor assumed that she would once again raise a child. She did not mind apart from the fact that Diane and Rob never seemed to ask her, they just assumed that any arrangement that suited them also suited Eleanor. They would go out some evenings without saying where they were going or what time to expect them home.

Eleanor relished the chance of raising a new baby but was acutely aware that she must also see to Peter's needs and not make him feel alienated. She was sure to involve Peter in her daily routine with the baby. Peter would hand her the talcum powder or clean cloth nappy. He was also good about advising Eleanor if the baby was crying.

Again, time passed quickly. When Peter turned five the local school had a pre-school class that he was enrolled in. He wasn't due to start primary school until the September start of the school year, but this arrangement allowed Peter to have a period of a few weeks to adjust to the situation. Eleanor would walk Peter and push James, in the pram, to the school. Fortunately, Peter loved his new experience and a chance to mix with other children. Eleanor realised that Peter had had very little experience with other children and blamed herself. However, her devotion to her grandson had prepared him better than some of the other children. He knew his alphabet, could count to twenty and knew his colours. He would learn to read quickly with Eleanor's help.

70

Eleanor's memory of current events had started to wane, and she was aware that she was losing things or forgetting where she had put them. She did not consider her forgetfulness as worthy of a visit to the doctor, but all the same she thought that she was too young to be having this type of problem. She recalled that someone once said that the brain, due to short term memory loss, was like an onion. The outer skin slowly peeled away until you reached the core, but what it meant was that the outer layers were recent memory, and the inner were the earlier ones. That was why older people had such vivid memories of the past but could not recall what they had for breakfast.

Despite Eleanor's strong aversion to nicknames, when she did forget something, she would admonish herself by saying *Silly Mrs Onion Head*. She did, however, buy herself a diary for birthdays, anniversaries, appointments and things she did not want to forget. This became invaluable.

The next few repetitive years passed before Eleanor knew it. There was so much to achieve, during the day, with young children to care for. James had even started school in February 1977 and Eleanor now had a little more time to herself but was not making good use of it and did not understand why.

There was one niggling thought that rose time and again, with Eleanor, was the situation in her own home. She had been usurped, in her opinion. Diane and Rob had taken over her house and life. She was an unpaid housekeeper, nanny to their two adorable children and the gardener, having taken over Leonard's role and his beloved veggie patch. Diane rarely lifted a finger to help her mother instead praising her cooking and housekeeping abilities. They only paid half of the household bills despite using more of the utilities and of course, eating more food. When did this happen? How did it happen? Why did Eleanor allow it to happen? Eleanor was a lodger in her own home. Diane had always been strong-willed, but how could her own darling daughter be so callous?

There had been a golden opportunity, to buy, when the house next door came on to the market, after Gertie and Mildred both went into a nursing home together, but Diane and Rob said that they did not want to live so close. It would have been the ideal set-up, especially for the children, thought Eleanor at the time, and she would have gladly helped them if money had been an issue.

It was time for a showdown with Diane and Rob, but not in front of the children. She would pick her time carefully and especially her words. Oh yes, and there was the question of using her larger car for transporting the family around, occasionally, and saddling her with the old car which they bought to drive to and from their teaching jobs.

71

Eleanor chose the week before school was due to return in February 1978. The weather was cold, and it was pouring with rain and forecast for the next few days. This meant that Diane and Rob would not be out gallivanting and leaving her to look after the children, as they regularly did at weekends. James was upstairs having a sleep in his bed. Peter was reading one of his Enid Blyton '*Secret Seven*' books, which Eleanor had introduced him to, in his own room, which had recently been redecorated, by Rob, with an outer space theme.

Sitting in the lounge, Eleanor had made a pot of coffee and a light Victoria sponge cake with a slice cut and ready to be removed. She called Diane and Rob down from their bedroom where Diane had been resting and Rob planning his schoolwork, for the new term. Diane often said how tiring it was raising two small children. She never mentioned the hard work and long hours she put in teaching other children as tiring.

Having given the confrontation much thought and knowing that she would be catching Diane and Rob off guard she commenced by asking

'How's the house hunting going?'

Diane and Rob looked at each other.

Diane spoke first 'why are you asking that Mum?'

Eleanor then let them have it

'I am giving you notice to vacate my home'.

The look on Diane and Rob's faces was priceless.

'You cannot do that, this is our home' said Diane.

'You agreed that we could live here', said Rob.

Eleanor countered with

'I agreed to you staying, only because you led me to believe that it would be a temporary measure. How many years is it now?'

Silence

'Basically, I want my home back. I want to live my life my way and do the things that I want to do. I have loved bringing up the Peter and James, but I now think it is time that you two accepted the responsibility of parenting'.

Silence. Diane and Rob shaking their heads in disbelief.

'I accept that I have not given you time to think things through, but I am serious that I want you out of this house. I will not turn you out into the street, but I want to know that you are taking steps to find a house in the near future.'

Diane looked at her mother and said angrily 'We will be out by the weekend. Rob's parents will put us up there for the time being'.

'Suit yourself' said Eleanor 'just remember that I offered for you to stay in the meantime'.

Taking herself into the kitchen Eleanor realised that she was shaking, but there, it was said now, and nothing could take it back. She felt that this day would have driven a wedge into her relationship with her daughter but hopefully time will heal any rift that she had created.

Eleanor made sure that she was not home at the weekend. She had contacted David and decided to drive herself, in the old car, to Bristol and stay overnight with the family. She had not seen the twins for a few months. The journey would take about two and a half hours, but she would make sure that she took plenty of rest breaks at the roadside facilities. She had not told David about the situation at home but thought that Diane probably had, and it would be interesting to see if he mentioned it.

Deciding not to drive home until Monday morning Eleanor was not surprised to find the house empty. Diane and Rob's pieces of furniture had been removed as had the children's. Eleanor felt a pang of remorse, but deep down she knew that she had done the right thing. Diane and Rob would probably tell the Winter's and their friends how they had been 'thrown out' which was far from the truth, but it did not matter now.

72

A new year, a new beginning. Eleanor would start by thoroughly cleaning the two back bedrooms and the nursery and then closing the doors on them. She would not be needing to use the rooms and wanted to reduce the need to do cleaning in them.

Looking through a local newspaper she saw that there were some courses offered and thought that she might try learning a language. She opted for French and was delighted to be accepted. The class was held in the evening, and it would be an opportunity for her to meet new people and hopefully make some new friends. By looking after the children every day she had sadly neglected some of her women friends who used to love to go out for lunch once a month, but she was never able to.

Driving to and from the classes improved Eleanor's night driving but she was still lacking in confidence and sometimes forgetting the road rules. Luckily her memory lapses never caused her to have an accident.

Monsieur Trebert was the French teacher, with an excellent command of English but with a slight French accent, which Eleanor found attractive. He was tall and slim with dark brown hair, greying at the temples, clean shaven and wore black rimmed glasses, not unlike Hank B Marvin, guitarist with The Shadows, thought Eleanor. He had lived in England for many years and taught French in schools but now he was retired he wanted to help others to learn the language that he so loved. Eleanor had already made up her mind that she would go to Paris in the Spring and although she had learned basic French when at school, she had forgotten a lot of it and so was desperate to get a few common phrases under her belt.

The other class members seemed to be a variety of ages and both genders. There was one woman that Eleanor thought she recognised from the shorthand and typing classes of years past. Her name was Daphne. Over the next few weeks Eleanor and Daphne began practising their new-found knowledge and were continually being corrected by Monsieur Trebert as to the pronunciation. This caused Eleanor and Daphne to giggle behind his back.

Remarkably Eleanor's long time forgotten French language came to the fore and in April she was able to travel, to France, with Daphne. April in Paris, how romantic, she thought. Sharing a room, they stayed in a small hotel not far from the *Sacre Coeur*. Each day of their week's holiday they would walk along boulevards and eat French pastries with black coffee, all the time trying to speak French, even to each other. They visited all the usual tourist sights starting with lunch in the Eiffel Tower and Eleanor was thrilled when she could look at the *Mona Lisa* in the Louvre. The painting was smaller than she imagined, but so amazing to see. A cruise on the river Seine followed by a visit to Notre Dame was special. Eleanor was moved by the sheer size of the interior, the Rose Window and some of the wonderful sculptures. A trip to Montmartre was another highlight, especially when an artist offered to do a caricature of her. She thought the drawing was quite good and paid him well.

On their return to the evening class Monsieur Trebert was astounded by Eleanor and Daphne's command of his mother tongue. He asked them if he might give them private tuition as they were so more advanced than their fellow students. He also wanted to introduce them to his favourite 19th century French author, Guy de Maupassant.

With this first trip together a success the two women decided that they would travel more, in the future. Daphne was also a widow and with a pension from the company where her husband had worked, was financially independent. Eleanor did not let on that hers was an inheritance. Daphne's daughter lived in Surfer's Paradise, Queensland, Australia. Eleanor told her that her daughter Diane had spent two years in Adelaide, South Australia, so they had something in common in that respect.

With more time on her hands Eleanor and Daphne saw each other a couple of times a week and Eleanor re-engaged with her women friends. She introduced Daphne into the group and so lunches, dinners, cinema trips and weekends away became the new normal for Eleanor and she relished every minute of her new-found freedom.

Eleanor and Daphne accepted Monsieur Trebert's offer of private tuition at a modest cost. Eleanor would drive to Daphne's house and then they would drive to Monsieur Trebert's flat at Brixton Hill. The weekly sessions became enjoyable and now they were on first name terms with Louis Maurice Trebert. Eleanor or Daphne started by taking a packet of biscuits to have with a coffee during the evening. This developed into a competition between the two women when it came to cake baking, both trying to impress Louis. All three became close friends and the tuition fee was waived. Daphne sometimes teased Eleanor, on the drive home, that Louis fancied Eleanor. Eleanor would laugh it off saying 'don't be stupid'.

As Christmas approached, that dreaded time of year, thought Eleanor, Louis invited both ladies out for a celebratory meal. Unfortunately, Daphne came down with influenza and had to decline. Eleanor was ready to ask for a postponement, but Louis asked her to come as he had made a special reservation at a French restaurant that he wanted her to try. It was his favourite.

Leaving the hairdressers, in her car, Eleanor started to think about the evening and narrowly missed a pedestrian, whilst lost in her thoughts. Unsure of what to wear Eleanor opted for black trousers, black patent court shoes and a black top with tiny seed pearls scattered in the stitching of the yolk. She added a string of pearls, that Leonard had bought her, and the matching earrings. Her black topcoat had seen better days, but she knew that she would be removing it at the restaurant.

The Christmas post was on her doormat as she opened the door. Amongst the Christmas cards was one from Diane. She had not had contact with her daughter for almost ten months, refusing to make the first move, as she felt that she had been the one wronged.

Diane's Christmas card was not special, just a run of the mill one from a packet bought at the supermarket. On the inside Diane had written their new address in St Albans and telephone number. Mmm, thought Eleanor, a small step forward, but still a chill in their relationship. She would buy a special Christmas card for *Daughter and Husband* and send the boys a special Grandson card, too. She could not stay annoyed with them for too long as she was genuinely missing the boys. At least she had a telephone number and in the New Year might swallow her pride and contact them.

Reading between the lines Eleanor knew that the train from St Albans stopped at Loughborough Junction, near the school, so they obviously had not changed their jobs with the move and were commuting on a daily basis during the week.

Louis arrived, as planned, in his car and looked rather resplendent in a dinner jacket and black bow tie. Eleanor was glad that she had chosen a classic look.

The restaurant was in Central London, and they had a short walk from where Louis parked the car, in a side street, to the restaurant. Eleanor's coat was taken from her in the foyer and a ticket given to Louis. The Maitre d' showed them to their table which was a half-moon booth with a curtain behind them. Looking at the menu Eleanor was not fazed by the dishes offered as her French was almost fluent now and she and Daphne had tried a few, new to them, French dishes when they were in Paris, including frog's legs but they both stopped short of eating snails.

Starting with an aperitif they sat in silence, each waiting for the other to speak. Deciding that she would be led by Louis in choices, they then discussed the merits of the courses, and Louis ordered for them both and a bottle of champagne.

As the weather was cold Louis decided on warming dishes. They started with Vichyssoise, a soup made of leeks and potatoes. This was followed by *Coq au Vin*, chicken in red wine. Finally, *Crepes Suzette* with orange liqueur, served at their table by a waiter who added the pancakes to the orange juice and butter in the pan, pushed the pancakes to one side, poured in the liqueur before setting fire to the fumes. When the flames died down, he spooned the sauce over the pancakes and served. The whole experience was enjoyed by Eleanor. Although she was a good cook, she had never attempted to flambe anything.

Making small talk during the meal Eleanor felt that it was all leading up to something. Over coffee and petit fours Louis spoke

'As you know, I lost my wife some years ago. I loved her dearly and no-one was ever going to take her place' he paused momentarily before continuing 'until I met you'.

Eleanor did not know what to say. She placed her hand on top of his which was on the table.

'Louis, I know what you are saying about your wife as I had the most remarkable husband. However, I do have feelings towards you and would gladly be a companion if that is what you are asking'.

Louis took her hand in his and kissed the back of it. Oh, so French, Eleanor mused.

They spent the rest of the evening talking about their late partners, the fact that he was ten years her senior and retired. He and his wife had no children despite wanting them. A medical problem, with his wife, thwarted their attempts to become parents. Eleanor told him of her three children and Derek's tragic death. They spoke of the possibility of moving on with a relationship but stopping short of talking marriage. They both had a love of the outdoors especially walking and gardening although Louis had to contend with window boxes whilst living in a flat. They both like crossword puzzles, too. Eleanor remembered that Leonard hated crossword puzzles.

Next day Eleanor rang Louis to thank him for the wonderful evening and his excellent choice of food and to say how honoured she was to be asked for her companionship. For the next few days Eleanor felt like a lovesick schoolgirl. Yes, she really did like Louis and had never thought that she could feel so elated about a man again.

In fairness, Eleanor thought that she should let Daphne know what had occurred, but not all the nitty gritty. Daphne was still suffering from the 'flu but she sounded happy for Eleanor and hoped that she might still be included in their three-way friendship from time to time. Eleanor assured that she would be.

Eleanor, Louis and Daphne attended a New Year's Eve party at the home of one of their fellow students from the French class. Eleanor and Daphne had made a few new friends from the class and often attended the theatre or cinema with some of them. On the stroke of midnight Louis made sure he was alongside

Eleanor and away from other females. He wanted her and her alone. Watching a television set of the celebrations everyone charged their glasses to drink a toast to the New Year. As Big Ben started to strike there was a loud cheer and '*Happy New Year*' rang out in unison. Louis took Eleanor in his arms and gave her a firm kiss which she thought would never end. Pulling apart slightly, to catch her breath, Eleanor returned the kiss.

'Happy New Year', said Louis.

'Happy New Year to you, too' Eleanor replied, looking longingly into his eyes.

'Perhaps this might be our year' he added.

'Could be' she replied.

Daphne finally made her way over to hug and kiss them on their cheeks and wish them both a Happy New Year. It was such a lovely party and Eleanor felt that she had turned a corner in life and was ready for a wonderful future.

73

1979 did prove to be yet another turning point in Eleanor's life. She still missed Leonard but knew he would understand her need to move on with her life and he would approve of Louis, she felt sure.

Social events for three of them gradually dwindled until it was just Eleanor and Louis going places, seeing places and enjoying each other's company. Eleanor and Daphne never did get another holiday together. Daphne was happy for them both.

Louis suggested a trip to France to his hometown, of Beaune, famous for wines and one of the oldest hospitals in Europe. Driving a hire car from the airport in Paris, Louis drove, sedately, pointing out places of interest to Eleanor during the journey. She marvelled at the extent of vineyards. On arrival, Eleanor found the small town quite fascinating. The hospital had a patterned tiled roof that reminded Eleanor of coloured building blocks. It had been founded in 1442 by the Duke of Burgundy and his wife. There was a market with stalls and a quaintness to the whole place. Louis told Eleanor that he no longer had family there but drove around the streets pointing out where he lived, where he went to school and generally gave her a background on his early life. They stayed in separate rooms at a small local hotel.

Not tied to a schedule, Louis suggested that they drive to Monte Carlo, part of the principality of Monaco. Known as the playground of the rich and famous and the home of Prince Rainier III of Monaco and Princess Grace, previously Grace Kelly, an American film actress. Eleanor thought it was a wonderful idea but then deep down recalled how Leonard always wanted to visit the South of France and he never got the chance. Eleanor did not mention this to Louis.

With wonderful warm weather and clear blue skies, the drive was most pleasant. Eleanor was stunned by the magnificent views of the coastline as they drove down into Monaco. Louis found a reasonably priced hotel and suggested sharing a room, but Eleanor declined again, this time thinking of Leonard. The hotel was away from the Casino, and the more expensive parts of Monaco, but it was comfortable and having a car allowed them the opportunity to see Monaco.

One evening, after dinner in a restaurant, over-looking the Marina, they took a stroll to the Casino. Debating whether or not they were suitably dressed to enter and they decided against it. They opted to have a drink at a nearby bar and watched the parade of very expensive cars drawing up outside the Casino's front entrance. Beautifully attired people alighted and then a Casino valet, in livery, parked the vehicle elsewhere. Even Louis could not believe the amount of expensive machinery that he was looking at.

After a few days they commenced the drive back to Paris, but Louis chose a different route so that they might have more experiences of the fantastic country-side of France. Each town that they stopped at seemed to have a character of its own.

Back home life returned to normal. Eleanor found plenty to occupy her during the day but found time for Louis most evenings and weekends. They attended concerts and art galleries, enjoyed lunches and picnics by the River Thames at Ham, near Hampton Court.

Life was good again.

74

Eleanor's relationship with her two remaining children was strained and she decided that she must rectify the problem. She started by visiting David, Pauline and the girls every couple of months. She would drive herself there and stay at least two nights before heading home again, and spending much of the time with the twins.

Diane, Rob and the boys was a different kettle of fish. So unsure of Diane's reaction. She rang Diane one weekend and asked if she might come over for the day to see the boys. Diane, surprisingly, was amenable to this, to the point she invited her mother to stay a night.

On a sunny Saturday morning and deciding to take the train from Loughborough Junction, Eleanor had a pleasant train trip to St Albans and Rob was there to pick her up at the station.

The house was large and detached in a well-kept garden setting. Obviously, the years of living with

Eleanor had meant that Diane and Rob could afford an expensive home. Eleanor did not begrudge them this. Diane hugged her mother as soon as she walked through the front door. The boys were so pleased to see Eleanor and they both clung to her before dragging her upstairs to show her their rooms and the guest room where she would sleep. The family also had a small dog, a long-haired dachshund, named Hans, which seemed pleased to see Eleanor and when she sat down to have a cup of tea the dog sat at her feet. Eleanor recalled that they never did get a dog when they moved to Herne Hill. Eleanor now felt very comfortable in their home and Diane's presence. The past seemed to have been forgotten by both parties. *Tempus fugit*, thought Eleanor, time flies but it also heals.

The whole weekend went very well. Diane cooked some lovely meals and Eleanor was able to sit back and relax although the boys were always wanting her to kick a ball with them or go for a walk. The surrounding countryside was very pretty, and Eleanor did manage a couple of walks with the boys and the dog giving Diane and Rob some free time to themselves. Eleanor even offered to babysit the boys Saturday night if Diane and Rob wanted to go out, but they declined saying that they would rather spend time with her. Nice, thought Eleanor.

Eleanor was asked to stay Sunday night, too, and would take the train, with Diane and Rob on Monday morning to Loughborough Junction where she could get a taxi home. Eleanor accepted the invitation. Eleanor felt good and accepted Diane's apology for their behaviour when she asked them to leave her home. In fact, Diane told her mother, that she did them a big favour, as they were so comfortable in the rut that they had created they needed someone or something to move them on.

Diane had someone come in each weekday morning to supervise the boys and get them off to school as she and Rob left early. Eleanor did not mind the early start. The boys hugged Eleanor and begged her to come more often. She promised that she would.

75

Back home and feeling really good about life and having her family back, she couldn't wait to tell Louis about the successful weekend. She had deliberately not mentioned Louis to either David or Diane. She would visit a few more times before breaking the news of a very good friend.

It was Louis who broached the subject.

'I have been thinking Eleanor. Not wanting to foist myself upon you, but it would make sense if I lived here with you.'

Eleanor was taken aback. She enjoyed their platonic friendship, but it had not crossed her mind to ask Louis to move in. This was her domain and she guarded it carefully, doing what she wanted, when she wanted, eat and sleep when she wanted, etc.

'I could pay my share of all utilities and food, I could work in the garden, and we would both be saving on petrol by not driving to each other's homes,' he continued.

Silence. Eleanor had perfected the art of silence.

'Louis, as much as I like you and enjoy your company, we are such different people, as I found out on holiday with you. I do not think it is a good idea. However, if at some time in the future I change my mind I shall let you know.'

Louis looked hurt.

'Obviously I have offended you Eleanor, so I shall leave.'

With that he got up and left.

After he left Eleanor was angry with herself. She had strong feelings for Louis, but it was if she was afraid to give of herself to another. She was a de jure widow, she had independence and here was a man wanting to share his life with her. What was stopping her? Was it fear of the bedroom? What the neighbours might think? No, she decided it was what will David and Diane think.

Eleanor did not hear from Louis for over a week. She was determined not to make the first move and she felt well within her rights to set the record straight. She also gave a great deal of thought to his suggestion of moving in with her.

There was a knock at the door and a delivery man stood there with the biggest bouquet of red roses

Eleanor had ever seen. The note just said 'Sorry'. Eleanor took the bouquet and thanked the delivery man before closing the door. She took the flowers into the kitchen, set them on the table, sat down and sobbed. What a fool she had been.

Needing to collect her thoughts Eleanor did not rush to telephone Louis. After a cup of tea and her favourite sweet biscuits she picked up the telephone receiver. As soon as she heard Louis voice she could not speak. He kept saying 'Hello, hello'. She put the receiver down. Composing herself she tried again. This time she was able to speak.

'Louis, I am so sorry. I should have been the one to make the first move. Thank you so much for the beautiful roses'

'*C'est la vie*' he said, '*that's life*'.

Eleanor smiled. She wanted to make amends and invited him to dinner that night.

Eleanor had always been a good cook and decided to attempt some French dishes but nothing too complex, thinking back to the dinner they shared at a French restaurant. Her menu started with *Pistou,* a delicious vegetable soup from Nice in the south of France, which they had tasted during their trip to Monaco. *Steak Bearnaise* would be the main course accompanied by a fresh garden salad, from Eleanor's own veggie patch, as the weather was still warm. Trying to decide between a chocolate mousse or an apple tart Eleanor opted for *Tarte Tatin* served with a thick cream. Not able to buy petit fours locally they would finish their meal with freshly brewed coffee and chocolate mints. A bit of a cop out but what the heck, thought Eleanor.

On the dot of seven o'clock Louis rang the doorbell. Wearing a midnight blue cocktail dress, Eleanor checked herself in the hall mirror before opening the door. Louis looked resplendent in a black dinner suit and bow tie. Eleanor smiled at the sight. Louis bowed slightly and presented her with a bottle of champagne. The misunderstanding of the previous week dissipated in seconds. Opening the door wide Eleanor ushered Louis into the lounge, for a pre-dinner drink, but not before he took her in his arms and gave her a huge hug and kiss. They seemed to be in an embrace for quite a while, she thought, but enjoyed it immensely.

The meal went off splendidly. Eleanor had mastered the French dishes with ease. Louis complimented her on each course and made no comment about the chocolate mints with their coffee. Making a mental note that he would buy Eleanor some petit fours the next time he was in the West End.

Relaxing on the sofa side by side, Louis put his arm around Eleanor.

'What a silly old pair we are', he said 'surely, we can talk sensibly and find a solution. I think we can both admit that our deep friendship has developed into something a lot bigger than we originally thought *possible*' (pronouncing possible the French way).

Eleanor nodded.

'I have given this a lot of thought, too, Louis. This home is big enough for us both and we make a good partnership. I shall be so happy if you would consider moving in with me on a couple of provisos.'

'And they are?' he said.

Firstly, neither of us are to have memorabilia from our previous partners. Things are okay to keep but put away somewhere and not on show. This will be our home. Secondly, can I okay the furniture that you bring, please? There are a few pieces of your home that I really like, but there are one or two that I am not prepared to give house room to.

Louis laughed out loud.

'Eleanor, my dear, whatever makes you happy. Happy wife, happy life'.

Eleanor looked at him.

'What is that supposed to mean?', she questioned.

'What I mean my dearest, dearest Eleanor, is that it would give me the greatest honour if you agreed to be my wife'.

'Is this a proposal, Louis?' she asked.

'*Mais oui, Ma Cherie*'.

'Then the answer is *Oui, Oui, Oui*' she said and throwing her arms around his neck before planting a big kiss on his lips.

Holding on to each other for what seemed an eternity they finally pulled apart.

'I have not got a ring for you yet. I want you to choose one' Louis said.

The rest of the evening seemed to pass in a blur for Eleanor. She was feeling on top of the world and yet had a couple of niggling doubts. They were labelled David and Diane. Finally, Louis left and promised to return early the next morning to see if she had changed her mind or if they could go ring shopping.

76

Shopping for the ring reminded Eleanor of her time with Leonard but decided to put all thoughts of Leonard aside, she was now with Louis. Louis took Eleanor over to the West End to look in jewellery shops. He had previously browsed the area and had an idea of the type of ring that he would like to buy for Eleanor, but she must choose.

Finally, they found a jeweller in The Strand, one that Louis had in mind, and looked for a while in the window. Eleanor could see a pretty, triple stone diamond ring that was within Louis' price range, but she did not know it. Entering the shop, they were met by a charming, young man, who despite his young looks knew about jewellery. He took the black velvet pad of rings out from the front window and put the tray on a piece of green baize cloth. Eleanor selected the triple stone diamond and tried it on her ring finger over her wedding ring, which she still wore. It was too big. She then tried another ring which was too small.

Eleanor began to think that she was one of the Three Bears. The young man called to a young female assistant sitting out the back of the shop and asked her to bring the new design rings. The pad of new design rings was so varied, and many had coloured stones, which reminded Eleanor of the *DEAREST* bangle. As much as Eleanor liked solitaire diamond rings, she was attracted to a square emerald surrounded by small diamonds. Voila, it fitted perfectly. Looking at her hand and admiring the flashes of colour and light she just knew that this as the ring. Louis approved of her choice but would need to talk to her about leaving off her wedding ring. Snug in a ring box and safely tucked into Eleanor's handbag they went home to Herne Hill as they had a lot to discuss regarding the big move.

77

Growing up just after a war and during the Great Depression Eleanor had never had a birthday party. The family were just too poor to make a fuss plus her father's health had a sobering effect on the family. Thinking back, Eleanor had not attended any birthday parties, either.

Eleanor made sure that her three children did have birthday parties when they were growing up and in turn, they attended numerous birthday parties of friends. Eleanor enjoyed making small sandwiches and small cakes as well as having plenty of ice cream and jelly on hand. She also served the children fruit juice as opposed to fizzy drinks which her children wanted

In November Eleanor would turn 60 years of age. Perhaps this was the ideal time to have a birthday party of her own. Perhaps she and Louis could announce their engagement, too. She would need to talk to Louis and get his thoughts, but the question of, if, and when, to tell David and Diane about Louis kept nagging her.

After a celebratory dinner at Louis' the day they bought the ring, Eleanor broached the subject of when to announce their engagement.

'Do we need to tell anyone?' he said 'Can you not just start wearing the ring?

Eleanor then told Louis of her dread of telling her children about him, the engagement and him moving in.

'Ring the children and make a place and date somewhere in between where they both live and we will turn up and break the news together'.

The next morning Eleanor contacted David and Diane and suggested that as the weather was still fine and before it started to get too cold why did they not all meet up, on a Saturday, at Henley-on-Thames for a picnic. She told them that the twins and the boys would probably love the chance to be together again.

So, on a beautiful Saturday morning, late in September Louis drove Eleanor, in his old car, to Henley-on-Thames, roughly midway between Bristol and St Albans. Eleanor was getting nervous and twiddled the beautiful emerald ring on her ring finger having removed her wedding ring without being asked and putting it in the same box as her precious bangle.

Eleanor deliberately chose an earlier time for David, Diane and their families to be at the grassy bank of the river, agreed to, so she and Louis could arrive holding hands. Expecting a reaction, when Eleanor and Louis were a few feet from the seated family both David and Diane jumped up and greeted Eleanor warmly with hugs and kisses. David held out his hand to Louis and Diane kissed him on the cheek without being introduced. Eleanor and Louis just stood there.

'This is fantastic' said Diane 'what a lovely surprise. So, who is this gorgeous man?'

Eleanor was blushing now.

'This is Louis, and we are engaged'. There, she had said it and it had not been as hard as she had been imagining.

'Congratulations' chorused David, Pauline, Diane and Rob. Hugs and kisses all round. The four children seemed a bit bewildered and wondering what all the fuss was about.

'Can we have lunch now?' said Peter 'I'm hungry'.

'Me, too', said James.

The twins said nothing.,

'Let's eat, then talk' said Eleanor, sitting down on the picnic rug that Louis had laid out for them.

Both Pauline and Diane had provided all the food required and Eleanor and Louis had brought some drink with them including champagne.

As soon as the younger children had eaten, they took off to play games. It was time to talk. It did not take long to explain how they met and how things had progressed to an engagement and Louis about to move in. Instead of David and Diane rebuking her they seemed genuinely pleased. What had she worried about? As David pointed out, it was not as if both of them had just lost their partners. Time had passed and time heals. *'Tempus fugit'* thought Eleanor.

Eventually Eleanor and Louis were back in her home. It had been a long day, tiring but enjoyable. Eleanor felt so good about everything. Her children had taken the news better than she could have hoped. Now they needed to sort out the move.

78

Eleanor and Louis toured his flat to see what furniture would be moved and what could be disposed of. Louis' wife had liked antiques and Louis would put some in store until he could part with them as he was a sentimentalist at heart. Eleanor, likewise, had looked around her home looking to see what she could part with to make room for the extra furniture coming in.

David and Rob came on a Saturday morning to help with the removal even though removalists had been engaged. With the extra assistance, the actual removal from one flat to a house went very smoothly and Eleanor, Louis, David and Rob were sitting down to lunch before they realised. Eleanor had tried to stay out of the way of the men, preferring to stay in the kitchen, but occasionally had a look to see that everything was going into the right rooms.

Louis' bed had been put into David's old room, next to the master bedroom. David had removed his bed when he got married.

Late in the afternoon David and Rob both left, having declined to stay for an evening meal, preferring to get home to their own families. This actually suited Eleanor and Louis who later would buy some fish and chips and eat at home.

Following their fish and chips Eleanor decided to take a bath whilst Louis opted for a shower after she had finished in the bathroom. They both sat cuddling and nuzzling each other, she in her silk nightdress and he in his pyjamas, on the settee. Eleanor had made them both hot chocolate which they sipped as they cuddled.

'Well?' said Louis 'what now?

Eleanor knew what he meant. She had thought about this moment and to her own surprise was looking forward to being in bed with a man for the first time in many years.

Dirty chocolate mugs were placed in the kitchen sink, to be washed in the morning, and Eleanor took Louis, by the hand, upstairs and into the master bedroom. She had bought new sheets and changed the bedside lamps in order to change the look. She had thought about buying a new bed but decided against it.

Snuggled together in bed, with the lights out, Eleanor allowed Louis's hands to feel her body, through her silk nightdress. She reciprocated. At their age she did not expect things to go any further, plus she had almost forgotten what intimacy felt like. Without rushing, Louis sat up and removed his pyjama top, then fumbling in the bed, removed his pyjama bottom. Both items were discarded on the floor his side of the bed. He laid there naked awaiting Eleanor's move.

'In for a penny, in for a pound' she said.

'*Pardon?*' said Louis with a French accent.

Eleanor sat up and removed her nightdress, dropping it to the floor. Loving hands caressed warm, fragrant smelling bodies. It did not take long before they were together, and intimacy took place before sleep overcame them both. Neither had realised how much the removal day had exhausted them.

Next morning Louis brought Eleanor a cup of tea, in bed, and one for himself before climbing back in. They reviewed the events of the previous day and how well it had gone. They had not bothered to put their nightwear on again so now had a chance to look at each other's bodies. Eleanor was pleasantly surprised at Louis's trim body considering his age. Louis also thought how well Eleanor had looked after her body, but neither of them made comment.

It did not take long before intimacy took place again. Louis was quite virile for a man of his age. Eleanor admonished herself for enjoying the experience, but she was oh so happy.

Sunday was spent rearranging some of the furniture and sorting out some of the wardrobe and drawer space for Louis's clothing. Eleanor had decided to cook roast beef and Yorkshire puddings for lunch and then buying some seafood for tea.

Life fell into any easy rhythm for them both. Slowly they both revealed their respective past lives to each other. No skeletons in eithers closets. Despite Eleanor's initial reservations, Louis was very easy to live with, made no demands on her and was a great help with house and garden tasks. Louis never questioned her financial situation, and she never revealed the inheritance or the bangle.

79

Eleanor talked to Louis about a 60th birthday party for her and he was in total agreement especially as she had missed out on so many birthday parties in years past. Eleanor started by drawing up a list of people that she would invite. Immediate family, of course, Daphne, Frank Gold, Gwen and Doris. With themselves that would make fourteen. There were a couple of others that she could invite but held back for now. She would send out invitations soon, the venue being her home and she would do the catering. Food and drink were soon sorted.

On the day of the party David, Pauline and the girls came over as did Diane, Rob and the boys. The men helped Louis put up lots of coloured lights and some banners whilst Diane and Pauline helped Eleanor in the kitchen. The children were very good and played board games in an upstairs bedroom and Eleanor kept them happy with pieces of fruit and juice.

Eleanor's guest list eventually grew with the inclusion of her old friends whom she used to see often and have lunch with. Everyone started to arrive at seven o'clock. She was shocked when Daphne arrived on the arm of a young, handsome, young man.

'This is Tony' said Daphne 'he is my lodger, and escort when needed'.

Eleanor hugged her friend and told her that excuses were not necessary. She was entitled to happiness whatever the age difference.

Eleanor charged the boys with taking people's coats and putting them on a vacant bed upstairs. She had the twins taking around small trays of canapes whilst Louis was getting their guests their choice of drinks. David, Pauline, Diane and Rob mingled with the guests. Although Eleanor requested everyone not to bring gifts, she received an assortment of beautiful things, from toiletries to photo frames and bottles of wine. A selection of hot foods was brought out and everyone commented on Eleanor's ability to please everyone. Louis had bought the birthday cake from an expensive bakery, along with some petit fours. Eleanor was amazed at the cake when Diane and Pauline brought it from the kitchen. Everyone sang Happy Birthday and Eleanor made a wish as she cut the cake, being careful not to let the knife touch the base. Cake distributed and glasses raised to make a toast Louis stepped up and announced their engagement. In the fun of the festivities few had notice the beautiful emerald engagement ring on Eleanor's ring finger. Congratulations rang out around the room. The women all wanted to see the ring. The men told Louis what a lucky man he was.

Finally, everyone left. Eleanor's family had been good helping with the cleaning up. The four grandchildren had flopped into beds halfway during the evening and were still asleep when carried out to their respective cars for the drive home.

In bed Eleanor could not wipe the smile off her face. She had had a wonderful birthday and she had to thank Louis for being by her side. As she cuddled into his back, she let out a small laugh.

'What are you thinking? Louis asked.

'No need for condoms' she said laughing. He joined her laughing.

'One of the few benefits of old age' he said.

On that note they both decided on what would end the perfect day.

80

The next few weeks were spent buying presents for Christmas and deciding on the menu as the whole family were going to be together at Eleanor's home for Christmas lunch before disappearing to their respective in-laws for tea and Boxing Day.

A large artificial Christmas tree was purchased and set up in the front lounge by the window. Eleanor and Louis decorated the tree with lights and small ornaments before placing presents for everyone around the base. In the week leading up to Christmas they turned the tree lights on, at night, so that they could be seen from the street.

Christmas Day morning both Eleanor and Louis were up early. After a quick breakfast of tea, toast and lime marmalade Eleanor set about getting the turkey in the oven and preparing the vegetables. It would be a traditional Christmas lunch with all the trimmings. She had made both a Christmas pudding and a Christmas cake some weeks before and on Christmas Eve she had made two dozen mince pies and some shortbread. She really enjoyed baking.

A special effort was made to make the dining table look extra special with her mother's, newly laundered, damask tablecloth, matching linen napkins, red candles in silver candlesticks, expensive bon bons from a West End store, crystal glassware and silver cutlery. Eleanor placed some baubles and lengths of ivy on the table, too.

With her whole family and Louis around her Eleanor felt the happiest that she had been for years. She had put a lot of effort into making this Christmas special and she had succeeded. There was so much food that a lot was left over which would get used up on Boxing Day, Eleanor had planned.

Peter and James were given the job of handing out the presents, but everyone had to open their present and show it around before the next one could be given out. Needless to say, this task took a bit longer than anticipated but was good fun and everyone seemed to like their presents.

With a bit of encouragement, the family members were ushered out of the front door, loaded with presents. Eleanor had ensured that not too much alcohol was drunk by the adults knowing that they had long drives to their respective in-laws.

Flopping down on the settee next to Louis, Eleanor was feeling elated and yet aware that there was a pain in her chest. Indigestion she thought. 'Knew I should not have eaten so much' she thought. She did not mention it to Louis but would take something for it next time she went upstairs to the bathroom.

The table was cleared, chairs put back in place and the dining room generally tidied. In the kitchen the washing up was tackled by them both and they made short work of it. Thank goodness Eleanor had plenty of storage space to put everything away again. Catering for ten is no mean feat.

Later in the evening Eleanor made turkey and cranberry sauce sandwiches for Louis and herself. They washed them down with a glass of shiraz. Even later they had a mince pie each and a hot chocolate.

Time for bed and now Eleanor's indigestion had worsened, and she had to make mention of it to Louis. He agreed with her, it was just indigestion and she had been putting herself under a lot of stress. A good night's sleep would sort things out.

Climbing into bed Louis made the first move towards love making but Eleanor had to push him away.

'Not tonight, Louis' she said, 'I'm just not able to'.

Louis said that he understood but she must wake him if she felt any worse during the night. She said that she would.

Lying on her back watching dawn lighten the room Eleanor thought she had an elephant on her chest. The pain was unbearable, and her left arm felt as heavy as a lead weight. Listening to her own breathing she realised that she had a shortness of breath. Whether it was thinking about the symptoms, Eleanor broke out in a cold sweat. Time to wake Louis.

Louis acted swiftly and ran downstairs to call an ambulance.

Tucked up in a hospital bed wearing an oxygen mask and all colour drained from her face Eleanor did not look at all well. A heart attack, the doctor had said. More tests would reveal the amount of damage to her heart, but she would need to wait until after Christmas. She would stay in hospital for the duration.

Eleanor apologised profusely to Louis for spoiling his Christmas and she asked him not to tell the children until after Christmas, not wanting to spoil their holiday and have them rushing to her bedside.

Before the New Year Louis contacted David and Diane and told them what had happened. They both wanted to see Eleanor in hospital, but Louis persuaded them that it was not necessary at this stage and until they knew more there was no point. Reluctantly they both agreed with his request.

It seemed to Eleanor a never-ending round of doctors, specialist, x-rays and reading material on heart attacks in women. The cardiologist finally told Eleanor and Louis that she had been very lucky. A few more hours and it would have been too late to do anything for her. Her heart was in a very bad shape, and she could die almost without warning. He prescribed medications but was not prepared to talk about surgery for her. She could and should continue living a normal life but would always need to be on her guard and watch for warning signs, such as over-exertion or stress.

Back home again and the children managed to visit but David and family came one weekend whilst Diane and her family came the following weekend. They did not want to burden her with too many visitors at once. Everyone was very concerned and wanting to know what they could do to help her in her situation.

81

After discussing it with Louis, Eleanor decided to get a house cleaner to come in once a week and she also wanted a dishwasher. The sheets, pillowcases, tablecloths, towels and Louis's shirts could all go to a weekly laundry service. Everything else Eleanor could manage with her washing machine and Louis pegging the clean washing out and bringing it back in when dry.

Louis placed an advertisement, written by Eleanor, in the local newsagent's window. A telephone call came soon after. A woman named Myra Tomkins said that she would like to see the house and discuss hours and rates of pay. She only lived two streets away and admitted to needing the money.

Louis suggested that he go looking for a dishwasher whilst she interviewed the person who was coming around and left.

Myra Tomkins was a very large lady, both in height and body. Quite formidable. She reminded Eleanor of

Hattie Jacques, an actress in many 'Carry On' films. Eleanor felt somewhat intimidated. Sitting in the kitchen and drinking tea Myra Tomkins was quite overpowering in her manner and dictated the terms of her employment in no uncertain terms. Eleanor wished that Louis could have been by her side but summed up enough courage to say to Myra Tomkins that she would let her know as she had others to interview.

After Myra Tomkins left, Eleanor felt quite exhausted. If anyone was to come into her home, she had to feel a lot more comfortable with them than the woman who had just left. Not usually one to stereotype people, Eleanor could not stop herself from thinking that Myra Tomkins was a cross between a hospital matron and a prison warder. It was the only way she could describe her. Not very flattering, but that was her impression.

On Louis's return Eleanor told him what had happened. He gave her a hug and said that she would soon find someone that she felt comfortable with. He told her that he had bought a dishwasher and that it would arrive the next day. He had also arranged for a plumber to come later in the day to plumb it in for them.

Two days later Eleanor sat across the kitchen table from Meg Jones, a lovely little Welsh woman with a strong Welsh accent and about the same age as Eleanor. Louis was sitting in the lounge in case he was needed. Mrs Jones started by telling Eleanor of her cleaning experience and the hours she would be prepared to work. Unfortunately, this caused her to launch into the reasons why she could only work on certain days and certain hours. Fred. Her husband Fred was a demanding man who expected her to wait on him hand and foot and wanted to know where she was at all times of the day when she was not within his sight. She would fit in the house cleaning at such times as Fred thought that she was out shopping. This revelation sent alarm bells ringing in Eleanor's head. The last thing Eleanor needed was an irate husband. Like Myra Tomkins Eleanor said that she would let Meg Jones know of her decision.

'Will I ever find a house cleaner?' Eleanor lamented to Louis.

'Third time lucky, *Ma Cherie*' he replied. Eleanor loved the way he would drop the occasional French words into his speech.

A timid knock on the front door revealed Phyllis, when opened. Not a terribly tall lady, older than Eleanor but she had a certain charm about her. Within minutes of sitting talking to Eleanor it was obvious that this was the right person for the job. Phyllis had the unfortunate surname of Phillips, making her Phyllis Phillips, a bit of a mouthful, so she preferred to be known as Flip. Ugh, thought Eleanor, another nickname. She was a widow and drove her own little car should Eleanor need to be taken anywhere.

After a few more questions and a tour of the house Flip told Eleanor that she would work the days and hours of Eleanor's choice and they agreed on an hourly rate. Flip started the following week.

82

Hating herself for being a semi-invalid Eleanor looked for things to occupy herself whilst Louis was in the garden or out doing some shopping. The answer came in a piano. She had told Louis that she used to play the piano and he had previously suggested that she take it up again. It would not be the old, upright type piano that her family had had all those years ago, no, it would be a compact, spinet type piano in shiny black. Not wanting to stress herself she tasked Louis with finding one for her. He was delighted to help and could not wait for her to start playing for him.

A few weeks later the piano arrived and found pride of place in the lounge. Louis had also purchased a piano stool to match. Seated, Eleanor tentatively lifted the piano lid and gently ran her fingers across the keyboard to feel the smoothness. With Louis beside her Eleanor touched the keys and started to play. It was if she had never stopped playing. The notes were there, her deftness and her ability to keep time had never faltered. She was amazed by her own abilities. Remembering some of the tunes her mother had taught her, such as '*The Maiden's Prayer*', Eleanor launched into a medley. Louis was also amazed and applauded her when she finished.

The onion layers are still there, she thought to herself. The past will stay with me for longer than the present.

Piano playing became part of Eleanor's new daily routine. Louis bought her some sheet music that she wanted and gradually she added new, modern tunes to her repertoire.

Eleanor also felt that she wanted to exercise a little more and Louis started taking her out walking locally. She had lost weight and strength since the diagnosis and was now determined to try and get back to her old life as much as possible.

By Spring Eleanor was feeling so much better. Louis had been working very hard in the garden in the past few months and his efforts were on show. Eleanor loved to sit by the French doors and look out into the sea of multi-coloured blooms. There were daffodils, bluebells, jonquils, freesias and other bulbs that Eleanor could not readily bring to mind.

83

Louis suggested a short holiday to Cornwall, breaking the journey at Bridgwater in Somerset for a couple of days. He felt that the climate might be a bit warmer, for Eleanor, at Land's End. Eleanor had never been to the West Country before and was looking forward to seeing Devon and Cornwell and especially Land's End which she had been reading up on in readiness for the trip.

Eleanor told Louis that she had a little bit of savings and would like him to sell his car and buy another for their trip. Louis was surprised by her offer but agreed that it was probably time to change vehicles. He searched the newspapers and checked out car sale yards until he found a reasonably priced car which fitted the bill. Right car, right price.

On a lovely sunny April morning they set off for their holiday. Smooth sailing, with occasional stops for refreshments, until they reached Bridgwater where the car died on them. It had been acting strangely during the trip and Louis was trying to work out why but did not want to say anything to Eleanor. Louis was not too alarmed, at least they had reached their destination for the next two nights, at a comfortable hotel, in the heart of the town.

Whilst Eleanor rested in a cosy hotel room, Louis contacted the motoring organisation, of which he was a member, who sent a mechanic out to look at the problem. He lifted the bonnet and carefully looked around the engine.

'It's a lemon', said the mechanic.

'Pardon?' said Louis in his French accent.

'This car is ready for the scrapyard. It has been botched up to make it look better than it is and hide its faults', said the mechanic.

'What do I do?' said Louis.

'I'll get the tow truck around here and take it away for you. There will be a charge' continued the mechanic.

'Sacre bleu' said Louis, shaking his head.

With their personal effects removed and the car towed away, Louis went to tell Eleanor the bad news. He had to break the news carefully for fear of causing her heart rhythm to falter. She was shocked but fine.

'But the car salesman seemed such a nice man' she said.

Louis was feeling bad, especially the fact that Eleanor had paid the balance of the money for the car after he sold his car.

Eleanor was as usual pragmatic.

'We will stay here, as arranged, until the weekend. Meanwhile we will contact David and see if he can get us home on Saturday. I do not think we are too far from Bristol.' Eleanor stated.

The next few days Eleanor and Louis made the most of their time in Bridgwater, a large historic market town on the edge of well-wooded country. They walked and found plenty to interest them. Eleanor especially loved the history of the town. She had always been interested in history even in school.

Home again, thanks to David, who said he enjoyed catching up with them both and how well he thought Eleanor was looking.

Back to square one looking for a car, but Daphne's friend Tony said he could help them, with his knowledge of car mechanics. Still happy with the model of their choice, Tony found a very reliable car in less than a week for them. Eleanor paid for the car and Louis said that he was indebted to her. She said that she would not hear of it.

84

Flip had been house cleaning for them for many months. Eleanor was more than pleased with her thorough cleaning. After her sessions the house was gleaming. Kitchen and bathroom shone. Furniture was highly polished. Everything was in place. Newspapers and magazines were neatly stacked under the coffee table. Dirty clothing was in the laundry basket.

Eleanor had even recommended Flip to some of her friends, and she had taken up cleaning for them, too.

Eleanor was often heard to say in jest

'Do not leave anything lying around or Flip will have it picked up and in its rightful place before you know it.'

Louis had suggested that he and Eleanor go to a hotel, by the sea, for a few days over Christmas. He did not want her stressing about presents and food and hoped that she might get some rest. They told David and Diane of their plans and would send money to them to buy the children Christmas presents.

Eleanor knew she had memory problems but on a couple of occasions when she was sure that she had put something down it she could not find it again. It started with small change. She clearly remembered putting two pounds worth of money on the hall table in readiness to pay the laundry man when he came. She asked Louis if he had picked it up, but he said that he did not.

Eleanor bought herself a small brown leather handbag, to take away at Christmas to the hotel at Brighton. She could not find it to show Louis a couple of days later. She was getting cross with herself and calling herself '*Silly Mrs Onion Head*' again. This is stupid she thought.

When a crystal and silver vase went missing, she was seriously worried. Was Louis trying to make her seem as though she was losing her mind, she wondered. Would he be that cruel? She hated herself for even thinking such a thing of him.

Trying to rationalise the situation Eleanor started to look around her home and see what else was missing. She found more evidence of items no longer in her home. Time to either confront Louis or seek his advice.

Deciding to talk to Louis rather than confront him she told him about the missing items.

Louis was silent.

'I did not know how to tell you this, *Ma Cherie*, but the gold cufflinks that you gave me last Christmas I can no longer find'.

A terrible thought raced through Eleanor's head, and she ran upstairs, stopping at the top puffing hard, trying to get her breath. Not a good idea with the state of her heart. I should not have done that she thought. Going into the master bedroom she went to her bedside cabinet. Pulling the drawer almost out she reached towards the back for a box. It was not there. The bangle had gone.

Returning downstairs Eleanor told Louis that she had inherited a valuable bangle from her father's aunt many years previously. When she had found it in Leonard's drawer there was a valuation certificate and photograph. She knew that she should have got it insured, especially as she had worked in an insurance brokers and probably should have had it deposited in a bank vault, but neither of these things happened. She was angry with herself now. At least she still had the valuation certificate and photograph.

Eleanor did not need to be a detective to work out that they had been robbed. She admonished herself for her next thought. Flip must be confronted.

Eleanor and Louis discussed the best approach and decided that they would both tackle Flip before she started work the next day. Louis also wanted the Police involved now that he knew about the valuable bangle.

Eleanor wanted to sleep on it and think of how she would confront Flip, but Louis over-ruled her. This is one for the Police, he said and went to the telephone to make a report. Eleanor did not stop him, knowing that he was right. The Police said that they would send someone around the next morning before Flip started work and wait in the lounge initially.

Eleanor hardly slept that night. She worried about wrongly accusing Flip and the fact that she might never see the articles again, particularly the bangle. If she did get it back, she would insure it and deposit it at the bank.

The Police car was parked along the road and the two officers duly arrived at Eleanor's and after introductions positioned themselves in the lounge with the door ajar.

Punctual as usual, Flip arrived. Opening the front door with her own key. Cheerfully she greeted Eleanor and suggested getting the kettle on before she started work. The two officers emerged from the lounge.

'Hello there Phyllis. Long time, no see' said one.

Flip turned at the sound of the voice and was shocked to see two policemen behind her.

'Up to your old tricks again, I see' said the second officer.

Flip looked bewildered and tried to make a run for the front door, but a strong arm stopped her.

'Let's all sit down in the kitchen and talk about this' said the first officer.

'Where are the items that you have stolen Phyllis?' said the second officer.

'Okay, fair cop. How did you know it was me?' she said looking at Eleanor.

Eleanor did not answer.

The first officer took Phyllis's comments as an admission of guilt and duly arrested her. In handcuffs Flip was led away to the waiting Police car along the road. Neighbour's curtains were twitching but Eleanor did not notice.

Later a female Police officer called to take statements from Eleanor and Louis. She told them that Phyllis Gray, not Phillips, was a habitual criminal and had not been out of gaol long before they employed her. The reason her cleaning was of such a high standard was due to the years of cleaning in gaols. Eleanor and Louis were shocked. They had no idea of her past and felt duped.

A few days later the policewoman returned to say that numerous items had been retrieved from a pawn shop, including the bangle. The pawnbroker had only given Flip twenty pounds for it not knowing its true value. Eleanor was so relieved. However, the items were evidence and would not be returned to them until after the court case. Eleanor advised the police officer of her friends that also employed Flip and provided names and addresses. They too may have had items stolen which would add to the charges against Phyllis Gray.

Eleanor rang David and told him what had happened and how it would result in a Court case down the track. David sounded concerned but just hoped that everything would turn out alright.

When Eleanor rang Diane, she received a different kind of response. Diane was more than concerned. She asked about her mother's health and if there was anything she or Rob could do to help in any way. Eleanor reassured her that the Police had everything in hand and although the stealing had taken place within their home the Police suggested putting in some security to protect them from a possible house break, especially as Phyllis Gray knew the layout of their house and might still have a duplicate front door key. They would need to call in a locksmith to change the front door lock and possibly add a deadlock.

85

After the incident, Diane invited Eleanor and Louis to her home for the weekend, as she was keen to learn more about the bangle. Her interest had heightened regarding the story of the Indian Aunt.

Arriving mid-morning on Saturday Eleanor and Louis had stopped on the road for some flowers and cake. Diane was so pleased to see her mother and hugged and kissed her soon after opening the front door. After lunch Eleanor went to their room for a rest whilst Louis, Rob and the boys went to watch St Albans City Football Club play a home match at Clarence Park. Diane made herself busy in the kitchen getting food ready for their dinner that evening.

After a short nap Eleanor went down to the kitchen to be with Diane. As they sat drinking tea and sampling a small piece of the cake Diane could not help herself.

'So, Mother, tell me about this bangle. I am all agog'.

Trying to remember facts in chronological order Eleanor began with the story of her father as a small boy. The story of the Indian Aunt. His father's death at Waterloo Station. Mr Sully and the inheritance. The mystery of Leonard's acquisition of the bangle. The house cleaner and thus brought her up to date.

Diane had not said a word all the while that Eleanor had been speaking. In fact, her own tea had gone cold as she had intently listened.

Eleanor suddenly had a flashback to sitting at her mother's knee listening to family tales and here she was passing them on to the next generation.

'Fascinating' said Diane 'I had no idea of your early life and my grandparents' struggles. I want to know more. Please write a book, Mum'.

Strangely enough, Eleanor felt a sense of relief having relived parts of her life again. It was so good that Diane was genuinely interested. She would show her the photograph of the bangle next time Diane visited her.

Dinner that night was a very chatty affair. Diane kept asking Eleanor to repeat some parts of the story, for Rob, but Eleanor was aware that Louis had never heard some of it before, so he was learning a lot that evening. He was listening but not saying anything.

Sunday, after a lie in, Eleanor and Louis went for a walk, hand in hand, in a nearby park.

'Why did you not tell me this Eleanor? I thought we promised to tell each other about our previous lives and yet you held back', Louis said in a serious manner.

'I cannot explain', said Eleanor. 'The inheritance was a shock to me, and I do not know why I have not made mention of it before now'.

Louis shook his head

'I am deeply hurt' he said 'it will take a little while for this to sink in. Your family will think I am a gold miner and only after your money'.

'Gold digger', said Eleanor.

'*Pardon?*' he said with his French accent.

'A gold digger not a gold miner' she said, laughing.

'Are they not the same?' he questioned.

'No, and I know you want me, not my money. You have proven yourself over and over again'.

With that Eleanor threw her arms around Louis's neck and kissed him hard on the lips.

They sat on a nearby park bench in silence. Eleanor moved closer to Louis. He did not move.

'Sorry' she said 'friends?'

Still not happy Louis shrugged 'S'pose so' he replied.

The rest of the day went off without incident, but it was obvious that Louis was still hurting, and the family sensed it, too. Eleanor could not think of any way to cheer him up.

The drive home to Herne Hill was in relative silence.

Monday morning Louis made the first cup of tea, as usual, and took it in to Eleanor.

'I am the one who should be apologising' he said 'I acted like a spoilt child, and I am indeed very sorry. I do not want your money, only you, and hope that we can pick up from where we left off prior to going to your daughter's, for the weekend'.

'If only we could turn back the clock' thought Eleanor regretfully, remorseful for upsetting Louis so badly.

Eleanor accepted his apology and after drinking their tea, cuddled up and both went back to sleep.

86

Months passed and Eleanor and Louis had to attend Court when Phyllis Gray's trial started. A number of her friends were also called as witnesses as they too had had items stolen. Eleanor felt bad that she had recommend Flip to them all.

Phyllis Gray pleaded guilty and told the Magistrate that she had felt bad, this time, in stealing from her employer. She said how Eleanor and Louis had been so good to her, but old habits die hard and selling to the pawn shop was easy money. She was duly imprisoned, and her prior convictions did not help her when the time came for sentencing.

'What a waste of a life' Eleanor said to Louis as they left the Court.

As soon as the stolen items were back with Eleanor, she and Louis went to Frank Gold to have the bangle insured. Frank was taken aback when he saw the photograph and valuation. He arranged insurance immediately. Giving Eleanor a wink he told her that he was now divorced. Their secret was safe.

The bank manager was happy to take possession of the package that she handed him. He would have no idea of the contents, but it would be safely stored in the vault he assured her.

87

Having decided to spend Christmas at a Brighton seafront hotel, Louis made all the necessary arrangements, including their arrival on Christmas Eve afternoon. Although the weather was cold, windy and bleak, the hotel was very comfortable and provided an excellent Christmas lunch and dinner and similar again on Boxing Day. Eleanor and Louis, although not big drinkers, enjoyed the fact that they could drink more and not have to drive.

On Christmas morning Louis presented Eleanor with a gold chain identity bracelet and it was inscribed '*Je t'aime*' on the flat area, which translated as 'I love you'. Eleanor gave Louis a Rolex watch. Now that the source of money was out in the open Eleanor felt more comfortable in spending it.

Eleanor arranged for herself and Louis to spend New Year's Eve at a London hotel and stay the night. She was not wasting money, but still felt that she had to make it up to Louis. As they alighted from the taxi, at the hotel entrance, Louis shook his head.

'You did not have to do this, Eleanor' he said 'please do not throw your money away on me. It is for your children and grandchildren. An inheritance, remember?'

Their room overlooked the river Thames, although it was hard to see in the dark, but the lights along the Embankment threw across the water. At the hotel they were treated like Royalty. They took dinner in their room before going downstairs to the ballroom for an evening of dancing and drinking. As Big Ben struck twelve, balloons fell from the ceiling, champagne corks popped, blowers, whistles and cheers went up before 'Auld Lang Syne' started. The atmosphere was wonderful as 1981 was heralded in by a very happy and noisy crowd. Sleep came easily to them both that night, not used to late nights and alcohol. Next morning, they were intimate. Louis said that they should not miss the opportunity as they would probably never stay there again. Eleanor agreed.

88

The next few winter months passed without incident. Life had fallen back into an easy rhythm. Eleanor had a couple of appointments with the cardiologist but all he could tell her was that she could die at any minute, so just enjoy life.

Armed with the knowledge that life could be short Eleanor and Louis flew to Rimini, Italy and stayed at a hotel, on the beach, with its own lagoon. Two weeks of sunshine would do them both a lot of good.

One day they took a bus trip to San Marino, the fifth smallest country in the world. As they alighted from the bus a young man approached them and handed them a flyer. In a Cockney accent he said

'Want some English fish and chips?'. The flyer gave details of his shop nearby.

Eleanor and Louis looked at each other and laughed. Fancy coming all this way for English fish and chips. They strolled the medieval walled old town and narrow cobblestone streets and marvelled at The

Three Towers, castle-like citadels dating to the 11th century on neighbouring peaks. A most enjoyable and worthwhile experience, they agreed.

In Rimini, there was a dressmaker's shop opposite the hotel, where they were staying, and Eleanor found that the female proprietor would make her a dress, in twenty-four hours, for a reasonable price. Selecting two beautiful silk materials, one a turquoise floral whilst the other a myriad of tiny blue squares, not unlike mosaic, Eleanor decided that she would buy two dresses. The woman, called Maria, then sketched the dresses she thought might suit Eleanor. They were both slimline, short sleeve and with a vee at the back. When the two dresses were delivered to Eleanor at the hotel, whilst she was having dinner, she could not help herself but open the boxes. To her delight the turquoise dress had a cape that could also be tied around the waist making it look like a peplum or over-skirt. The blue dress had a similar cape but with two tiers that could also be tied as a peplum.

Other female guests commented favourably on them and wanted to know where she got them. She readily told them. Business would be good for Maria.

Next day, wearing a very full, predominantly white, skirt scattered with large orange flowers, Eleanor went to pay for the dresses. Maria said that she would only charge for one dress as she had admired Eleanor wearing the skirt before and would very much like to have it. Deal done, Eleanor went back to the hotel and changed. Returned to the shop and handed Maria the skirt. Two happy ladies.

Someone told them of a venue, in nearby Viserba, where they could dance under the stars. Wearing one of her new dresses and a pair of new leather sandals Eleanor and Louis took a taxi to Viserba. The taxi driver knew exactly where they were headed. The venue was indeed open air, next to the beach and decorated with hundreds of small electric lights. The small, live band with a singer, played music that was varied and seemed to be energetic to begin with and slower and more romantic as the night went on. One of the last tunes played would stay with Eleanor. It was '*Till*' and a young woman sang it in Italian.

Viserba was not too far from their hotel, so Eleanor and Louis decided to walk back along the beach, splashing their feet at the water's edge as they went. Eleanor, swinging her new sandals in one hand and holding Louis's in the other, gently humming '*Till*'. She would try to find the record on her return to home and perhaps an English translation.

Days of lying on the beach and eating ice cream served by a young man wearing swim trunks, a white cotton jacket, neatly pressed and white gloves made for some happy memories. Eleanor nicknamed him '*Gelati Joe*', against her better judgment, but he was now etched in her memory.

89

Amongst the mail awaiting their return there was a wedding invitation from Frank Gold. He was marrying Elizabeth Masters, in a few weeks' time, at their new home in Tunbridge Wells. Frank had enclosed a small note saying that he had retired after selling his business. However, the new owner had kept Gwen and Doris on as employees. He and Elizabeth had bought a bungalow just outside the town and would hold the wedding and reception in their large garden.

Eleanor smiled at the note. Thinking back to how she had burst in on them years previously, never suspecting anything untoward about Mrs Masters numerous visits to the office. How naïve of her.

Driving to Royal Tunbridge Wells, early on a Saturday morning, Eleanor raised the subject, with Louis, of whether she should sell her home. Perhaps it was now too big for their needs and the large garden was demanding more and more time of Louis. He was quiet for a while and then asked her what had caused this thought. Eleanor said that she did not know, but a move to the country or the coast might benefit them both. Louis asked if he might think on it for a bit longer before giving his response. The subject was dropped.

Frank and Elizabeth's bungalow was situated not far from the Pantiles, a Georgian colonnade of small shops. Eleanor and Louis stopped off there to stretch their legs and have a cup of coffee. They were early for the afternoon wedding and decided that Eleanor might benefit from a short rest. One of the shops was a real estate agent and browsing the homes for sale in the window they were surprised at how cheap homes were in the area.

Arriving at Frank and Elizabeth's house a few minutes early they were greeted by Frank with a glass of champagne each. Elizabeth would not make an entrance until the ceremony began. Chatting to Frank was so easy as he showed them around his home. He had always been a charmer, thought Eleanor, and she could see why Elizabeth fell for him.

A celebrant conducted the ceremony under an arch of roses and ivy. Frank looked resplendent in a morning suit, with tails, and a striped, silk cravat whilst Elizabeth had chosen a mid-calf length cream dress, with three quarter length sleeves and a round neck, to which she added a pashmina for her shoulders. The silk material of the dress fell gently over her hips. With her blonde hair swept up Elizabeth looked as stunning as she always had. The reception was more like a cocktail party with two waiters continuously walking around with trays of canapes and bite sized sandwiches. Prawns were on cocktail sticks. Champagne was plentiful but Eleanor and Louis soon switched to soft drink. Neither were big drinkers.

Before they left the reception Elizabeth Masters, now Mrs Frank Gold, managed to talk to Eleanor, alone, in a secluded part of the fragrant rose garden. Surprisingly Elizabeth asked Eleanor if she would like to buy her full length, genuine mink coat. Eleanor was taken aback. She had never ever thought of owning a mink coat even though she had more than enough money to buy one. Elizabeth confided that she did not have as much money as Frank thought she had and had spent more on her wedding outfit than intended. Eleanor was shocked. She could not believe what she was hearing. Elizabeth thought that she and Eleanor would be of a similar size, and she wanted one hundred pounds for the coat. Eleanor was in a dilemma. Elizabeth asked her to go into the house with her and into the master bedroom where Eleanor tried on the coat. It fitted perfectly, and it felt good as Eleanor hugged it to herself and paraded in front of a cheval mirror. The decision to buy was quick. With an agreed price of ninety-five pounds the coat was packed in its original box and quickly and secretly, taken out to the boot of Louis' car. Louis was wondering what the 'cloak and dagger' action was all about, but Eleanor said that she would explain later. Eleanor promised to post a cheque to Elizabeth in the following week and she was true to her word.

90

A visit to the cardiologist showed Eleanor's heart was still slowly deteriorating but he was happy to learn that she had not allowed it to interfere too much with her life. He was surprised that she was still travelling abroad but congratulated her for not giving in to her problem.

Winter came early that year, but Eleanor ensured that the mink coat got worn to combat the cold, and with Christmas looming Eleanor and Louis had to make a decision as to how they wanted to spend it. Both David and Diane had extended invitations to them, but they decided to be home-bodies, and enjoy each other's company. Eleanor sent money to David and Diane for them to buy presents for the children.

Another year that Eleanor decided not to put up Christmas decorations. She asked Louis if he minded, and he said he did not. Who will get to see them? He had asked her.

Christmas morning Louis cooked eggs, bacon and toast and together with Eleanor's favourite tea, took it all up to their bedroom. Eleanor was surprised but delighted with his actions. They stayed in bed for quite a while as outside was looking dark and threatening to snow.

'So glad that we decided to stay home' said Eleanor 'I would not want to be out driving in this weather'. Louis agreed as they snuggled down for another sleep.

Showered, dressed and back downstairs Louis presented Eleanor with a beautiful cameo dress ring. It fitted perfectly. Many years earlier she had commented on a similar ring in a jeweller's shop, and he remembered. Eleanor produced a Christmas wrapped, package. Louis frowned. When he opened it he found the complete works of Guy de Maupassant, his favourite French author. Two very happy people who hugged and kissed each other for such thoughtful presents. Later David and Diane each telephoned them to wish them a Merry Christmas.

An intimate lunch for two comprised roast chicken and vegetables followed by individual Christmas puddings and custard. They drank a Sauvignon Blanc with their lunch. They spent the afternoon watching television, doing crossword puzzles and generally relaxing.

Meanwhile it had started to snow outside. Eleanor loved to watch snow falling and how the garden was transformed into a Christmas wonderland at least until it thawed and there was slush in the streets.

91

New Year was celebrated at home. Toasting each other in champagne Louis said that 1982 was going to be another good year for them both. Eleanor frowned.

'I have been thinking, *Ma Cherie*, maybe it is time for you to sell this house, but there is no rush, you need to think of where you would like to spend your next twenty years', said Louis, planting a kiss on each of Eleanor's cheeks.

'Oh, and when are *we*, emphasizing the word we, going to get married?' he added.

'Why, aren't you happy with our current arrangement?' said Eleanor.

'*Non*', said Louis abruptly.

'Okay then, when we move into our new home' she promised.

Just then the telephone rang. It was Diane wishing them a Happy New Year and as Eleanor hung up the receiver David rang to wish them a Happy New Year, too.

Whilst Louis was in the kitchen making a cup of hot chocolate, to take up to bed with them, Eleanor thought about her house. She had been living there for almost 35 years. Happy years. *Tempus fugit.* A great deal of family history was wrapped up in this house. It would be a big wrench to move, but she admitted, to herself, that the thought had crossed her mind on more than one occasion. We'll start looking in March, she decided when the weather improves, gardens will look better, and driving will not be hazardous. She informed Louis of her decision on his return from the kitchen.

True to her word Eleanor started searching real estate in a number of different areas, she really did not know where she wanted to live. Did she want a sea change or a tree change? She had read this line in a magazine recently.

One weekend, two months later Eleanor and Louis took an early, leisurely drive from Dover to Brighton after Eleanor thought a sea change might be in order. Starting with real estate offices and newspapers for the area they quickly decided that Dover was not for them, particularly with the ferry crossings.

Driving on further they looked at Deal and a couple of other small towns and repeated their tour of real estate offices and checking newspapers. Still nothing appealed to them.

Lunch at Eastbourne was taken in a seafront hotel with their table overlooking the Promenade. They both chose locally caught fish and chips, together with a shandy. The real estate offices had a few homes that might suit the bill, but they talked about staying there or moving on to Brighton where they had booked in at the same seafront hotel again as previously. They drove on.

Spending time in their room reading newspapers, and colourful brochures picked up, they found three houses in Eastbourne that might fit their requirements. They had talked at length as to what they wanted. It would be a bungalow with a tiled roof, no thatched cottage for them. Three bedrooms would allow the occasional visitors to stay, especially the grandchildren, during school holidays, now that they were getting older.

Early on Sunday morning the first real estate agent, a woman, arrived to take them to a viewing of the first house in Eastbourne, twenty-one miles east. Very nice, but on a busy main road, which Eleanor and Louis had not considered, when drawing up their criteria.

The second agent collected them mid-morning, from the hotel again, and took them in a different direction to Eastbourne, more inland, but unfortunately there was a three-storey block of flats that backed on to the rear garden. Another point, they had not considered previously.

Eleanor's disappointment showed clearly on her face.

Louis put his arm around her and said 'third time lucky. Remember?'

Eleanor nodded.

Having checked out of the hotel, Louis told the real estate agent that they would follow him to the house. It would give them a chance to look at the area at the same time.

The third house was close to the road to Beachy Head, a chalk headland in East Sussex, but not situated on a busy road. The bungalow, and its attached single car garage, was bathed in sunshine when they arrived, with a very pretty, front garden. The houses either side were well cared for and had nice gardens. Walking through the front door Eleanor suddenly felt comfortable, almost at home. The rooms were bright and spacious and tastefully decorated. The rear garden was not as big as their current garden but had been well laid out with a small sunroom and a fishpond, off to one side leaving room for changes such as a veggie garden should they require. There was a mature lemon tree, too. Eleanor thought of all the jars of lemon curd she could make. The kitchen was blue and white. It reminded Eleanor of Wedgewood or Delft. Either way, she liked the colour scheme.

Not wanting to influence Louis, Eleanor sidled up to him and asked 'well?'

'*Certainment*', he replied nodding.

Feeling really positive, they told the agent that they were very interested and would be in touch as they had a house to sell. He advised them not to wait too long as he believed the property would sell quickly and the price was realistic. Louis said that he agreed, but a few hours to talk things through was needed and they would give him an answer on Monday morning. They shook hands and the agent drove off.

With their luggage already in the car, Eleanor and Louis drove around the area to familiarise themselves with such things as shops, schools, not they needed one, the local hospital and walking areas. The house was only a short walk to the seafront. Then they set off for home again. Eleanor could hardly recall the drive back to Herne Hill as she and Louis never stopped talking about the house and what they would do with it.

The first three telephone calls Louis made on Monday morning were to local real estate agents in their area asking them to call and value the house for selling. All three said that they would be there that day. The fourth call was to the real estate agent selling 4 Mulberry Crescent, Eastbourne.

The rest of the day went in a whirlwind, with three different agents walking around her house and taking measurements. All three valuations came in within a few thousand pounds of each other, but only one agent said that he believed he had a client ready to buy the house. Although his valuation was the middle of the three Eleanor and Louis decided that they would prefer a quick sale and lose a few thousand pounds rather than wait until someone wanted to buy. There would still be more than enough money for the bungalow.

92

It was June before the sale of Burbage Road and the purchase of Mulberry Crescent was finalised. Rather than ask David and Diane to help them move, and with money from the sale of Burbage Road, Eleanor engaged a firm of removalists as the removal could be done in one trip. She had boxed up much of the smaller items and given away a lot of china and glass to a local charity shop. All the while Louis was watching Eleanor to make sure that she did not overdo it and took regular rest breaks. Louis was proving helpful, too, selling some of his furniture that he no longer felt sentimental about. There would not be room for everything in the new house. Downsizing, recalled Eleanor, quoting from another magazine.

The day after they moved into the house there was a knock at the door. Louis opened it to find an attractive, grey haired, elderly lady standing there and holding a cake.

'Welcome to Mulberry Crescent' she said 'I'm Margaret Bunton and I live next door' indicating number 6.

'Do come in' said Louis and called for Eleanor.

Over a cup of tea and a piece of Mrs Bunton's Madeira cake, and all three seated in the lounge, Mrs Bunton informed them that she was a widow and had lived in Eastbourne almost all her 85 years. She was proud of the fact that she still drove herself around the town and if they needed to know anything they only had to ask her. She also told them that she used to serve on the local council for many years.

A handy person to know thought Eleanor. Mrs Bunton also told them that Jeff and Cathy lived at number 2 but spent much of their time in London and only came down at weekends. She kept an eye on their house and had a house key, in case of an emergency.

After she left Louis commented on what a nice person she was. Eleanor had to agree. Nice neighbours were so important to them both.

Next day Mrs Bunton was back again.

'Do you need anything from the shops?' she said. Eleanor thanked her but said that they had everything they needed.

Day 3 and Mrs Bunton was knocking on the front door again.

'There's a concert in the town next week and I thought you might like a flyer' she said.

'Thank you' said Eleanor, taking the flyer but not asking her in.

Eleanor turned to Louis.

'We need to nip this in the bud, we do not need her constantly bombarding us with offers, but she is obviously lonely so I must think of a way to wean her off of us'.

Louis agreed.

The constant daily visits went on for two weeks before Eleanor felt ready to tell Mrs Bunton to stop calling by. Eleanor had made enquiries, in the town, as to activities for elderly people and found that there were quite a few clubs, depending on Mrs Bunton's interests.

Armed with a plethora of brochures and flyers Eleanor asked Mrs Bunton in for tea, home-made scones, jam and cream. Louis had taken himself out for a walk. Talking, in general, Eleanor started to probe Mrs Bunton's interests. She liked knitting, reading and used to play cards with her late husband. Ah, thought Eleanor a couple of possibilities.

'I was thinking' started Eleanor 'of joining the local library and perhaps a book club, would that interest you?'

'Oh yes, but I would not know how to go about it' replied Mrs Bunton.

'That's easy' said Eleanor 'I shall take you with me. Also, do you play bridge or canasta?'

'Actually, my husband and I used to play poker. I love it but have no one to play with' said Mrs Bunton'.

This revelation stumped Eleanor as she had no information on poker, but undeterred she would start with the book club at the local library.

Monday afternoons was the time set aside for the book club and the other enthusiasts readily welcomed two new members. Driving home from their first meeting Mrs Bunton remarked on how friendly everyone seemed and she could not wait to read the recommended book and go back the following week with her opinion. Great, thought Eleanor. I shall keep this up for a week or two then find an excuse to no longer attend. Her ploy actually worked, as Mrs Bunton was so engrossed in reading books, for the book club, that she hardly had time to call on Eleanor, but Eleanor made sure she found time for Mrs Bunton at least once a week, mainly to check on her welfare and to see how her new friendships were developing.

On separate weekends David and his family came down to see the new house and spend the weekend with them and the following weekend Diane and her family did the same. Already Diane's teenage boys were planning on spending some school holiday time there and loved racing each other up to the top of Beachy Head.

Since moving into their new home Eleanor and Louis had spent many happy hours walking the seafront and finding places of interest. Louis had walked up to the top of Beachy Head but would not let Eleanor climb due to her heart condition.

No more mention had been made about getting married, despite Eleanor's promise, which suited Eleanor. She was very happy with life and just loved her new surroundings.

Louis had thumbed through the brochures and flyers that Eleanor had picked up for Mrs Bunton, and found a chess club, which he joined and now spent one afternoon a week with a new-found group of friends, mainly men, but Eleanor thought that it would be good for him to enjoy male companionship.

Eleanor, meanwhile, had taken up flower arranging, which she found that she thoroughly enjoyed. Always a lover of flowers she found that she had a creative streak in her. One of the ladies, Edna Croft, regularly did the flower arrangements for All Souls Anglican Church, a polychromatic Byzantine building with a prominent campanile, built in 1882. When Eleanor first saw the church, she was impressed. It was such a striking building unlike anything she had seen before. She told Edna that she was not a church goer but would love to help her with the flower arrangements each week. Edna said that she would love the help. So, now Eleanor had an interest, too. Life was really oh so good. What could possibly go wrong?

93

At the beginning of December Eleanor started her Christmas preparations. She bought, wrote in and posted her Christmas cards to friends and relatives, including one to Daphne who had telephoned her to say that she would be spending three months in Australia with her daughter and family, over the Christmas. She would be staying in Surfer's Paradise, Queensland. The name conjured up an exotic location in Eleanor's mind. Daphne promised to take lots of photographs and tell her all about Australia on her return.

In some of the cards she enclosed a small letter giving an update on family, such as David and his family now living in Newcastle, after the bank transferred him in November, and snippets about Diane and Rob's family. She also told of her happiness with the new home.

As part of her preparations, Christmas cake and the Christmas pudding were made and stored in the pantry. A small turkey was ordered at the local butcher shop. She had written out her menu for Christmas Day and Boxing Day, together with the food shopping that she would need. Presents were going to be in a monetary form again this year due to distance and the cost of posting parcels to grandchildren whose tastes and interests she no longer knew. She and Louis had invited Mrs Bunton to spend Christmas Day with them and invited Jeff and Cathy to Christmas drinks on Christmas Eve. Eleanor had bought a new, four-foot, artificial Christmas tree to set up in the lounge with lights and baubles from a previous Christmas. A present for Louis was causing her some consternation but she was positive that she would find something he would like.

A week before Christmas and Eleanor was nursing a very bad cold. The doctor told her it was not influenza and would be gone in four to five days, with warmth, rest and lots of fluids, which was good news. Louis insisted that Eleanor stay in bed as the weather was cold and miserable and it was easier to keep the master bedroom warm for her rather than heating the whole house, whilst he went out to his chess group. Encouraged to drink lots of fluids there was a large jug of lemon drink on the bedside table together with a glass, a box of aspirin and vapour rub to help her breathing. Fortunately, thought Eleanor, the Christmas preparations are done.

There was a telephone on the bedside table on Louis' side of the bed. They had had the extension installed in case Eleanor required help when Louis was not around. Lying back, dozing, Eleanor was startled by the telephone ringing.

'Is that Eleanor?' a male voice asked, 'this is Tony, Daphne's friend'.

Eleanor visualised Daphne introducing her young male friend Tony at her 60th birthday party.

'Yes', replied Eleanor.

The was a slight pause.

'I am ringing to tell you that Daphne has had an accident, in Australia, and unfortunately has died' he said.

'Oh no' exclaimed Eleanor 'not Daphne, please not Daphne' and tears started falling down her cheeks. 'What happened?

Tony, choking back the words, told her that Daphne was crossing busy Pacific Highway, to meet the family on the beach, and was knocked over by a speeding car. Her death was instant, according to the doctors. Her daughter had her cremated in Australia and would retain her ashes. At some stage the daughter would return to England to wind up her mother's affairs, but in the mean-time Tony was welcome to live in her house.

Eleanor dared to believe the Christmas Curse.

94

Cathy and Jeff came, as invited, on Christmas Eve. They brought a bottle of red wine and some cheeses with them. As they were in London all week there had not been a lot of time to talk, in depth, with them. They were married, had no children, and were both violinists in an orchestra. Eleanor commented that she had not heard them playing their violins. Jeff smiled, that's because we have one bedroom sound-proofed, he said. Oh, said Eleanor. Even Mrs Bunton had not provided that information, so perhaps she was unaware.

On Christmas Day Eleanor and Louis rose early to spend a leisurely breakfast with each other and exchange gifts. Eleanor had allowed plenty of time to cook the lunch. Although Louis enjoyed eggs and bacon Eleanor bought croissants and yoghurts to have after their muesli. Louis handed Eleanor a small, Christmas paper wrapped box. Inside Eleanor found a crystal necklace lying on a bed of red silk. The colours flashed all around the room as she held it up to admire it. Hugging Louis closely she thanked him and kissed him. In exchange, Eleanor handed Louis a small box and inside he found a keyring fob. Louis frowned, puzzled, unable to make sense of the gift.

'What is this?' he asked. 'I do not have a luxury car like this'.

Eleanor laughed. 'You do now' she said.

'Please explain, *Ma Cherie*'.

Eleanor explained that she had been thinking it was time to treat themselves to a top of the range new vehicle. She still had plenty of money in investments and at their age they deserved some luxury. She had not actually bought the car yet but had spoken to the dealer and after Christmas they could go together and select the vehicle of their choice, colour, model and year if they chose a used vehicle.

He was overjoyed. He did not know what to say apart from '*merci, merci, merci, Ma Cherie*'.

Eleanor made telephone calls to David and Diane wishing them and their families a very Merry Christmas. Each of the grandchildren also spoke to thank Eleanor for the presents received.

Mrs Bunton arrived on the dot of twelve noon brandishing a bottle of sherry and a box of chocolate mints. Louis and Eleanor looked at each other, and smiled, when they saw the mints remembering some from many years earlier.

Lunch for the three of them went well. Eleanor, as usual, had surpassed herself with her cooking and presentation. Louis made sure that their glasses stayed filled. Tea was a lighter meal with a choice of small items to pick at or make a sandwich, followed by a rich, fruit Christmas cake that Eleanor had made earlier in the month.

Mrs Bunton went home about eight o'clock, looking flushed and a little unsteady on her feet. Louis walked her to her front door and watched her go in, safely.

Flopping into bed that night they reviewed the day and congratulated themselves on another success and within minutes were both fast asleep.

Boxing Day was a much more leisurely affair. After a cup of tea in bed they talked a while then turned over and managed to have more sleep.

95

Eleanor was already cooking breakfast when Louis came down from his shower. He was still in his dressing gown.

'You look worried Darling' Eleanor said.

'I am a little' he replied.

'Do you want to share your problem with me?' she then asked.

'No, not yet' he responded, 'but it is a man thing'.

Eleanor knew not to push Louis, but it now caused her some concern. She knew that whatever it was, a visit to the doctor would put both their minds at rest. Unfortunately trying to see a doctor over the Christmas and New Year period was hopeless unless it was a true emergency.

Eleanor and Louis spent New Year quietly and did not toast 1983 in, preferring to go to bed early. Louis was reluctant to travel too far due to the weather and his health issue. Again, Eleanor did not push him.

The purchase of a black luxury car went smoothly. They had been dealing with a local car dealer and he had found them a very respectable vehicle, only three years old, with low mileage, and in an excellent condition. Wearing her mink coat Eleanor felt like the Queen whenever they went out for a drive.

In March Eleanor had to see the cardiologist. Again, he was amazed that Eleanor was keeping so well and apart from medications he told her to 'just keep on living'.

With such good news Eleanor suggested to Louis a trip to Hong Kong. If she was going to die, Hong Kong was a good a place as any she said.

Louis was reluctant due to his health issue, so Eleanor said that it was time to see the doctor and sort it out. She would go with him if he wanted her to, but he declined.

The doctor's visit should have been made weeks before. Louis had heard men at the chess club talking about prostate cancer and the symptoms. He had convinced himself that he, too, had prostate cancer and would therefore die soon. His doctor listened to him, examined his prostate, pronounced everything was alright and then told Louis that he was, in fact, suffering from a recurring bladder infection, which was soon remedied with medication. The doctor told him not to delay making an appointment in future. He was annoyed with himself for not facing up to a problem instead of stewing over it and imagining the worst. He told Eleanor when he got home, and she was in agreeance with the doctor.

'Louis, we must share our health issues' she said. He nodded sheepishly.

The trip was planned for Easter. Eleanor had read numerous travel brochures and fancied an expensive hotel in Kowloon. It was a five-star hotel which opened in the nineteen twenties. Apparently the rich and famous stayed there. On the opposite corner was a more modest hotel with a glass walled lift that travelled up the outside of the building. Louis had said that he preferred this one.

'This hotel will send a car and driver to pick us up at the airport' Eleanor said, referring to the expensive hotel.

Louis looked over the top of his reading glasses. I do not think we would feel comfortable there, *Ma Cherie.* I know we can afford it, but I would prefer not to stay there'.

Eleanor disagreed but said nothing before adding 'they have afternoon teas, perhaps we can have one of those'.

'Maybe'.

Eleanor and Louis consulted a travel agent and two days before Easter flew to Hong Kong. Eleanor had not realised just how far it was and felt exhausted when they finally arrived. She was overawed at the high-rise buildings and throngs of people everywhere.

The hotel was beautiful and with modern lines. There was an exterior glass walled lift, as described in the travel brochure, and their superior room was elegant. They had a wonderful view of the Harbour, too.

Deciding that they both needed to rest they took dinner in their room that evening.

Next morning, much refreshed, they went downstairs for breakfast and were amazed to see small white picket fenced enclosures in circles around the foyer. In each of the enclosures there were either baby rabbits or day-old chicks. There were also huge Easter eggs dotted around and one of the staff handed them an Easter egg each. The concierge said good morning and referred to them by their title and surname. Louis was most impressed.

A buffet breakfast almost made their eyes water. There was just so much food and a chef who would cook eggs any way you requested. They had their own waiter, too, who fussed over them.

They had booked a Kowloon tour in the morning and a Hong Kong Island tour for the following day. The morning tour showed Kowloon and up to the New Territories. The next day tour meant that they had to use the Star Ferry to the island before boarding a bus for sightseeing. The views from Victoria Peak were magnificent and Eleanor could hardly put down her camera. When the tour visited Aberdeen there was a bustling market and in the Harbour they saw the massive floating restaurant that opened in 1976. They decided that they would try it one night.

Eleanor was so keen to try out the nearby hotel's afternoon tea that they made their way there, after booking through their concierge, the next day. The hotel itself boasted classical colonial curves, shiny marble floors, elegant, gilded columns and expensive artwork adorned the walls. Afternoon tea had been a part of the hotel since opening. There was a small musical ensemble playing. All of this surpassed their expectations. There were dainty, assorted finger sandwiches, filled with cheese or cucumber, with the crusts of the white bread removed. The freshly baked scones, stuffed with raisins were served with jam and Devonshire clotted cream. The presentation of sandwiches and scones were on a tiered silver platter. The waiting staff fussed over them like Royalty, whilst they ate. Everything was of an impeccable standard, but they both agreed that they were glad that they chose not to stay there.

The next evening Eleanor and Louis received directions from the concierge, to the floating restaurant on a huge Chinese junk In the middle of Aberdeen Harbour. He had made a booking for them and arranged the transport. Once seated in a truly magnificent Chinese setting, they quickly decided to have a banquet between them. They both enjoyed Chinese food from a small shop in Eastbourne but did not expect the enormous array of dishes that were served up. Both feeling quite full they dawdled over coffee and fortune cookies. If the cookies were to be believed, they would both have very long lives.

Most evenings they chose to dine in one of their hotel restaurants but always had pre-dinner drinks in the lounge on the top floor. The views out of the city were magnificent. Both Eleanor and Louis enjoyed the nibbles on the low tables, usually bowls of deep friend cuttlefish balls and bowls of salted peanuts.

Calling it 'slumming', one evening they ventured into a less affluent area of Hong Kong and found a rice kitchen in a back street. Looking in the window the place seemed packed with Chinese. Deciding to take a chance they entered and found that the food was displayed in pictures over the counter. They indicated the dish of choice and found it to be very cheap, no wonder the locals were dining there. The meal was delicious and just as they left it started to pour with rain, so they waited in the doorway for a while hoping it would ease off. Across the road an elderly Chinese woman was trying to collect rainwater in an open weave basket. Of course, it leaked like a sieve. Another memorable moment thought Eleanor.

To finish on a high note Louis had decided that on their last evening at the hotel they would dine in the most expensive of the hotel restaurants. When making their own booking the booking clerk pointed out that 'sir must wear a jacket'. Louis was in shirt sleeves at the time of making the booking. Louis responded by saying that 'sir had a jacket'.

On the dot of seven o'clock they arrived at the restaurant entrance. Eleanor in a very classic, knee length, black dress with pearl accessories. Her hair in a bun at the nape of her neck. Louis in a black dinner suit with bow tie. When watching Eleanor dress for dinner Louis had to remark,

'*Tres chic*' and presented her with a small, black satin clutch bag, which he had bought whilst in Hong Kong. Eleanor was surprised and delighted, kissing him for his thoughtfulness.

The Maitre d' greeted them and presented Eleanor with a long-stemmed red rose. They were shown to a table for two just off the dance floor in the middle of the restaurant. The lighting was subdued but as her eyes became accustomed to the low light Eleanor could see a large contingent of Arab men, in robes, to their left. When she nudged Louis and indicated the group, he was of the opinion that it was a Sheik with his male entourage.

On the table were two small red books of matches. The name Trebert stamped in gold lettering on them. The Maitre d' presented them each with red covered menus and again the name Trebert was stamped on the front in gold lettering. Eleanor and Louis looked at each other and shrugged. Eleanor noticed that there were no prices in her menu and showed Louis. He showed her his menu with the prices.

Eleanor could not believe her eyes when a chef with the tallest white hat, or *toque,* as she remembered from her crossword puzzles, came to their table. He had an array of medals hanging around his neck. He announced, to Eleanor, that he had created a chicken dish just for her that evening. Eleanor thanked him and said that she would look at the menu and then decide.

Eleanor's choice of food did not include the special that had been created for her, but she enjoyed her chosen dish. With a dessert each and two bottles of wine consumed they both felt good. The band had been playing for some time and when Louis and Eleanor got up to dance Eleanor reached the raised floor first. She felt a hand take her elbow and help her up on the dance floor. At first, she thought it was Louis, but it was a staff member standing nearby. They danced for a while before returning to their table for coffee and brandy. Louis had made a mental note of the bill and told Eleanor, very quietly that they did not have enough money on them to pay. Eleanor joked that she should have brought her rubber gloves with her so that they could wash up the dishes.

Undeterred, as they left the restaurant Louis told the Maitre d'

'Charge it to our room' and they left giggling.

Early the next day, as soon as the bank was open Louis was withdrawing money in order to pay for the meal and any outstanding charges they had incurred during their stay. After all, said Eleanor, what is money for?

Spending two weeks in Hong Kong meant that they got to see so much and spent so much. There were shopping malls and so many restaurants catering for all types of food from many different nations. The whole town seemed to be alive twenty-four hours a day. However, Eleanor and Louis were always ready for bed at the end of another exciting day.

96

On their return to Eastbourne, life seemed so slow and tame. Just right for them though. The high life was fun whilst it lasted but they considered that they were too old to live that sort of life.

Eastbourne became very busy in the summer months with visitors, but Eleanor and Louis didn't mind having to queue for an ice cream or not being able to sit at their favourite café. They knew that visitors brought a lot of money into the town and in the winter they could have it all to themselves again.

It was a lovely, warm sunny day, midweek, but neither Eleanor nor Louis had their clubs to attend. Eleanor decided to call in at Mrs Bunton's and take her some German apple cake that she had made. Louis said that he would go for a walk along the seafront but be home by 5pm at the latest. Eleanor told him to be sure to wear a sun hat and thought how nice he looked as he strode down the path wearing cotton shorts and an open necked cotton shirt and carrying his white fedora hat.

Margaret Bunton was always glad to have company. Her involvement with the library had helped her make some new friends and her social life had taken a turn for the better, often being invited out to lunch with one of the book group members.

Sharing a pot of tea together plus a piece of Eleanor's delicious cake the two women chatted about many things. Eleanor commented on the knitting that Margaret had put down on Eleanor's arrival.

'Oh' said Mrs Bunton 'that's for Karen's new baby girl'

'Who is Karen?' asked Eleanor.

Mrs Bunton went on to explain that Karen was one of the librarians and she and her husband lived at number 20. Karen recently had a baby girl, and they called her Lucy. Their surname was Farmer. Mrs Bunton was making a number of knitted cardigans for the baby with the cooler months coming.

The two women spent all afternoon together and it was close to 5pm when Eleanor said that she must go and start getting a meal organised.

Six o'clock came and there was no sign of Louis. Not too concerned, Eleanor assumed that he had met a friend from the chess club and perhaps decided to have a drink together. Luckily they were only having a ham and egg salad for tea and some strawberries from the garden.

Eleanor turned on the television set and watched the news. There seemed to be problems all around the world, so Eleanor turned it off again. Although she was interested in current affairs, on such a lovely day she wanted good news.

By 7.30 pm Eleanor started to get worried. This was so unlike Louis, a stickler for time and he would not do anything to cause her worry. She did not want to bother Mrs Bunton and thought that David or Diane might think she was becoming paranoid, so she plucked up courage to walk along the street to number 20 and speak to Karen. At least it would be a good opportunity to meet her neighbours.

A young woman answered the door and when Eleanor asked if she was Karen, she said that she was. Eleanor introduced herself and said that she knew her name from Mrs Bunton but wondered if she might be able to help her with a small problem. Looking puzzled, Karen asked her in and showed her into the lounge.

'This is my husband Matt' said Karen introducing Eleanor to a young man, sitting on the sofa, wearing a police uniform and reading a newspaper. 'He's shortly off to do a night shift'.

Eleanor was taken aback. She had not expected to see a policeman. In fact, she did not know what to expect.

Karen asked her to sit down and tell them what her problem was.

Later, Eleanor could not recall exactly what she said and thinks it all came out in a jumble.

The baby, upstairs, started to cry and Karen excused herself to go and attend to her. Matt had put down the paper and gently asked Eleanor a few pertinent questions such as where was Louis going, what was he wearing, did he often come home late? Eleanor thinks she gave accurate information about what Louis was wearing but could not be sure.

Karen came back downstairs, holding the baby, and asked Eleanor if she would like to hold her whilst she put the kettle on. Matt said that he had to leave but he was sure Louis would be home soon and that she should try and relax. Spend some time with Karen and Lucy before going home.

Back home Eleanor was now very worried. It was getting dark, and she considered ringing the local hospital in case Louis had had an accident.

Whilst looking up the telephone number in the local telephone directory there was a knock at the door. Louis had installed a spyhole in the front door, but Eleanor did not use it. Instead, she opened the door to see Matt Farmer and a young policewoman standing there. Her heart sank. Vivid memories of police on the doorstep when Derek died. Eleanor fainted.

When Eleanor opened her eyes again, she was lying on the sofa and Matt was talking quietly to her. Telling her that an ambulance was on its way.

'Where is Louis?' she asked.

'He's at the hospital' Matt replied, lying in part, as Louis was in the hospital mortuary.

The ambulance team were very caring, and Eleanor made them aware of her serious heart problems. Matt had alerted them, out of Eleanor's earshot, to the fact that Louis was dead. They nodded and said that they would handle the breaking of the news to her at the hospital.

Eleanor was kept in the hospital overnight but not discharged until Diane arrived, the next day, to take her home and stay with her for a few days.

David arrived at the weekend to help with making funeral arrangements and Eleanor was grateful that he was there when Matt came to tell them of the circumstances of Louis' death.

Louis had been sitting in a deckchair overlooking the beach and towards France. No-one knew how long he was there, but it was only late in the evening that a man, who had been walking his dog along the seafront, realised that it was the same elderly man who had been sitting there in the morning when he passed. He remembered the white fedora. He gave a cursory check of the man and thought perhaps he was dead but thought better than to touch him. The man then called into the nearest still open shop and asked them to ring the Police.

An ambulance arrived together with the Police as it was possibly a sudden death, and it was confirmed to be. Unfortunately, due to the lightweight clothing that Louis was wearing and the lack of a wallet there was no identification on him to assist in finding his family. He had a set of house keys but nothing else. The Police then had to wait until someone telephoned in about a missing person. It was sheer coincidence that Matt had met Eleanor just before going on shift, so he was able to solve the mystery of the man within minutes of arriving at work.

An autopsy showed that Louis had suffered a massive heart attack and his death would have been instant. He certainly would not have suffered, which was a relief for Eleanor.

Eleanor and Louis had discussed funerals and she knew he wanted to be cremated. Like Leonard, it was a small, private affair, conducted at the funeral director's premises. The only stipulation that Eleanor would not be able to meet was the fact that Louis wanted to have his ashes scattered from the top of Beachy Head, when the wind was blowing out to sea. Eleanor would not be able to climb Beachy Head even for Louis, so David and Rob promised to take on the task.

97

Alone again, Eleanor had to think about her future. She had lost another good man, in Louis, and her family had returned to their own families. She dared to wonder if Louis had been looking at France when he died and if his ashes might drift as far as the coastline of his homeland.

Time to take stock of life. She had a lovely home, freehold and manageable, even the garden. She had a car, which she loved to drive, that she might consider selling in order to buy something smaller, but there was no rush. Holidays were now over. She could not see herself going any further than her front gate. She would not travel anywhere on her own, especially overseas. Her family were supportive but not close. Would she consider moving to be nearer to them? She decided not. She had some good friends and could immerse herself in voluntary work in the community. All of this can wait, she decided. She did not have to think of anything apart from the good times and happy memories of a life of wonderful experiences. I shall make a fresh start on life in the New Year she told herself.

Mrs Bunton had a gardener and Eleanor soon arranged for him to take care of her garden, too. He was an older man called Stan and Eleanor would ply him with hot or cold drinks, according to the temperature of the day and cake or biscuits. Although Eleanor wondered if their friendship might develop, she firmly put it in the 'No' basket. Stan was happily married.

Winter was arriving fast, and that dreaded Christmas time again. Someone told Eleanor that there was a name for the phobia about Christmas. It was called Christougenniatikophobia. She doubted that the word would be in a crossword at any time soon but was fascinated to learn that such a phobia existed.

Since Louis' death, Eleanor had become quite friendly with Karen and Matt and had started babysitting for them when they wanted to go out. Eleanor had told Karen how she had brought up her own three children as well as two grandsons for her daughter and son-in-law, so understood the pressures put on young couples with a young family especially the need to work.

Turning down invitations to David and Diane's homes for the Christmas period, citing weather and road conditions Eleanor was delighted to receive an invitation to Karen and Matt's together with Mrs Bunton. Apparently, Karen's parents had moved to Spain, for warmer weather and had a hectic social life over there. It did not faze Karen or Matt not to be with family, so they told Eleanor, plus Matt had some time that he needed to be on duty over the Christmastime.

Christmas Day went off really well. Karen had cooked a tasty turkey dinner with all the trimmings and Eleanor had bought some of her home-made mince pies and shortbread to share. Mrs Bunton brought along some chocolate mints. Eleanor smiled when she saw them.

Being a librarian, Karen could not help herself but buy Eleanor and Mrs Bunton a book each. She assured them that they were by very good writers and perhaps they could swap with each other after they had read them. Eleanor tucked this thought away for the future. Eleanor gave Mrs Bunton some expensive hand cream and Karen and Matt a bottle of good French wine. She also gave baby Lucy a beautiful soft toy.

98

Eleanor went early to bed on New Year's Eve after telephoning David and Diane and wishing them and their families a Happy New Year. A recent visit to the doctor had diagnosed high blood pressure but with medication and not overdoing things her doctor reassured her, that like her heart condition, she could go on for years.

Waking much later than usual and not feeling herself Eleanor rose gingerly to go to the bathroom. It was daylight. Her body did not want to respond. Her right side felt heavy. She decided that she would go downstairs first and make a cup of tea before having a shower. Feeling unsteady on her feet she made for the top of the stairs. When she opened her eyes, she was lying in an awkward position at the bottom of the stairs. Unsure of how she got there and why she made a futile attempt to get up. Her mind was not functioning properly, but functioning, whereas her body was not.

As she lay there a terrible realisation came over her. 'I have had a stroke. The doctor warned me about high blood pressure but with medication I should be alright'.

Try as she might, Eleanor could not move herself to the telephone, so she tried calling out. Despite shouting, nothing was coming out of her mouth. Again, realisation told her that the stroke was massive and that she had lost most of her bodily functions.

Whether it was exhaustion, from her efforts to move to a different part of the hall, away from the stairs and near the 'phone, she would not remember. She did not have a watch on and no way of knowing the time. Finally, she noticed the light fading and wondered if anyone would ever find her.

Falling asleep again she was awoken by a loud knocking on the door. Unable to call out she hoped that the person would not walk away. More knocking and someone calling out to her. She recognised the deep resonant voice. It was Matt. He had come to return a plate that she had left at their house on Christmas Day.

Although not a religious person, Eleanor started to pray that Matt would find her and save her.

Matt pushed open the letterbox in the front door and thought he could make out something on the floor at the foot of the stairs. Unsure, he returned home for a torch and shone it through the letterbox. That's when he saw Eleanor lying there in a contorted fashion.

He called the Police and ambulance. He told his Police sergeant that they needed to break down the front door. The Police responded and the ambulance people were soon there, too.

In the Emergency Department at the hospital Eleanor was aware of people around her although she did not know where she was. She could hear voices but could not move or respond to their commands. She thought she heard the word stroke but thought that her problem must be with her heart even though she had thought stroke when she first realised that she could not move.

After numerous tests Eleanor was moved to a ward occupied by three other women. She kept slipping in and out of consciousness or was it sleep? Eleanor was confused.

At some stage Diane and Rob arrived. Both had very concerned looks on their faces. Eleanor could not communicate with them, but her mind was screaming out to tell them that she would be alright.

David and Pauline came to her bedside and tried talking to her and asking questions but to no avail. Eleanor realised that people were talking about her as though she was either deaf or not there. She wanted to speak out and tell them 'I'm here, I can hear you'.

How many days Eleanor laid in the hospital bed she would never know. Doctors and nurses came to her bedside and spoke amongst themselves. Nurses came and tried to feed her, but swallowing was very difficult.

David, Pauline, Diane and Rob stayed in Eleanor's home for a few days whilst trying to find out the prognosis of Eleanor's condition. Karen and Matt sent flowers and a Get Well Soon card. Mrs Bunton sent a card, too. Other friends sent cards and flowers, but Eleanor's mind was muddled and she could not recall who the people were.

Eleanor felt totally useless. She felt that her body was no longer hers and started to hate the fact that other people had to do everything for her. She greatly objected being a burden to the staff, despite their caring ways.

Days, weeks or was it months before Eleanor was a resident at Lady Rawlings Home for the Elderly? Again, she would never know.

The room began to feel a little chilly. Eleanor could not call out for a nurse, and she could not pull the knee rug up that had slipped towards the floor.

It was then that Eleanor became aware of an elegant young woman standing at the French doors. She seemed to have an aura about her. She was dressed in pale grey clothing to the floor, elbow length pale grey kid gloves and wearing a large expensive looking hat with ostrich feathers. A small grey silk bag hanging by a chain from her wrist. Eleanor thought she could detect the smell of ginger.

Eleanor was not afraid or alarmed but more curious as to who this woman was and where she had come from.

The woman held out her hand towards Eleanor, then beckoned her to go with her. Eleanor did not resist, feeling very happy and light in her body.

'Wake up Eleanor' said the young nurse rushing into the room, 'sorry I did not come back to help you with your tea. It must be stone cold by now'.

One look at Eleanor's marble-looking features told the nurse all that she needed to know.